The Guests

ALSO BY ADRIANE LEIGH

My Perfect Family
The Perfect Escape
The Guests

THE GUESTS

ADRIANE LEIGH

JOFFE BOOKS

Joffe Books, London
www.joffebooks.com

First published in Great Britain in 2024

Cover art by Nick Castle

ISBN: 978-1-83526-797-4

To the quiet heroes.

PROLOGUE

This wasn't the plan.

    I was never supposed to kill my husband.

    But sometimes plans change.

CHAPTER ONE: COLE

Last summer

"Mm, I forgot how well you ring all my bells." Lyra adjusts her lacy neon-pink bra as she speaks. "Why did we break up again?"

"Because you went to rehab and your dad threatened to cut you out of his will if you didn't get sober this time," I remind her.

"Right." She pouts then leans over and presses her lips to mine. "Worth it, but barely."

"What happens when he finds out you're banging the help again?"

"I do have a thing for the help." I let it go, even though I know she means it. Lyra is spoiled rotten and unbearably pretentious, but that's what makes her fun. I'm used to her back-handed compliments because I know, deep down, she loves me, as much as a girl like that can love anyone, anyway.

"Same time tomorrow?" I ask as I pull the T-shirt over my head.

"Maybe. You've got a new group of tourists coming, don't you? A new batch of entitled, spoon-fed housewives to flirt with?"

"How do you know me so well?"

"Please, we've been friends for almost a decade. I know you have a thing for brats."

I only shrug. "This group is different. I know most of them. It's a reunion of sorts."

"Ugh. Reunions and funerals. I hate them both."

I huff. Lyra *would* equate the two, of course. "Well, this week is an odd little mix of both."

"Oh? Do tell."

"It's a will reading. The lawyer already arrived on the last boat. He's drinking cognac on the beach, and he'll probably be toasted by the time they arrive. It should be interesting to watch."

"A will reading, huh? That is unusual. I wonder if Dad knows about that."

"Oh, he knows. I told him when he called me to chew me out. *Again.*"

"He forgot to mention that to me." She sighs. "He's so up his own ass."

"As he should be. He's the reason I'm here, so I can't complain."

"Well, I can."

"He's bailed you out a time or two. Can you blame him for feeling so strongly about keeping us apart? We've put the old guy through the wringer."

"Ah—" she waves off my comment — "I like keeping the old man on his toes."

"And me." I pull her down into my lap, cupping her cheeks in my palms as I trail hot kisses down her neck.

"Mm, just how I like it." Her tongue tangles with mine languidly before she pulls away and pushes her designer bag over her shoulder. "Catch you next time, cowboy." She opens the door of my cabin and calls over her shoulder, "And check your phone once in a while. It's hard to keep you on your toes with sexy text messages when you're not answering them."

I roll my eyes. "Reception has been shitty all summer. The fucking underwater cables to the mainland are still severed after the ice last winter, and the only cell tower up on the hill is too far away to make a difference on this side of the island."

"Ah." She nods. "Just one more reason for you to be a grouchy asshole, I guess." She blows me a kiss and then waltzes out the door. The heavy wood bangs against the jamb, and I wonder if she'll ever learn to treat this old place with kid gloves. It will be hers one day, after all. The rich bastards I'm waiting on to arrive all own a small slice of this old estate, but it's her dad who owns the largest piece of the pie. The day he kicks off, Lyra will be a very wealthy woman, and part of me thinks that's why she likes to keep the old guy on his toes — the sooner he's gone, the quicker she can blow through her inheritance.

At that moment, I hear the telltale echo of a ship's horn from the cove. I shove my feet into a pair of old leather sandals and stalk out of the cabin on quick strides.

I've got a gaggle of entitled guests to cater to this week, and the tips won't be as good if I keep them waiting. Besides, Lyra's dad has already warned me multiple times that if I slip up even once this summer, I'm out on my ass for good. I may be the only local on this tiny island, but I owe the old man a debt that he insists on holding over my head.

I can't have a repeat of last summer. If anyone dies this tourist season, I'll be the one they blame.

CHAPTER TWO: RYLEIGH

"How's the bird's-eye view?" Kerrigan settles herself on the bench next to mine, the small catamaran slowing as we approach Stonecliffe Island.

"Gorgeous and windy," I offer. "I didn't expect so many little islands."

"It's beautiful, isn't it? We need to explore at least one of them this week — they're so removed from the world its almost spooky. It's easy to get lost in a place like this."

"Sounds like an adventure," I comment. "Why do you look so sad?" I frown as I take in her expression.

She shrugs. "Kip told me to get lost. He's working below deck, and I asked him if he was planning on ignoring his wife the entire week while he works."

"Oh." I'm not surprised. Kip and Kerrigan are always fighting and making up. "He's probably just trying to get a few last emails in before we hit shore and lose service."

"Oh, Kip never loses service. Not even in no man's land. He activated StarLink so unless there's a big storm, he'll be fine. While we lose service, he'll still be tapping away on that keyboard and talking to the guys at the office. He never would have survived up here as a kid. It's only been a few years since the island got internet, and it's never worked very well."

5

"When's the last time you were here?" I ask, knowing it isn't recently.

Kerrigan's eyes cast off to the fast-approaching shoreline. Chalky limestone cliffs bookend a white stone beach nestled in a small cove. It's breathtaking, and I can't imagine why anyone would stay away from a place like this.

"It's been years, I guess," Kerrigan murmurs. "Kip never wants to take the time to get out of the city. The last few summers, I've been begging him for a week away. Even with his dad passing, he never missed a day of work. I wouldn't be surprised if my father-in-law requested the reading of his will here just to force Kip into taking some time off. Joke's on him, even in his grave. Kip's success is built on technology, but it's like he's become fully integrated with his computer at this point."

I only nod, knowing that Kerrigan isn't interested in hearing me play devil's advocate. She only wants to vent. She *always* only wants to vent.

Daniel huffs softly at my shoulder, as if he's reading my mind. He's scratching furiously at his notepad, eyes casting up to the blue waves once in a while as he works on his next great story. Daniel is my other best friend, but this is the first time these two bubbles have touched. Coming from the same small town, Daniel and I understand each other on another level because of our humble beginnings. We both live in Chicago but in truth, it seems like our friendship relies more on our shared history than it does actual rapport these days. Lately, Daniel has been distant, and I suppose I have too. Maybe we've just outgrown each other, maybe our lives have taken different paths that no bridge could ever reconnect.

Kerrigan has always lived a life of luxury and only dips her toes into rural living for chic summer getaways up the coast of Lake Michigan. Her father was a famous yachtsman, and most of her summer days as a child were spent on a boat, traveling to and from this island — a tiny rock in the middle of Lake Michigan dotted with evergreens, limestone pebbles, and shorebirds. It's quiet, simple, and rural enough to feel like another world away from the hustle of the Chicago streets.

While Daniel is my oldest friend, Kerrigan is my newest. From the moment we met two years ago we became fast friends. I would even go so far as to call her my best friend because we talk every day and just seem to click in a way that Daniel and I never did. While my friendship with Daniel is solid, we go weeks without talking sometimes. Daniel spends a lot of time alone with his work; disturbing him with my petty dating dramas feels almost disrespectful lately.

"Almost there, lovelies! I can't wait to open a bottle of bubbly. I brought the Clicquot — I can't imagine they stock it on this tiny little rock." Mika seats herself in a chair in the row in front of us and lifts a golden-wrapped bottle of champagne from her designer tote bag. Her colorful silk caftan and oversized sunglasses belong more on the pages of *Vogue* than in this tiny Northern Michigan setting, but I like it. This is the first time we're meeting, and so far, Kerrigan's description of her "quirky and fabulously pretentious" fashion designer friend has been accurate. Kip's and Mika's fathers were co-investors and friends for decades before Kip's father passed away.

"Mika, *love*, at least wait until we reach shore," Stavros purrs in his softly inflected accent as he places a hand on his wife's back and rubs a moment before settling next to her in a hard-backed seat. He crosses his legs at the ankle, sun-kissed skin shimmering in the evening sunlight.

"There's nothing wrong with a little before-dinner aperitif." Mika taps his cheek with her palm. Stavros catches her wrist in his hand and places a chaste kiss on the underside.

"Whatever you say, darling."

"Everyone, meet my gorgeous husband, Stavros." She pecks him on the cheek.

"Nice to meet you." Stavros holds out his hand to me.

"I'm Ryleigh." We shake hands before he does the same to Daniel.

"I didn't believe her at first when she said she was married after knowing the guy for only two weeks," Kerrigan says to me.

"Well, when you know, you know." Mika laces her fingers with Stavros's and pecks him on the cheek again. "This man treats me like a queen."

"You are my queen."

I catch Kerrigan rolling her eyes.

I wonder what it's like to be so doted on. And then I wonder if Stavros's affection for Mika is real. Something about him makes me think he likes to put on a show. The silk button-down, open at the collar to reveal a smattering of dark chest hair, gives him the air of a Mediterranean playboy, which is only accentuated by his sockless feet wrapped in brown Italian-leather loafers. Stavros is startlingly handsome, in an alien sort of way. He's not someone I would be drawn to as a friend or lover, but I like that he's here, adding his own personal pizzazz to our getaway.

"Kerrigan, who is the handsome gentleman waiting for us?" Mika croons.

"Gentleman?" Kerrigan's gaze whips to the shoreline, where a tall, sandy-blond man is waving at us. "Oh, that's no gentleman. That's just Cole. He's the caretaker of Stonecliffe and will be at our beck and call this week."

"He's cute!" Mika's eyes sparkle. As soon as the boat slows, she stands, tote over one shoulder and bottle of Veuve Clicquot in the other hand as she moves across the deck in her Gucci slide sandals. Stavros follows, looking as interested in the new addition of the caretaker as his wife. Kerrigan is behind him, and I fall into step behind her, eager to plant my feet on solid ground again.

"That was the longest thirty minutes of my life," Kip grumbles behind me, and the hairs on my neck instantly stand on end. Kip has been on edge all of this trip. From the moment we left Chicago — him driving and Kerrigan in the front seat, with Daniel and me in back — it's been a cold war between them. I've been tempted to ask Kerrigan what's up with them lately, but I know if I wait long enough, she'll tell me herself. Kerrigan lives her life like an open book — her carefree judgments and inconsiderate comments filling the space between us like thunder-clouds on an otherwise calm summer day.

"Cole!" Kerrigan's voice simmers with insincerity. "It's so good to see you."

"Likewise." Cole looks uncomfortable when Kerrigan air-kisses his cheek. I wonder if she's indifferent to the effect she has on people, or if she has no concept that they can see through her sickly-sweet tone.

"What time is dinner? We'd like to open this *champs* and have a little cocktail before the food is ready." Mika winks at Cole and raises the bottle to him. "Handsome strangers are always welcome."

Kip breezes by all of us, his leather sneakers thumping along the wooden dock and then off into the sand. "Cole, my man! Have you given any more thought to what we talked about on the phone a few months ago?"

Cole's face darkens. "Nope. Still not interested in selling."

Anger flickers in Kip's eyes before he continues. "You're missing out on a life-changing opportunity — don't say I didn't warn you. So which villa are we in? I've got to finish a few emails before I can even think about drinking."

Mika seems oblivious to the shade Kip is throwing, her hands too busy hovering at Cole's shoulder as she steps off the dock and into the sand.

"Wi-Fi isn't working," Cole announces.

"No internet at all?" Stavros pouts.

Kip huffs, already making his way up the rocky trail.

"You'd think he'd offer to take a few bags," Kerrigan says under her breath. The tone of her words chills like a winter wind.

"I've got them." Cole throws Mika's duffel over his shoulder and then lifts Kerrigan and Kip's luggage easily before

9

nodding for us to follow him. We work our way through the sand and up to a trail that weaves around boulders and wildflowers before ascending to the grounds of the estate. Stonecliffe Manor dominates the view. The stately Tudor-style mansion with its gables and gardens looks plucked from the English countryside. Vibrant green hedges flank the gray stone path that leads under the old carriageway and entrance. A half-dozen smaller stone villas, obviously the newest additions to the property, anchor the expansive gardens on the north side. Kip is already moving in long strides to what looks like the largest villa.

"All the villas are guest suites," Cole explains. "The pool is heated and available to you twenty-four seven. I can schedule a masseuse or anything else you'd like this week — just let me know. Dinner is at seven every night. We can do some day trips, or if anyone wants to go fishing, I can take you to some secret fishing holes and then prepare the catch for dinner." Cole chances a glance over his shoulder. Stavros and Daniel, the only two of our group who might be interested in a chartered fishing trip, aren't paying attention.

"Which villa has the best view? I'll take that one." Stavros wraps an arm around Mika's shoulders as they walk.

"They all have a great view, but the Chippewa has the best view of the bridge." Cole points at the green suspension bridge in the distance that spans the waters where Lake Michigan and Lake Huron meet.

"Perfect." Stavros kisses Mika. I think how lucky they are to share their love so openly.

"So, how long have you lived here, Cole?" Mika asks.

"All of my life, short of a few summers I spent working on the cargo ships in the lake."

"Longshoreman, huh?" Stavros comments. "Tough job."

Cole nods, seemingly uninterested in the conversation. "Tougher than I could have imagined. Found out quick that boat life isn't for me."

"Ever get down to the big city?" Mika's eyes never leave the broad stretch of Cole's back as he walks.

10

"Spent time in Chicago, Detroit, Cleveland, Buffalo. All the major hubs when I worked the lakes."

"Bet you know these islands inside and out."

"I've fished, camped, or worked on just about every stretch of shoreline this state has," Cole confirms.

"Worldly," Daniel comments under his breath so only I can hear.

"Shh." I elbow him quickly.

"Ow, Rye. Stop being abusive," my friend complains, pretending to block my next blow with his notebook.

"The hot tub is next to the pool, and you'll find towels and other pool things under the pergola," Cole interjects.

"Ooh, I'll be at the pool. Catch up with you later," Daniel says.

"But what about the tour?" I have to raise my voice because Daniel is already jogging off in the direction of the infinity pool that overlooks the bluff.

"Fill me in later!"

I frown. I practically had to twist Daniel's arm to come this week. He complained about deadlines, but he always has deadlines. Plus, he can write in paradise just as well as in his one-bedroom walk-up in the city.

"You brought us a shy one," Stavros hums as he watches Daniel, who's just reached the pool and is peeling off his T-shirt before settling into a lounger.

"He's a classic introvert."

"Are you telling me he's not going to warm up to us?" Mika cocks an eyebrow at me. "You're bold to bring him. Like throwing him to the wolves once we've had a few drinks."

I laugh, but something tells me she's not kidding. Mika has been watching Cole like she's a wolf and he's her prey. I wonder if Stavros has noticed or if he's indifferent to her flirty innuendos.

"I'll get him to open up. I've got a week. I can get anyone to open up to me in a week. I just need a little time to draw him into my web." Stavros is positively glowing, and it's the

11

first time I actually believe what he's saying. He strikes me as the kind of pretentious asshole whom everyone hates until they get to know him. He's friendly, unfiltered, and handsome in that Greek lothario sort of way. I see why Mika married him after just two weeks.

"You make it sound like we're part of an evil cult or something." Mika waves him off.

"A kinky cult, maybe." Stavros rubs his palms together eagerly.

"Leave the boy alone, or he'll never come back," Mika says as she comes to a stop behind Cole.

"This is the Ojibway villa." Cole points. "Two queen beds, full en suite bath, kitchenette, plus a Jacuzzi."

"Daniel and I will take this one," I offer, already setting my backpack and travel bag on the brick walkway in front of the polished teak door.

"You two got plans for that Jacuzzi?" Stavros winks at me.

Kerrigan stifles a giggle. "Daniel and Ryleigh aren't dating. She's got a boyfriend back in the city. Right, Ryleigh?"

"Oh, really?" Stavros narrows his sparkling eyes at me. "So, Daniel is single?"

"Uh . . . yes?" I'm wondering why Stavros is so interested in Daniel's single status when his wife is inches away.

"Shh, baby. Let the kids be this week." Mika giggles, and I bristle at her words, probably because I do feel like a child next to the success and ostentatious wealth she and Kerrigan exude. Daniel and I are definitely the odd pair out in this group. We're both struggling artists — him a freelance journalist, and me trying to catch my break in theater. I have dreams of working as a director's assistant or production manager someday, but so far, I can't land anything more than a job as a backstage grunt painting sets and taking coffee orders for everyone else. In fact, hustling as a receptionist at the athletic club where Kerrigan and Kip are members is how we met, and it's her connections that landed me temporary work at the Park Theater in Chicago's South Loop. I'd been passed over for every position I'd applied for before that. I have no doubt Kerrigan called in a favor to get me on the playbill. Before that moment, I'd always been a nameless stagehand, but in my first production at the Park Theater, I'd shown enough initiative behind the scenes to be listed as assistant to the artistic director.

I'm thankful Kerrigan put in a good word and only a little bitter that even behind the curtain, it still matters who you know.

"Looks like Kip has already set up shop in the Chippewa—"

"Bastard took the biggest villa," Stavros interrupts Cole.

"Well, he is the reason we're here," Mika reminds him.

"You two can take the Mackinaw." Cole indicates the villa next to mine. "On the other side of Kip, just beyond the grove of cedars, you'll find the Keweenaw. It hasn't had the same updates as the others, and it's taken this week by a film crew."

"A film crew?" I question.

Cole nods, rolling his eyes. "They're investigating paranormal activity on the island. They asked to stay in the manor house — the locals have lots of stories of hauntings and ghost sightings over the years — but Stonecliffe Manor needs a lot of work. The entire top floor should be condemned after all the water damage we had this spring."

I follow Cole's line of sight to take in the mansion, four elegant gables shooting into the sky. A sun-faded sign at the front gate reads, *Welcome to Stonecliffe Manor*. In truth, the building looks out of place in this beachy paradise, like something out of a gothic novel. It gives me a shiver, and I glance away. It isn't hard to imagine a spooky face appearing in one of the upstairs windows on a dark night.

"The Mackinaw is fine for us." Mika interrupts my thoughts as Cole sets her duffel next to the door of her villa. She smiles at him and then asks, "And where are you staying this week?"

Cole raises one eyebrow and then mumbles, "Other side of the bluff and down the stone path is the caretaker's cabin. I'll see you tonight at the cliff's edge for dinner. If you need anything before that, you can pick up the phone at the pergola — it rings my cell directly. Or you can dial 911 for an emergency."

"The only emergency we're gonna have this week is if the champagne runs out," Mika quips.

"Good. Because service hardly works on the best of days since the ice tore up communication lines under the lake this winter. I've got a satellite phone, but that only works if there isn't cloud cover."

"It sounds like you're telling me we're cut off from the outside world." Mika's face falls.

"Unless you want to pony up a half a million for repairs. Stonecliffe is low on the priority list because it's uninhabited most of the year," Cole says. "You wanted rest and relaxation." He shrugs as if being cut off from the outside world is normal. "Oh, and the lawyer is waiting to read the will at the outdoor bar under the pergola whenever you're ready."

Mika arches an eyebrow at Kerrigan before picking up her bag and slipping into her villa. Stavros follows her, leaving Cole, Kerrigan, and me standing in the yard. I feel something unspoken pass between them, like two people with a secret shared history.

Cole's voice drops an octave. "Good to see you back on the island, Ker. It's been a long time."

"Thanks." She pauses awkwardly. "I'm just going to freshen up after that choppy boat ride." Her tone is clipped, and I know instantly that she's blowing him off. "Can you drop my bags at my villa?"

She's already stalking off across the yard. Kip steps out of their villa then, phone to his ear, concentrating on whatever conversation he's having.

Cole's eyes gleam as he watches Kerrigan go.

There's definitely something going on between them. Kerrigan's icy glare is all the evidence I need. A thrill runs through me as I wonder how this week will unfold.

So many new personalities. So many new secrets.

CHAPTER THREE: KERRIGAN

"You're vibrating," I mutter. Kip's eyes dart to his phone rattling on the table in our villa. Mika's name lights up the screen. He hits decline and turns the phone over. I can't tell if he meant for me to see her name or not, but I did, and it only stokes my anger.

"This is our chance to reconnect, but I don't know how I'm supposed to do that when there's a computer screen between us."

"Stop being dramatic, Kerrigan."

Kip knows I hate being belittled. Even worse, I can't stand being ignored, so why he chooses to do it so often is beyond me.

"I have so many good memories on this island, and you're ruining them." I tuck the last of my sweaters into the bureau and then slump into a chaise in the corner of the room opposite my husband.

He's still ignoring me, typing furiously. I sigh, realizing I can't even provoke him into paying attention to me. I wonder what his reaction would be if he knew Cole and I hooked up when I was in high school. It was casual, a few summers of fun with a childhood sweetheart. Our nights might have been fueled by beer and cheap wine back then, but our passion wasn't. From the moment we met, something crackled and hummed between us like a live wire. I still remember every stolen second we spent together on Stonecliffe. If I'm honest with myself, it's probably the reason I never pushed Kip to spend time here.

I bite back angry tears. "You know it's pretty hard to make a baby when we don't even fuck anymore."

Kip's gaze turns dark. He glances over the top of his screen long enough to land a single death blow. "It's pretty hard to make a baby when you're so cold I can't even get my dick hard."

And there it is.

My husband's true feelings. They rarely make an appearance nowadays.

"You're a selfish asshole. I can't believe you fooled me long enough to get a ring on my finger."

"I fooled you?" He chuckles, and it turns my blood to lava. "More like you bagged a sugar daddy to support your pathetic art gallery. You know my work is the only reason you have a career. It's not like you have a skill or any inherent talent beyond bedding wealthy assholes like me."

I think of Cole. I'm tempted to tell Kip that the man I've always held a flame for is now the caretaker of this estate we're staying at, but there's no point in poking the bear. Flirting with Cole this week will do that job for me. And I don't even think Cole would mind being used as a pawn in my little game of revenge. I saw the way his eyes lingered on my cleavage, memories of a younger us probably flashing through his mind.

"Why don't you go out to the pool with your friends and sip mimosas?" Kip's tone is dismissive and uninterested. I'd gladly take his anger over this indifference.

The ache lodged in my throat is undeniable. I want to scream, hurl insults his way, but deep down, I'm afraid he's right. My creativity waned in college when the real world hit and I realized I'd never be able to keep a roof over my head as a working artist. Oil pastels, charcoal, and watercolors don't pay the bills.

"You act like I'm just some bored housewife with a hobby." My voice cracks on the last word. I think of my first gallery showing, when Kip bought me a diamond tennis bracelet to celebrate. He was so sweet and thoughtful, but at some point between there and here, he changed into someone I never would have married. I wonder if that's the normal course for most marriages, or if I had a hand in changing the man I'd vowed to spend my life with.

Kip and I never had a traditional arrangement. His appetite for variety was the only thing he refused to compromise on, and I was okay with that . . . under the condition that he be discreet. But the longer we're married, the less and less he seems to care about my feelings or reputation, or discretion.

"Everyone knows art galleries and charities are just high-end money-laundering schemes. I support your dream, Kerrigan, but when it stops making money . . ."

I think about a time not that long ago when he wrote a check for the down payment on my gallery and said you can't put a price on dreams. "My art is the only thing that gets me by some days."

"Then it sounds like it's time to schedule your therapist twice a week." With that, he's back behind his computer screen, leaving me crushed and more determined than ever to make him pay for the pain that he's inflicted.

I struggle to pinpoint when the unraveling of our marriage began. But it can't unravel now; I've invested too much into this.

Before I can respond, there's a knock at the door of the villa. I can see Cole's profile in the reflection of the mirror over the bureau, and my heart thrums in my chest.

I jump to my feet, swiping at tears as I cross the room and swing the door open wide. "Hi."

"Hey." My skin tingles with awareness as Cole's eyes pass over my form quickly, and then he averts them entirely. "The lawyer is waiting to read the will. He's anxious to get off the island."

"Is everyone else ready?" I ask. Cole quietly smolders. "Ready and waiting on two."

"Great." I leave the door open and return to the bed, grabbing my bag and not bothering to utter a word to my husband. "I'm ready."

Following Cole down the walkway, I stumble on a brick when I hear Kip slam the door of our villa, feet scuffling on the stone behind us.

Cole's cheap cologne lingers on the breeze and sends a rush of memories through my veins.

I already know my husband is cheating on me. What's the harm if I have a little fun with an old flame this week? Kip will be so buried in work, I don't think he'll even notice. And if he does . . . Well, I'll cross that bridge when I get there.

CHAPTER FOUR: RYLEIGH

"And the last order of business . . ." The lawyer turns over the final sheet of paper in his stack as the evening sun splits through the olive branches clinging to the pergola. "*This place.*"

I tune back in to the lawyer's words as Kip sips his drink across from me, a mix of bourbon, grapefruit juice, and honey, eyeing on the last paper in the lawyer's hands.

"There's no lien on the property," the lawyer reads. "It looks like profit from the rental of the villas offsets upkeep, plus a little extra each year, so that's good news. And the ownership breakdowns . . ." He scans the text. "Kip, Kerrigan, and Mika each own twenty-two per cent of the shares of Stonecliffe. Jon Caruso, your father's best friend—" he looks at Kip — "owns twenty-three per cent."

"Come again?" Kip's eyes flare. "What about the remaining eleven per cent?"

The lawyer shrugs. "Cole Mayer, the caretaker, owns five per cent as he always has . . ." He's still working down the page. One eyebrow arches then, as if he's just stumbled across a surprise. "Everything looks standard, with the exception of one inheritor." The lawyer reaches the end of the page and then flips the sheet over and adds it to his stack. "Ryleigh Halstrom."

Kerrigan turns to me with accusation in her expression. "*Ryleigh?*"

"Me?" I'm positive I've misheard him. My focus has been all over the place today. From the moment I told Kerrigan I would come on this trip, I've been wondering if I would live to regret it. The thinly veiled tension that simmers between Kip and Kerrigan is annoying at best, but now, well . . .

"Are you Ryleigh?" The lawyer's forehead crinkles with annoyance as he looks at me.

"Yes," I admit. Why Kip's father would mention me directly in his will is lost on me.

"He left you six per cent of the estate."

"Why?" Kip and I ask at the same time.

Kerrigan's normally cold and distant expression hardens in a way I can't quite place.

"Looks like he thought highly of you. I can't say why he did it, but he did mention that 'Ryleigh deserves it.'"

"What does that mean?" Frustration laces all of Kerrigan's words.

"You must have misheard. I only met Mr. Lange a few times. I wouldn't think he'd even know my name."

"Well, he did. And he was looking out for you." The lawyer smiles.

"You must have read it wrong." Kip swipes the paper from the lawyer's stack. "Where's the deed? He would have to update the deed and get permission from the other shareholders to transfer ownership shares of Stonecliffe."

"Not when it's in a trust and the slice he's transferring is his. If he were proposing to amend the shares and taking from some of yours, he would need permission, but since he's passed away, the shares are split between the other owners, outside of the last six per cent. The final six per cent is Ryleigh's."

"This doesn't make sense," Kerrigan murmurs.

"This is bullshit. Selling this fucking rock is going to be impossible." Kip stands, the feet of his chair clattering across the clay tiles as he pushes away from the table. "There has to be a way to undo this. Can I just buy her out?"

"If she wants to sell." The lawyer shrugs, then stands up himself. "Do you?"

Everyone's eyes fall on me then. "I-I . . ."

"You all look so shocked," Mika purrs as she pours more champagne into her glass, "but there must be a reason Kip's father wanted Ryleigh to have a piece of the island."

"And what reason could that possibly be? To take one more cheap shot at me from the grave?" Kip says with indignation. He doesn't leave time for anyone to respond. He's already stalking to his villa, back turned to us and a string of curses in his wake.

"Well, my work here is done. If you have any questions, you can call me." The attorney tosses a few business cards on the table, leaves the stack of paperwork, and then pauses to speak to Kerrigan. "Make sure he signs these when he calms down from his tantrum. I'll need the signed copies once you're back in the city."

Kerrigan rubs a hand over her face and then nods. "Thanks for coming all the way up here. I know my father-in-law would have appreciated it."

"Henry didn't give a shit about anyone else. I was surprised when he asked me to amend the ownership of this place, but it's not my job to question him."

"I understand," Kerrigan sighs. "He must have had his reasons."

Maybe he did. But for the life of me, I can't figure out what they are.

"Have a great week — please don't forget to drop these off at my office when you return to civilization."

"*If* we return," Stavros says under his breath.

Mika elbows him once. "Why would you say that?"

"Kip might take off all our heads first. Saying he's bent out of shape about the reading of his dad's will is the understatement of the century."

"Don't be so dramatic. He'll calm down, and until he does, we'll just stay out of his way." Mika waves him off and then brings the champagne glass to her lips.

21

"I've never been happier to be poor," Daniel grunts at my side as he stands. I don't think anyone else heard him, and I wouldn't care if they did. Right now, I can't say I disagree.

I follow him as he walks in the direction of the pool that flanks the pergola. The Olympic-sized pool stretches to the edge of the limestone cliff that rises at least one hundred feet above Lake Michigan. To the east and spanning the sparkling waters of both Lakes Michigan and Huron hangs the five-mile-long Mackinac Bridge. The island lies far enough away that the traffic traversing the distance between the Lower and Upper Peninsulas of Michigan is noiseless. Just a reminder of the rural tranquility this little slice of island paradise offers.

"I don't know how you stand these people. They're so pretentious." Daniel's scathing words pull me from my thoughts.

"They're not so bad. They've just been going through a rough time," I defend.

"That was intense." Kerrigan walks up behind us. Daniel doesn't bother to turn, but I do. "I can't figure out why Henry Lange would leave you a piece of this island."

"Me either." The announcement still has me reeling. I now own a bigger share than Cole, and he's lived here all his life, from the way Kerrigan talks.

"Kip's probably right. One last posthumous *fuck you*." Daniel is doodling in the margins of the open notebook in his lap.

"No, I don't think so. That old man was a brilliant businessman. He did this for a reason," Kerrigan reveals.

I squirm on the pool lounger, feeling the spotlight on me.

"I spent so much time on this island as a child," Kerrigan begins. "You've never even been here before. Don't you think it's weird?"

"Yes," I answer honestly.

A pregnant pause lingers between us. "My best memories are of playing in this bay," Kerrigan watches the waves in the distance. "When our fathers bought this island, they wanted to preserve its natural beauty for future generations. It was the

1960s. They were all barefoot, free-love hippies building their own little slice of paradise. Livin' the dream." A sentimental smile turns her lips. "I used to imagine my own kids playing on this shore, Kip showing them how to fish, like my dad showed me. He always liked to wake up early, before the sun rose and while the fog still blanketed the water. He'd row us out into the bay, light a cigar, and drop our bobbers in the water. And then he'd ask me how things were going. He was so patient as he told me about the different types of fish, his dreams for the family and the future of the estate — I always wanted to marry someone like him. Guess I missed the mark with Kip."

Sadness creeps into her words. "Mom always complained that Dad worked too much — always out on the water away from the family — but he wanted to give us a better life. He invested in multiple properties over the years that still pay dividends into the trust every month. He was a dreamer, a total romantic, but he also knew how to execute and strategize his way to success. I think my mom resented him sometimes for being so smart and capable — whatever he put his mind to, he achieved. And the funny thing is, Kip reminded me of my dad when we first met, all big dreams and ambition. Now, instead of living happily ever after, it looks like I'll be planning a divorce in paradise. Kip's been so difficult lately. I'm trying to be patient, but I think we're both at our limit."

Daniel huffs, closing his notebook and tucking it under his chaise before standing and peeling the T-shirt over his shoulders.

I watch his lean form dive into the deep end of the pool, slicing through the water with precise strokes.

"I was always scared to swim, scared of the water, unless I was with my dad. He made me feel safe. I used to crave the smell of fresh rain and cigar smoke in the air. Even after he died, I swear I could smell it at random times in the house. But now . . ." She swipes at tears in her eyes. "Now, every day with Kip feels like I'm drowning."

23

CHAPTER FIVE: COLE

"Sunscreen, ladies?" I approach the small group gathered at the pool with a sideways smile.

Kerrigan's face falls. She's probably wondering if I heard her talking about the state of her marriage. I did, but I won't let on. I'm glad to know that somewhere under that chic facade, she's a broken mess just like the rest of us.

The only difference between people like her and people like me is that she prefers to hide her pain, whereas I wear mine on my sleeve. Some might call it a chip on my shoulder, but I like to think of it as stubborn authenticity. Most people put on some kind of pretentious air to avoid sharing their pain, but I'd hoped Kerrigan wouldn't be one of them. Growing up, she was always so open and carefree, easy to laugh and always down for some flirty fun for the few weeks of summer she spent on the island. Life seems to have taken a toll, though. Where light used to sparkle in her dark-brown irises, a bitter edge now shines.

Without waiting for a reply, I squirt a dollop of the cream into my hand and begin to smear it across her shoulders.

"Cole!" she shrieks, but a smile is already playing on her lips.

"Protection is protocol at Stonecliffe." I grin, rubbing the lotion along the exposed angles of her back.

"I wish we would've known ahead of time about the film crew. They're not going to be filming us, are they?" Kerrigan asks. Something tells me she'd probably like the attention, but I don't say so.

"No, they've been told to leave the guests alone. They should be out of sight this week, but if you're bothered, let me know, and I'd be more than happy to have words with them."

"Couldn't they come in the off season?"

"I told them we were booked through Halloween outside of one villa this week only. I was hoping they'd choose not to come, but they arrived last night. They did a Halloween investigation last year, and apparently they captured enough evidence on their little gadgets that it warranted a return trip. I think they're hoping to sell the special to Netflix or one of the other big streaming companies, but it seems like a long shot. Not because Stonecliffe isn't haunted — I don't know anything about that — but because there doesn't seem to be a working brain cell between the three of them. They already tried to sit me down for an interview."

"You didn't do it?"

"What can I tell them? Nothing they don't already know. I told them they'd be better off talking to one of the old fishermen or someone else from one of the other islands. I don't want to be a part of whatever bullshit they're trying to conjure."

"You don't think Stonecliffe is haunted?" Ryleigh asks.

I think of all the silly, over-the-top paranormal activity shows I've seen on late-night cable television.

"If Stonecliffe is haunted, it's never bothered me. I don't take care of the manor house anyway, and it's hard to see much of anything at night once the fog obscures everything." I think of Kip's dad. He hadn't been to the island in years, but that didn't stop him from taking an active role in its promotion. "Remember the ghost hunts Kip's dad used to host when we were kids?"

Kerrigan laughs loudly. "He was such a horror junkie. His ghost stories around the bonfire were always so creepy, and remember when he set up the film projector and screen so we could watch classic horror movies near the cliff? Those are some of my best memories — terrifying and mesmerizing at the same time."

"I think that's why he wanted to buy the island, because of all the ghost stories that follow this place. Stonecliffe has a lot of bizarre history, but I don't think it's spooky — just weird human shit." I shake my head. "Remember he compiled that book of hauntings and sold it at the local gift shops? *Ghosts of Mackinac* or *Haunted Great Lakes* or whatever?"

"He sent my dad signed copies of both! I still keep them on my bookshelf." Kerrigan giggles. "He was crazy, but it was fun."

"Well, that crazy old man is the reason the film crew is here. He contacted them to do an investigation years ago. I think they only came because . . ." I pause, unwilling to say the next part. Being with Kerrigan feels as easy as when we were kids, and already, I find myself wanting to reveal more than I should about my sketchy past. "Well, let's just say tragedy draws a crowd."

Silence lingers, and I feel like I've stuck my foot in my mouth.

Kerrigan turns her head to the side and pulls her dark waves over one shoulder to give me better access. She's wearing a one-piece black swimsuit with a flimsy cover-up over top, and I take it upon myself to slip my fingers under the edge of her bathing suit to apply the cream. Goose bumps race across her skin, and I imagine her turned on, nipples poking through the delicate fabric of her suit as I run my fingertips across her warm body.

She may be carrying a few more chips on her shoulder than when I saw her last, but she's more beautiful than ever. Kerrigan seems to have aged in reverse. I can only imagine the expensive treatments and skincare routines she probably employs to make that happen.

"Oh! We should explore one of the deserted islands this week! You'll take us, right, Cole?" she asks.

"Sure. Whatever you want," I mumble, thinking I haven't been to one of those islands in years — probably not since the last time Kerrigan was on this island with me.

"You have magic hands," Kerrigan purrs, voice throaty and low, and I know I've done it. She's as turned on as I am. I know, because that's how it's always been between us. Flirty glances and simmering sexual tension.

"The better to serve you with," I reply, every word laden with innuendo.

"Mm. So, how have you been? Really. How's island life treating you?"

I'm not sure how much to reveal or just how much she knows about what happened last summer. Most people don't venture to ask me this question because a simple internet search will reveal everything they want to know. I imagine Kerrigan knows exactly how I've been, but I appreciate the pretense of the conversation that most people around here don't afford me.

"It's been a good start to the summer. Never thought I'd find myself living full-time on this island again — but hey, another day in paradise. I can't complain."

"Until winter ice takes out the power," Kerrigan comments.

"Right. Well, I mostly can't complain. I'm thankful Lyra's dad offered me the caretaker position. Not sure where I would have landed if he hadn't."

"There's nobody more qualified to take care of Stonecliffe than you."

Her statement feels laced with judgment. I'm not sure what to say, so I ask the question that's been lingering in the back of my mind since she arrived. "So why stay away from the island for so long?"

"That's a long and not very interesting story."

"Give me the quick and dirty version." I angle around her, sliding sunscreen from her shoulder to her wrist and back again.

27

"Well, I've spent the last few years getting my art gallery off the ground. I knew the art business was hard, but I didn't expect it to be almost impossible."

I nod, encouraging her to continue.

"And Kip's business requires a hundred-hour workweek."

"Sounds like he's in the wrong business," I comment, hoping she doesn't take too much offense, even though the edge in my voice is razor-sharp.

"He's committed. I can't complain."

"But it kept you away from the island."

"Well, I'm back now." She catches my eye, smiling softly.

"Is it everything you remembered?"

"Right down to the boy I had a crush on."

Something flips inside me — anticipation at spending so much time with her this week, I think. "Glad to hear that."

"Hey, crew." Lyra saunters up to a lounger and flops down in it. The air suddenly feels pregnant, like she's just stumbled into a situation where she doesn't belong. It's been years since Lyra and I spent so much time together and I wouldn't exactly say I've enjoyed it. Her haughty arrogance is hard to swallow on a good day. Lyra's outspoken nature has always made her intimidating; I confess it's one of the things that drew me to her early on. But now? Now it's the very thing that leaves me on edge in her presence. Something about her time here this summer feels suspicious and makes me feel like I'm under a microscope — like she's been sent to be my babysitter.

A heavy silence lingers in the air, and with the sunshine glinting off Kerrigan's hair and her full lips pressed together like she wants to say more, I can almost imagine that we're fifteen again, just back from swimming and lying by the pool as her parents drink champagne and my dad stumbles around the estate, making sure everything is perfect for them.

The apple hasn't fallen far from the tree, but of course, it never does. We've both turned into our parents, and something about that excites me, like we're strangers meeting for the first time, but also feeling a familiar twinge of déjà vu. "I'm surprised you didn't make it up for a few girls' weekends, at least."

"That sounds fun," Ryleigh comments, her gaze lingering on her friend as he backstrokes the distance of the pool. She's gnawing on her bottom lip like she's got the weight of the world on her shoulders. If I've learned anything taking care of the tourists who come to this island, it's that people always tell you who they are — just not in the way you'd expect. They often linger on superficial conversation and reveal their secrets in the things left unsaid.

"Oh! Can you take us to the main island tomorrow for shopping? I can't wait to show Ryleigh what life in Yooperland is like," Kerrigan says.

"Yooperland?" Ryleigh arches an eyebrow.

"Locals are called Yoopers — you know, the Upper Peninsula. The *U.P.*," Kerrigan explains.

"I don't know if you can call Mackinac Island the Upper Peninsula," I say.

"Oh, it is." Kerrigan nods keenly.

I smile. "All right, then. A shopping trip to the big island tomorrow. Do you think everyone will want to go? Because the catamaran you came in on is scheduled for service this week. Not sure when the crew is coming to pick it up, but once it's gone, we'll only have the four-seater or the Chris-Craft. It seats six, but that old engine doesn't have the power for open water like it used to."

"Hmm, girls-only field trip, then." Kerrigan seems to remember that Ryleigh is beside her. "Is that okay? Daniel won't mind staying back with the guys, will he? Kip will camp out in the villa all day, working. We'll be lucky if we catch a rare sighting of him at dinner, so it will just be Daniel and Stavros during the day tomorrow."

"He'll be fine." Ryleigh waves a hand toward him in the pool. "He'll swim, write, repeat. He's pretty low-maintenance."

"Perfect." Kerrigan claps her hands, and it makes me glad that she hasn't lost that childlike energy that once drew me to her. "Want to come with us, Lyra?"

Lyra grunts softly in reply, fixated on her phone as her thumbs move across the screen at fever pitch. It must be important, whoever she's sending a message to. My instincts tell me she's up to something, but I can't quite figure out what it could be.

Kerrigan frowns once she realizes that Lyra is ignoring her. She catches my attention for a moment, eyes widening with unspoken words. I wonder briefly why we lost touch. And then I think of what the guys at the Pink Pony will say when they hear she's back. I've spent a lot of time pining for this woman over the years, and while I keep my thoughts pretty close to the vest, with a few drinks, memories of her invariably slip out like lake water through my hands.

I don't make it to the big island often; the weekly delivery of supplies by boat means that I'm secluded on Stonecliffe for weeks at a time. But when I do make it to Mackinac, I always stop at the Pink Pony. It's the low-key watering hole the locals like to frequent, and I've been tossing back whatever's on tap there since before I was of legal age to drink. If I time it right, I can even catch up with my childhood best friend, Jake. But then, if I tell Jake why I'm on the big island — for a shopping trip with Kerrigan, *the* Kerrigan — I'll never hear the end of it.

"What time do you want to leave tomorrow? Right after breakfast?" I ask.

Kerrigan scrutinizes me, hand blocking the glint of sunshine coming from over my shoulder. "That sounds perfect, Captain."

Every nerve in me tingles when she calls me that. It's what she always called me when we were teenagers and I'd take her out on the boat. *Captain Cole.* Does she know what she's doing to me when she uses that nickname? I think she must, and for the first time since she arrived, I'm really fucking glad she's here. Lyra has been a fun distraction, but Kerrigan is back. And if I have it my way, she won't be leaving again.

I was sad to hear that her father died last year. I remember him vaguely — tall and broad with a gravelly edge in his voice from too many cigars. My father was the caretaker of Stonecliffe then, and I think how funny it is that I'm repeating the same cycle now. The Mayer family has haunted these islands for generations, first logging the woods and then fishing the blue waters. Mackinac Island and the mainland ports that service it have always been swamped with visitors coming for a taste of the old days. Outside of emergency vehicles, there's no motorized transport on these islands, and the powers that be are invested in keeping it that way.

The fact that Stonecliffe Island is still entirely privately owned is rare. Most of the islands around here are either protected state land, owned by corporations, or divided and parceled out for mansions and luxury estates that sit empty most of the year. With the way things are going, I'll probably be the last generation to work on these islands. And anyway, working with tourists is a world apart from commercial fishing or logging.

I'm grateful to still be here, but the fact that my future on this island lies entirely in Lyra's father's hands is a tough pill to swallow. He saved my ass from sitting in a jail cell, though. And it's only because of him and his team of lawyers on staff that he was able to beat the civil lawsuit the girl's family brought against the estate after last summer.

Without Jon Caruso stepping in, Stonecliffe Island would have been underwater and sold to the highest bidder long ago.

CHAPTER SIX: RYLEIGH

"Don't forget to get me something awesome, Rye!" Daniel's voice jerks me from my text messages as Cole eases the boat away from the dock. I wave at Daniel as he stands barefoot on the shore, seeing us off for our shopping trip.

"He's so adorable. How long have you been dating?" Mika gestures to my friend.

"Oh, we're not dating." I told her this yesterday, but I assume she forgot with all the champagne she was drinking. "We've known each other since elementary school." I glance down at my empty phone screen. "I'm seeing someone back in the city. He works all the time, though. He couldn't get the time off to come. Plus, it's sort of new. I don't want to be too clingy or whatever, asking him to come on a week-long trip so soon."

"Is your gaydar broken? Daniel likes boys," Kerrigan tells Mika flippantly. She was distracted at breakfast this morning, and I can't help but wonder if she and Kip are fighting again. He was absent, and at this point, nobody asks where he is because Kerrigan always has the same answer. Plus, it seems to put her in a bad mood.

"They're just so close. I figured he was probably bi, but kids these days don't get caught up with labels anyway. Love is love." Mika shrugs her off.

Cole aims the boat in the direction of the Mackinac Bridge. From a distance, the five-mile suspension bridge that connects the peninsulas is deceiving, but as we get closer, the staggering size of it is awe-inspiring.

Kerrigan's voice interrupts my thoughts. "I've been trying to nail down Ryleigh and her new man for a double date with Kip and me, but she's got herself a proper workaholic."

"Sounds like a keeper." Mika winks at me, and I blush. "I wouldn't mind being a kept woman. It's exhausting running a business."

I nod, listening to Mika as I watch Kerrigan. Her eyes are squarely on Cole's back as he maneuvers the boat.

I doubt Kerrigan would admit it to anyone, but she seems more attached to Cole than I would expect. She never mentioned that they dated at one time, and now I think it wasn't because it was insignificant. Maybe it was *too* significant. Maybe there's more to the story of Kerrigan and Cole that she wasn't interested in revisiting.

"So, how long have you been living in the city?" Mika asks, as the white lake cottages along the southern bluff of Mackinac Island come into view. From here they look more like mansions.

"Since college. I graduated with a degree in theater production and set design from Northwestern and never looked back. Daniel and I grew up in the same small farm town in Illinois. I think we were both itching to get out early on, so when opportunity knocked, we both answered. We were roommates for a while, but Daniel needs a lot of quiet time to write. We're both theater nerds and introverts, but he's on another level. We're the kind of friends that shouldn't live together." I end my explanation with a small shrug.

"So, you and Lyra are a thing?" Kerrigan is clearly addressing Cole.

He turns, arching an eyebrow. "Depends who you ask, I guess."

Kerrigan doesn't respond, digesting his words carefully.

We cruise around the north side of the island, and our destination comes into view. Frothy, whitecapped waves kiss the stony shoreline of Mackinac Island. We near the undeveloped side, and Cole eases off the throttle so we're moving slowly around the rocky outcroppings. Shorebirds dip and dive into the waves as they pluck fish from the freshwater. To the east, Lake Huron stretches into the sun-soaked horizon, and to the west, Lake Michigan sparkles and glimmers for as far as the eye can see. They feel more like small oceans than they do inland lakes.

"Fucking tourists leaving their junk everywhere," Cole grunts as we pass a small beach tucked between birches and evergreens. The currents have washed a pile of trash on shore, leaving an array of camping gear all tangled together and caught in the rocks. A tent, a little red cooler, and old beer cans all float in a massive tangle of fishing line.

"Who says it's tourists? Those crusty old fishermen leave nets and junk everywhere," Mika comments.

"Most of the fishermen do their best to clean up after themselves. This island is trashed every year by September — tourists just up and leave their tents and camping chairs and all kinds of shit when they're done like squatters, no regard for the fact that people live here. This is home to a lot of us — would you leave your trash in someone's front yard? These islands are small. If everyone who visited left some junk behind, it'd be a garbage dump by now. The locals spend weeks organizing volunteer clean-ups before winter comes." Cole shakes his head with disgust. "That's why a lot of the locals hate tourist season and the tourists that come along with it."

"But the money the tourists bring supports the economy," Mika says.

Cole just shrugs. "It is what it is. The only advice I have for you is if you stop in at the Pink Pony, avoid using the 'T' word and you'll get better service."

Silence falls as the pile of trash fades in the distance.

This place is paradise, but why does it seem like not everyone feels the same?

"Well, ladies. This is where I leave you." Cole's tone is low, rumbling like the boat's motor as we pull up to a weathered

34

dock at the end of the marina. Large catamarans, private yachts, and even a small cruise ship are anchored in the crystal-blue bay, while dozens of small boats are docked at the marina. Historic Victorian homes line the shore like rows of Easter eggs, elegant front gardens with sharply trimmed hedges flanking the entrances as tourists shuffle along the sidewalks. It feels like we've stepped into a time warp, and as I walk off the boat, the first thing that registers is the soft clip-clop of horse hooves.

"It's even more gorgeous than I remember." Kerrigan's eyes shift along the Victorian rooftops. "Most of the homes are inns and B&Bs now." She seems to be talking to herself more than us. "Business seems good." A frown flits across her face. "Maybe I should work Kip for an investment property on the big island. I bet it'd do well with my eye for interior design and his . . . *money*." She cracks a grin then as she nudges my shoulder like a schoolgirl with a secret.

"You should talk to him about it," I offer lamely. I've never been in a position to ponder future investments. It takes everything in me each month just to make rent. Kerrigan is very open about her wealthy lifestyle. I appreciate it because I feel like I always have more I can learn about financial things, but most days, it's so far out of my realm of experience that I can't help but be awkward.

"Well, I'm gonna run to the general store for a few things, and then I'll camp out at the Pink Pony until you ladies are ready to leave." Cole pauses at Kerrigan's side on the dock, his voice lowering. "Welcome home." Kerrigan's and Cole's eyes meet for a beat before he whispers, "Text me when you need me."

Kerrigan nods, unable to tear herself away from his icy blue gaze.

"Oh, a local leathermaker!" Mika adjusts her tote on her shoulder before heading off the dock and stopping at the first shop on the corner. "I'll take one of *everything*."

I laugh, wondering if she's serious as I trail behind her. The chemistry between Cole and Kerrigan is palpable, and

I can't stand to breathe it in a second longer. When I first met Kerrigan and Kip, I thought the sparks that flew between them were from sizzling chemistry, but now I realize it was deep-seated tension with moments of thinly veiled tolerance.

"Are you the designer?" Mika asks the shopkeeper.

"I'm all the things." The woman smiles broadly.

"Really? I own a storefront in the West Loop." Mika pauses, as if this should mean something to the woman. When she doesn't respond, Mika continues, "*In Chicago.*" Mika surveys the whole shop, leather handbags, totes, belts, and wallets decorating every available inch of wall space.

"Oh. Well, the leather I use is entirely repurposed."

"Is it sourced locally?" Mika asks.

"Mostly." The woman nods. "A lot of it I find right here on the island. Saddle leather always has a lovely worn patina that my customers seem to find desirable."

"Your craftsmanship is to die for. Do you ever do bulk orders? I'd love to sell something like this in my store." She's running her fingertips along the leather grain of the bag nearest her. It curves elegantly in the shape of a saddle bag. A strap with a rose-gold buckle holds it together, and while it's not my style, I can see why others would like it. It's a beautiful bag, hand-stitched, and every piece entirely unique from the next. I inhale the soft oiled-leather scent of the shop and grin when Mika purrs, "Isn't is lush, Ryleigh? You would wear this bag, right? It looks just like vintage Dior. Stavros would love this."

"It's beautiful," I agree.

"We'll take three." Kerrigan saunters in, cheeks flushed like a schoolgirl. Did she and Cole have words? I get the impression that if Kerrigan was interested, Cole would be ready and waiting to sweep her off her feet.

"Three, ma'am? They're $750 each."

"They're perfect. Plus, I know that sparkle in Mika's eye. She's bound to walk out of here with something anyway. This will be the perfect souvenir for the three of us to remember our day on the island."

"For us?" I stumble over my words. "I'm not accepting that."

"Oh, nonsense. I've taken you out for dinners in the city that cost more than that. It's a gift."

"Yeah, but . . ." The truth is, Kerrigan always pays when we go out for dinner, and she's got expensive taste. I knew the bottles of Veuve Clicquot didn't come cheap, but I never dreamed she was dropping $750 on a dinner tab when we went out.

"I want to do this." Kerrigan places a hand on my shoulder, smiling softly. "For my best friends."

"Kerrigan, inviting me up for the week is more than enough. If anything, I should be buying something for you."

"No, no. I cherish having you in my life. Both of you." She winks at Mika.

"Let her spend Kip's cash, honey," Mika interjects. "It's what she does best. Besides, if that man is going to work himself to death, someone might as well reap the rewards."

Kerrigan doesn't get angry, only offers an amused shrug. "She's not wrong."

"Plus, a bag like this is an investment. So much vegan leather bullshit out there nowadays. This is a classic."

I wonder briefly if I could sell it when I get home and pay my rent with the money, but then I think that Kerrigan is just the type to ask me where my bag is when I show up for our next lunch date with only my trusty old Coach crossbody in tow. I decide not to argue anymore. It's not my place to tell these women how to spend their money.

"So . . . three bags, then?" The shopkeeper smiles.

"Yes, dear." Mika winks. "We'll take these three. And I'll take your business card if you've got one. I'd love to place a special order and see if they sell in my store in the city. I bet they'll fly off the shelves."

"Okay, then. Thank you, ladies." The shopkeeper blushes, sliding a business card across the counter to Mika before wrapping our purchases in tissue paper and slipping them into three separate shopping bags.

"Well, this is a fabulous start to a great day," Kerrigan puffs as we leave the shop. The aromas of homemade fudge and caramel corn waft on the breeze as we make our way down the crowded main street. Horse-drawn carriages pass, shuttling tourists to their destinations like taxi cabs. "I forgot how much I missed the sweet simplicity of this island."

"Ohh, a cheese shop!" Mika veers into a small storefront on the corner where various selections of cured meats and cheeses are on display. "I'll take one of *everything.*"

I giggle as I realize that's exactly what she said in the last store. Shopping with an unlimited budget is a luxury I've never experienced before.

"Oh! Goat cheese! This would be the perfect pairing for dinner tonight . . ." I tune Mika out as she gushes over more local delicacies. I snort-laugh to myself when I realize I would have been better suited to hit the general store and the local watering hole with Cole. I've always been on a cheap beer and boxed wine budget, but it's fun to dip my toes into the lifestyle of a wealthy tourist's wife.

Ten minutes later, we're walking out of Mackinac Cheesemongers & Wine with three hundred dollars' worth of locally made cheese and cured meats and a bottle of sauvignon blanc from a local vintner. I've never felt more spoiled in my life, and I've only been here for less than a day.

"Oh! They do horseback riding!" I catch sight of a sign that advertises a local barn just off the main street offering rides for fifty dollars an hour. "We should try it."

Mika huffs, and Kerrigan visibly shudders. "Never in my life could you get me on one of those beasts. We may be in paradise, but that doesn't mean people don't die."

"What?" I laugh nervously, taken aback by her statement.

"Trust me, honey." Mika waves a hand. "These horses are so overworked giving rides to tourists who don't know the first thing about being on a horse. If you wanna ride, you should come with me to my father's estate in Tuscany. He breeds local mares and stallions and makes damn good money training them."

"Tuscany? *Italy?*" I'll never have the chance to go to Italy. I won't even bother dreaming so big.

"We go every year. You're welcome to tag along anytime. Bring Daniel too. Stavros would love another guy to hang with while I shop."

"But . . . I'm here now. And look! That horse is so pretty." I point to a dappled gray that's clip-clopping toward us.

"No, she's right, Rye. I've seen a lot of bad stuff happen here." Kerrigan cringes as the horse passes. "When Kip and I met again as adults, we were attending a destination wedding on the island — there were two deaths that weekend. Two!" She holds up two fingers for dramatic effect. "One of the groomsmen on the way to the reception in a horse-drawn carriage stood to make a toast, and it spooked the horses. They took off down the street and took a corner too sharp. The carriage tipped, and he flew off . . . right under the carriage wheel. The entire wedding party watched him bleed out in the street while his girlfriend cradled his head and cried. I'll never forget it, and I haven't ridden a horse since."

"Wow," I breathe. "That's awful."

Mika nods. "They look sweet, but they can kill."

"Sometimes the sweetest poison delivers the deadliest dose." Kerrigan giggles like she knows what she's talking about.

"So, what's the other story?" I'm curious what kinds of other horrors Kerrigan has witnessed in paradise.

"Oh, well . . ." Kerrigan hesitates. "That story is even sadder." She looks down in recollection. "One of Kip's friends, also in the wedding party, hooked up with one of the bride's cousins. He got drunk the last night we were here and tried to impress her by diving off the cliff that overlooks the bay. It didn't turn out well — he misjudged the leap and never surfaced again. We all stood and watched as a pool of blood colored the water crimson. It was horrifying."

"Whew." Mika whistles. "It's a wonder you ever came back to paradise."

"Maybe it's one of the reasons we stayed away so long." Kerrigan shrugs, then unwraps one of the blocks of goat cheese

39

she purchased. "I guess I have post-traumatic stress." She tears a piece from the corner and passes it over her elegant, red lips. "Mm, this cheese is delicious."

I frown, still reeling from her horror stories. "I don't think I'll ever ride a horse again."

"Attagirl." Mika pats my shoulder. "Pretty to look at, terrifying when you get too close. Like people, really."

I force a chuckle. I know Mika is joking, but then I wonder . . . *is she?*

CHAPTER SEVEN: KERRIGAN

"Wanna grasp the shaft and pop my cork, Ker?" Cole appears over my shoulder with a wink. His wayward smile is directed at me, and I hate that I like his attention.

"Excuse me?" I pretend to take offense, but really, I'm so turned on by him. The way his blond hair, slightly too long, curls around his ears makes him look boyish — just as I remember him. But he's taller, and he must work out now because his shoulders are broader and the muscles in his arms are more defined than I remember.

"You heard me," Cole purrs, then lowers his voice an octave so only I can hear. "Wouldn't be the first time."

"Cole!" I chastise, glancing over my shoulder to make sure Kip isn't coming up behind us. Everyone else is gathered around the outdoor table, grape vines twisting in and out of the pergola above our heads as we nibble appetizers and talk about our day on the main island.

"Don't hide that dirty mind from me." Cole presents a bottle of fruity champagne to me. "I was talking about the bottle, Kerrigan, but if you want to take this to a filthy place . . ." He winks and nods in the direction of his cabin.

"Hmm. Ever the pervert, I see." I feel my cheeks heat up. I haven't flirted with someone openly in years, since way before Kip and I were married. It feels good. *Correction*: it feels great. I suddenly wish I would have spent weekends up here alone before this. Seeing Cole again makes me feel alive. Makes me feel something I haven't in a very long time. Maybe ever.

"You bring out the worst in me." Cole pops the cork quickly and then pours me a glass. "Or maybe the best."

I don't answer him, but I feel his words from the tips of my toes on up. Why did we lose contact again? I'm struggling to remember why Cole and I never dated officially. I always thought of him as a fling and nothing more, but why? Why was I so insistent on finding someone who was marriage material, when nothing about the marriage that Kip and I share is exciting or fulfilling?

I sigh, thoughts bubbling in my mind as I sip the champagne. "It's good. Thank you."

"It's been aged for eighteen months right here at the estate."

"Do you have a vintner on site?" Mika sips from her glass, rolling the liquid around in her mouth before swallowing.

"The grapes are grown and processed here at a small vineyard on the west bluff before they're taken to the winemaker on the big island for bottling. Same guy that you bought your bottle from earlier today handles the bottles for the estate," Cole says.

"Mm," Stavros hums as he sips from his freshly poured glass. "Tangy."

"The cooler weather really adds a depth of flavor to the body of the fruit." Cole finishes pouring for the rest of the table just as a young guy holding a professional video camera walks up to us.

"Evening." He acknowledges everyone around the table before a woman with a clipboard steps up behind him. "I'm Jeremy, and this is my assistant, Kacey. I don't know if Cole told you, but we're filming a paranormal investigation at Stonecliffe Manor this week. We're wondering if you all would be willing to sign releases just to cover all the bases. To be clear, we don't plan on featuring any of you in the footage or anything, but I think it lends the piece real credibility to see guests at the manor."

"Ups the creep factor," Stavros agrees, eyes sparkling as he leans into the conversation. "I'm in. Where do I sign?"

"Oh, honey—" Mika puts a hand on Stavros's shoulder — "have I taught you nothing? At least ask about royalty rates before you sign your name to anything."

"Royalty rates. Uh . . . there are no royalty rates. We're on an indie budget. We'll be lucky to make any profit at all by the time Netflix buys the footage. We're operating on a shoestring here."

"Can you put my name in the credits?" Stavros is still all in, ever the opportunist.

"Uh, sure. But again, we're not planning to feature any of the guests this week — at least not the ones of this world," Jeremy quips.

"Where do I sign?" Stavros is eager.

Daniel and Ryleigh are watching, skeptical frowns on their faces.

"I'm not interested, and I don't think my husband will be either," I add.

"Okay . . ." Jeremy's assistant with the clipboard passes the consent forms to Stavros over the charcuterie board. "Well, I respect that you don't want to be on film, but it would just make it easier for us in postproduction if we aren't blurring faces in the outdoor shots."

"Well, guess you're gonna have to."

"I told you they wouldn't be interested," Cole grunts.

"Worth a shot." Jeremy shrugs.

"Ah, what the hell, I'll sign it. In the name of art." Mika takes the clipboard when Stavros is finished and signs her own name on the next page.

"Thanks, it means the world to me. This is my passion project. I've wanted to film at Stonecliffe for years, but the timing was never right. I grew up listening to my dad talk about his experiences here and on Mackinac. And, well . . . I really appreciate your support. I swear we won't be in your hair or anything. You won't even know we're here." Jeremy glances at Daniel, silently imploring him to consider it.

"Are you filming tonight?" Ryleigh finally speaks up.

"All night. We did some exterior shots today and some coastline I plan to overlay with a voice-over history of the island."

"I think that's enough, guys. I told you I can't have you harassing the guests." Cole is visibly annoyed.

"It's fine." Ryleigh speaks up, taking the clipboard from Mika when she's finished. She signs her name quickly and then passes it to Daniel. Silently, Daniel signs his name to the document, and I'm feeling like a loser for shooting Jeremy down so quickly. Especially in the name of art.

"Fine. I'll sign." I relent, knowing Kip won't like this. The only support Kip gives to the arts is listening to me prattle on endlessly about the gallery. I suddenly wonder why I married him at all; he's not my type. At least, not anymore. He used to be, I think, as I sign my name to the form. And he's generous financially. Without his support, I wouldn't even have the gallery. For the first time, I wonder if I should cut my losses — sell the gallery and leave my marriage behind. I shove the thought from my mind as quickly as it comes.

"Thanks." I pass the clipboard back to Jeremy's assistant, thinking I just won't mention anything to Kip about signing anything. And if he really has an issue with it, I'll tell him my signature must have been forged. Sometimes it's better to let a white lie slip out here and there than to rattle the beast.

"You didn't have to do that." Cole pauses, his gaze holding mine earnestly.

"I don't mind." I shrug, sip my drink, and then turn away.

"If they annoy you at all, just let me know and I'll have words. I don't like anything about them being here, but Kip's dad set this up before he passed, and I couldn't get out of it."

"It's okay." I smile, and adjust in my chair. His attention feels good, but can anyone else tell there's something pulsing between us?

44

"I'm gonna go check on the main dish with the caterers. Text if you need anything." Cole brushes my shoulder with his palm, and I feel his touch *everywhere*. "The Northern Lights are supposed to make an appearance tonight. If you're up late enough, this is the perfect spot to see them from."

Cole leaves, and I turn back to the table and catch Mika looking at me.

"Watch yourself, lady. Fucking the help isn't as good as it sounds. Trust me." Mika's comment jars me. She's being flippant, an amused smile of warning on her face.

"Shh, darling," Stavros interjects. "Fucking the help sounds fabulous. Leave Kerrigan be. A vacation without a little kink sounds like no vacation I want to be on."

Stavros gives Mika a knowing wink, and it makes me wonder if the two of them are swingers. If I've learned anything in life, it's that you can never really know a person. Everyone has secrets. Mika pushes her chair back from the table and excuses herself to the ladies' room, her eyes trained on Stavros as she moves in the opposite direction toward the row of villas that edges the garden.

At that moment, Stavros stands, sipping the last of his champagne before following Jeremy and his assistant away from the table. I see him lean his head into Jeremy and ask a question, and for the first time, I wonder if Stavros is more open than I even realized.

"Do you think Stavros is gay?" I ask out loud before I can catch myself.

"He's definitely something," Daniel quips. "Is something wrong with that?"

"Nothing is wrong with that," I defend. "Unless you're married to a woman."

"Please." Stavros is back. "I'd bang anything with legs for a green card, darling." He pats me on the shoulder as he passes me and returns to his seat at the table. "It's the American Dream."

He's sitting now, peering at me pointedly. I don't have a reply for him, because I realize that's maybe where Kip and I went off the rails long ago.

45

Mika returns at that moment, and I wonder if she heard what her husband just said. Or if she'd even care if she did.

"Food's here. I'm gonna go help the help." Stavros winks at his wife, pecks her on the cheek, and then rushes off in the direction of Cole, who's walking toward us with two large trays of food balanced in his hands. When Stavros reaches him, he takes a tray in two hands and winks at him.

"Do you think Stavros would ever cheat on you?" I blurt before I can help it.

"Oh, honey." Mika waves her hand at me. "Knowing him, completely. But I wouldn't ever want to put out his fire. It's that fire I fell in love with, and men with a fire like that can't be contained. My Stavros is a mustang, and sometimes you just have to let a mustang run."

CHAPTER EIGHT: COLE

Wanna party at the Pink Pony tonight, playboy? Lyra's text comes through just as I finish cleaning up after dinner. Kerrigan and her friends are out by the bluff, taking in the soft pink and green swirls in the sky.

I can't. Have to stay sober this summer. Getting my rocks off is the only kicks I can get this year. You know that. I type my reply quickly, then pocket my phone. Lyra knows I have to be on my best behavior. I'm practically on house arrest with her dad, chained to Stonecliffe until the last guest is long gone. I wish she'd stop trying to sabotage my success and sobriety, but then, it wouldn't be Lyra if she weren't looking for a good time.

Banging the tourists is bad for business, ya know ;)

I huff at her reply and promptly type out my own. *We can't all get our kicks from livin' off Daddy's money ;)*

Her reply comes quick. *Ha-ha. Sure we can. Spend the winter in Ibiza with me. I promise to make it worth your while. Every night. And every morning too ;)*

I let her message linger, unwilling to reply to her absurd offer. Spending the winter with Lyra would be a lot of fun, though I can't help but think that spending it with Kerrigan would be even more fun. Seeing her again is obsessing me. I can't stop thinking about making her mine, stealing her from that boring husband who ignores her, and showing her what she's been missing. I didn't realize how much I missed her until I saw her again. And being back on this island seems to remind her of who she was here — of who we were here together. Our history runs deep. Her relationship with Kip is superficial at best and certainly strained.

Hello? Lyra's next message pops up. *Did my last message go through?* Three little dots pop up on the screen, indicating she's typing another message. *Ugh. The lack of cell service on these islands kills me. How's a girl supposed to sext? We can only get our rocks off like cave people . . . talking in person.* She adds an eye-rolling emoji for good measure. I let her messages hang, because now, my thoughts are tied up with Kerrigan. I want to break down the walls she's built around her heart in the years we've been apart.

I chuckle to myself as I think about the hell the guys at the Pink Pony would give me if they knew I was fucking around with Kerrigan again. She messed me up when she left that last summer and never came back. The summer she met Kip. The summer two people in the wedding party died in freak accidents.

I drowned all my sorrows at that bar, mourning the loss of us for nearly a decade as the old fishermen took the piss out of me. They fucked with me relentlessly, said heartache was the price I had to pay for fucking around with a rich city girl. But Kerrigan and I were way more than a summer fling.

We were everything.

I make a point not to travel to Mackinac Island much, mostly because I don't like those crusty old fucks in my personal business — and that's just where they like to be. I'm dreading the moment they find out Kerrigan is back. I'll never hear the end of it. They've been ribbing me all summer to get a real job and quit catering to the rich tourists' wives. They treat me like I'm one of them, but the truth is, while I may have grown up here, I'm *not* one of them. I've been looking for my out for years, but the right opportunity just hasn't come up yet.

Until now. Until her.

Kerrigan has always been a pain in my ass. The memories of our time together are weapons that left wounds that never heal. From the moment we met on the beach at Stonecliffe as kids, I knew she was different. The way she talked to me, like I had a future beyond this place, left a mark that remains to this day. Kerrigan burns like a scar. For a time, she made me believe I could be more than these people — dared me to dream about being a charter boat captain in San Diego or a longshoreman in Monterey — but without her, I've floundered.

Instead, I'm here. Working off a debt I'm not sure I even owe.

I've spent too many of my days catering to tourists visiting the most popular vacation destination in the state. Mackinac Island feels lost in time. Venturing off these islands and into the city leaves me feeling anxious and on edge from the traffic noise and gas pollution that's impossible to escape. Impossible, until you come here. Sprawling white cliffsides bookended by forests of rich green pines and twisted beeches line these rocky shores. Our slice of paradise is unique, picture-perfect. And so intoxicating is the peace that it's hard to leave.

While Stonecliffe Island is smaller than neighboring Mackinac, this keeps the tourist traffic low and the serenity at a maximum. A few times a summer, a group of tourists arrive by boat at the marina and invariably wander the shores or climb the cliff path to get a look at Stonecliffe Manor. Built by a Detroit auto industry titan over a hundred years ago, it used to operate as the private playground for wealthy men and their families from the city. The main dining hall at Stonecliffe is wall-to-wall photos of Stonecliffe Manor in its heyday — like a scene from *The Great Gatsby*; dignitaries and socialites arrived by horse-drawn carriages to be greeted by a serving staff of more than twenty. Kennedys, Rockefellers, Astors, and even Winston Churchill are rumored to have spent time here before the market went bust and Stonecliffe was left unattended for more than two decades.

And then Lyra's, Mika's, Kip's, and Kerrigan's fathers came along.

My father lived in the tiny caretaker's cottage on the other side of the island because he was born there. He was born the only child of Stonecliffe's caretaker and one of the young kitchen servants. My grandfather stayed to take care of Stonecliffe after it was abandoned by its wealthy owners and raised my father after he was abandoned by his mother when she lost her job at the manor. She worked at the Grand Hotel on Mackinac Island for a while, but soon, she met a wealthy businessman from Chicago and never looked back.

When Stonecliffe Island was sold to Kip's and Kerrigan's fathers and their friends, my father negotiated his childhood home and the caretaking job into the deal.

And now here I am, still living off the fruits of his labors.

When Dad passed three years ago, I nearly lost my mind, and as much as Lyra annoys me some days, she saved me back then. She cared when no one else did, she held me while I tried to forget he was gone, she made me eat three meals a day, and sometimes, on the days I really needed to forget, she gave me a bump of cocaine to get me through.

I love her in my own complicated way — just like I love this island, I suppose. Some days, it feels like the only thing keeping me afloat, and others, it feels like it might be the final wave that drags me under for good.

CHAPTER NINE: RYLEIGH

"I'm not even sure why Kip came on this trip," Kerrigan grumbles.

I shrug out of my swim cover-up, bright morning sunshine warm on my skin. "He seems like he's under a lot of stress with work."

Daniel slides into the pool as I sit down at Kerrigan's side. We dangle our legs in the heated water, and I take a deep breath, then let the frustration exhale out of me.

"Well, he's piling on the stress by neglecting his marriage." Kerrigan uses my discarded cover-up to wipe at the tears forming in her eyes. She's not as talkative as she usually is, but maybe I'm reading into it more than I should. Or maybe she's sick of this getaway already. I can't say I blame her. In fact, I've been thinking this week would be easier if Kerrigan just wasn't here at all.

"Whew, that boy never skips a day at the gym, does he?" Mika is suddenly at my shoulder, gawking at Daniel, who's settled at the other end of the pool, back to us as he looks out over the bluff. Lake Michigan sparkles in the distance, and I have to admit, from this vantage point, he does look pretty good. Every muscle in his back is taut and glistening with pool water.

51

"If I would have known we were spending the week with another Greek god, I would have packed something a little smaller." Stavros gestures down at his fitted swim briefs with a frown.

"I'm surprised you brought anything." Mika winks and then places a kiss on her husband's cheek.

Stavros waggles his eyebrows, and a charming grin crosses his face. In the next moment, he's pushing his shorts down to his ankles and discarding them at the pool's edge. Mika laughs before he turns and dives in naked. His round ass cheeks surface first, and I can't help but laugh at the absurdity of it.

"You can take the boy out of Greece, but you can't take Greece out of the boy." Mika chuckles. "Ah, what the hell. Vacations are always better naked."

The next thing I know, she's shrugged out of her silk Pucci cover-up and is shoving her one-piece down her body. She dives into the pool as naked as her husband and swims off after him.

"They're crazy as shit, those two," Kerrigan says.

I nod. "They're cute together. A perfect match."

"Is that what a great marriage looks like?" Kerrigan muses as Mika and Stavros meet in the middle of the pool and tread water together, lips locked and hands roaming everywhere.

"For them, I guess."

We watch them make out for a while before Kerrigan says, "I don't think Kip and I ever really had that. I thought I loved him when we first got together, but we never had that *tear-each-other's-clothes-off-and-make-out* kind of love."

"Love doesn't look the same for everyone." I turn to face her, unsure of what else I can say. "Maybe you and Kip could rekindle that feeling."

A laugh bubbles out of her. "That's why we're here. Ironic, right? *We'll make a baby in paradise*, he said. Meanwhile, he's holed up behind that computer, ignoring me. He's been so focused on work, and I've been so focused on building a family . . . I'm afraid I've pushed him away. I feel like I'm a walking, talking womb and not a lover. Maybe Mika and Stavros are right, maybe an open marriage is better than whatever cold war standoff Kip and I have found ourselves in."

I look out at the couple kissing passionately in the pool. "I think everyone wants to capture that feeling."

"You don't have it with your man back in the city?" Kerrigan asks.

I turn, brows knit together. "I wish."

"Have you talked to your boyfriend lately?" Kerrigan squints through the sun at me.

"He's been busy." I shrug, fiddling with the rose-gold infinity band that rests on my left ring finger. Kerrigan and I may be best friends, but she rarely asks about relationships, or anything in my life really.

"You really caught yourself a workaholic. Consider my marriage with Kip as your warning," she half jokes. "Did he give you that ring?"

"Mm-hm." I twist in my seat, feeling under the spotlight.

"It's beautiful. How are things going with you two?" I can't tell if she's genuinely curious or just trying to make conversation.

"Great. We see each other about once a week."

"That's it?" Kerrigan frowns.

I don't answer her; talking to Kerrigan about boyfriends isn't my idea of a good time.

"Do you think he's the one?" she asks.

"It's kinda early to think about forever."

"Forever? Who said anything about forever?" She laughs.

I let her laughter hang in the air before I finally decide I need a change of scenery. "Think I'm gonna go for a swim."

I slide the band off my finger and tuck it into my beach bag before slipping off the Swarovski-encrusted sandals that Kerrigan bought for us during a girls' weekend away last summer. She was tickled that we had matching footwear. But the truth? I didn't have the heart to tell her that the glitzy glamour of the sandals isn't my style. I only ever wear them when I'm

53

with her, and the rest of the time, they collect dust on the top shelf of my closet.

As I'm dipping my toes into the water, Stavros and Mika are making their way out. They're holding hands, dripping water, and look like two horny teenagers with flushed cheeks and drunk smiles.

"Wanna see a trick?" Stavros whips his swim shorts up his thighs as he speaks.

"Not if it involves seeing your junk again," Kerrigan quips.

Stavros only laughs, slides his shirt over his shoulders, and then pulls a queen of hearts playing card out of the pocket. Mika rolls her eyes but takes the card dutifully.

"Steady, my love," he croons, and Mika's smile twitches.

She holds up the card in her right hand, and before I can register what's about to happen, Stavros is launching a small knife from the charcuterie board at his wife. I flinch when it lands squarely in the queen's heart.

"Holy shit," Kerrigan gasps.

"Really, dude?" Daniel exits the pool, shooting Stavros a glare as he does. "Maybe warn someone next time."

"Well, then it wouldn't be a trick." Stavros's grin is playful.

"That's quite the hidden talent," I mumble, wondering what else he's capable of that we don't know about.

"Safety first, always." Stavros's grin widens the more he realizes the rest of us are shaken by this violent skill he possesses.

"Did you grow up in the circus or something?" Daniel wraps a towel around his waist and collapses onto the nearest lounge chair.

"I wish. I was a deckhand on my uncle's boat in Greece before I went to Chicago. I wear deck shoes for a reason, y'know. I'm . . . how do you say . . . *authentico*?" He flexes his biceps like Popeye, and I can't help but laugh. "I learned how to survive on the high seas with a bunch of crusty fishermen. I'm as scrappy as they come. I'm not afraid to get a few scars on my knuckles."

"What a waste of a manicure." Mika waves him off.

He grins. "You like me scrappy, baby. Don't be afraid to admit it."

Mika pats his cheek and pecks him on the lips. "You know me so well."

"Afternoon, losers." A woman appears around the edge of the pergola. A pair of designer sunglasses holds back her golden waves, and she wears the tiniest triangle of a black bikini top underneath a lightweight shawl that dances around her shoulders with the breeze. "Whoa, what are you all looking at?" Her pretty face scrunches with annoyance at us. "This crew needs a total vibe check. Where's Cole?"

"At your service." Cole appears out of nowhere, two bottles of champagne in hand. "Can I pour you some?"

"Mm, good." Her face lifts in amusement. "Right on cue."

Cole spends a few minutes filling fluted glasses before passing them around the group. "Dinner should be ready in thirty minutes under the pergola."

"You should take them to the mainland. This catered food is the worst." The woman finishes her glass then steals another fresh one from Cole's hands. Cole indicates it was meant for me.

"I don't want any, thanks." I wave him off.

"Some of you know Lyra, but for everyone else, meet Lyra Caruso. She's a pain in the ass, but her dad Jon owns a piece of this rock, so . . ."

"Cute," she says witheringly.

"You haven't met before?" I glance from Lyra to Kerrigan.

Lyra scrunches her nose. "Daddy has investment properties all over the world." She sips, seeming totally disinterested in us. "The only reason I'm here is because I had a little issue in Dubai with a prince and a private jet last summer. It's domestic flights only for me, at least for now. I'm basically on house arrest." She pouts.

"You were in Miami last week," Cole quips.

"We've had a place in Miami since I was a kid. It's practically my backyard." She swirls her drink. "Ryan and Blake are in the Maldives right now, so trust me when I say North

America is house arrest for a girl like me." She sighs wistfully. I've never met someone like her, I realize. Someone who will settle for nothing less than the Maldives, while I'm just trying to carve out a weekend here and there.

Lyra whispers something that only Cole can hear and then sticks out her tongue playfully. I see him crack a smile, but he catches himself and steels his features quickly. She sips at her glass and then settles herself a few chairs away from the rest of the group. Daniel takes the lounger beside her, and after wrapping myself in a towel, I curl up in the lounger between Kerrigan and Daniel.

"Her waist is so tiny. I don't know how she does it," Kerrigan murmurs beside me. "Maybe I need to focus on more core exercises at the gym."

Cole is opening the second bottle of champagne to pour some for Stavros and Mika.

After he pops the cork, he leans between Kerrigan and me and tops up her glass.

"She paid for every inch you see. She got a boob job over the winter, and she's hell-bent on getting her money's worth. Or Daddy's money, anyway."

"Does she work?" I ask under my breath so only Kerrigan can hear me. She just grunts and shakes her head. I glance down the line of loungers. Lyra's perfectly bronzed legs are crossed, a delicate bracelet catching the sunlight and shining a prism of colors at her ankle. She exudes luxury, but just beneath the surface lives an insecure party girl who craves attention and validation. Lyra doesn't seem to know it, but money doesn't buy class like she thinks.

"Cole? Can I get a refill, baby?" Her lips are loose, each of the words slurring together.

Cole stiffens at my side a moment and then moves to Mika and Stavros. "Don't you think you should take it easy, love?" Cole calls to Lyra as he pours a flute for Stavros. "You'd think a stint in rehab would have taught her some restraint."

"Hard to teach lessons when Daddy keeps cutting checks." Mika nods at Cole as he passes her champagne.

Daniel barks a laugh then. It's such an unexpected sound, I shoot him a glance. He refuses to look at me, though, diverting his attention back to his notebook as Lyra's grin deepens.

"None of these bougie bastards would be here without my father's money," I hear her slur. If Lyra thinks she's being discreet, she's not. Far from it. I heard her statement as clear as day. I have no doubt Kerrigan and Mika and everyone else did too.

"Excuse me?" Kerrigan leans forward in her lounger and shoots Lyra a deadly glare.

Lyra giggles, stands up, and then empties her second glass. "You heard me."

"Our parents bought this together. We're here because of *all* of them," Kerrigan spits.

"Keep telling yourself that." Lyra adjusts her cleavage and turns her face up to the sun.

"I hate entitled assholes," Kerrigan declares.

"What did you say?" Lyra is clearly drunk, wobbling on her designer stilettos as she walks dangerously close to the pool edge.

"My father was a great businessman — he had investments all over this state. Not even my mother knew the extent of his holdings. My family trust still pays monthly dividends from all of the properties. My father was the greatest man I've ever met."

Lyra stumbles once, and I almost launch off the lounger to catch her from falling into the pool. "Your father and Kip's and mine were best friends — trust me when I say they had secrets you haven't even scratched the surface of." She laughs.

"Like what?" Kerrigan is boiling.

Lyra shrugs and hiccups. "Maybe you'll learn a thing or two about your old man this week."

"Shut up, you stupid, simple . . ." Kerrigan seethes, searching for the perfect insult, then she tips her chin and

grins. "The spoiled rich girl act doesn't look good on you."
Kerrigan exhibits more class than Lyra by a long shot.

"You no-good fucking b—"

"Hey! What did I miss?" Kip comes around the corner of
the pergola, planting his palms on my shoulders.

I lean away from his touch and turn, shooting him a
wordless glare.

"Oh! Damn, you look so much like my wife from behind
— same dark ponytail . . ." Kip shoots me an apologetic look.
"Sorry about that."

"I confuse those two all the time from behind, especially
after a little too much bubbly," Mika comments.

Kip plants his palms on Kerrigan's shoulders in the
lounger next to mine. "Hey, baby," Kerrigan croons. "I was
just taking out the trash."

Lyra's face turns the shade of a ripe tomato.

Kip freezes, eyes casting around the group. "Kerrigan —
be nice this week, eh?"

She doesn't reply, but she does shrug him off.

"Great. Still upset from earlier, then?" Kip says as his
demeanor shifts, and a dark cloud settles over the patio that
wasn't there moments ago.

"Ohh . . . trouble in paradise?" Stavros finishes his glass
and sets it on the table.

Kip shoots him the middle finger. "I'll have the staff
bring me my dinner in the villa."

Kip walks off as Mika quips, "There *is* no staff."

Stavros huffs. "It's like an episode of *Days of Our Lives* up
in here." He catches Cole's gaze. "I used to watch that show
dubbed in Greek with my mom as a kid. She even let me skip
school sometimes when something extra juicy was supposed
to happen." He clucks his tongue for dramatic effect. "Can we
get another bottle of the champs, good sir?"

"With pleasure." Cole bows dramatically in good fun.
"I'll be back in a moment with more." He turns, heading back
to the main house, where all the provisions are kept.

Kerrigan stands from her chair and follows Kip across the yard. I squirm watching them walk away. I anticipated a lovers-in-paradise kind of vibe this week, but the reality is more like being in enemy territory.

"Well," Lyra laughs, "there isn't enough champagne on this island to make me give a shit about these people. Where's my Cole?" And with that, she walks off on her wobbly heels. I notice Kerrigan flinch in the distance at Lyra's endearment of *my Cole*.

"What a dumpster fire," Daniel says so only I can hear. "I'd risk a limb to get off this island. I don't know how you talked me into this, Rye." Daniel sounds genuinely distressed. "I'm starting to regret any time spent with these people. These aren't your friends. You know that, right?"

"W-what do you mean?" I whisper.

Daniel squints at me. "Really? You think that woman has your back? She's so far up her husband's ass, she wouldn't know reality if it bit her in *her* ass."

"You mean Kerrigan? She's sweet. You don't think—"

"Sweet is the last word I would use. Jesus, Rye — really? I thought you were better at reading people than this. If you call these people friends, you need to think about what that means to you."

"I dunno. They're nice enough. They invited us here, didn't they?"

Daniel grunts.

"Come on, it's been nice. They probably just want to have fun. To get away. Something to distract them from the will reading maybe," I defend.

"Hardly," Daniel scoffs. "People like this don't do anything that doesn't benefit them somehow. I just have to figure out the *why*."

"The why?" I ask.

Daniel narrows his eyes. "Why they want us."

59

CHAPTER TEN: COLE

"Don't fuck with my guests this summer," I warn as Lyra nears me.

She huffs, crosses her arms, and cocks her head. "Come on—"

"I mean it." I'm firm, as firm as I've ever been with her. Lyra doesn't understand consequences in the same way the rest of us do. When a wealthy father is your safety net, things like rules and repercussions don't generally apply.

Lyra tries to swipe one of the champagne bottles from my hand. "You know, technically, they're *my* guests."

I shake my head. "Bitterness doesn't suit you."

"Bitter about what? They should be paying. We're losing money on actual customers."

"Please, the only difference between you and them is a lot more designer shoes and daddy issues."

"Obviously." She glares, coming closer to me. "That's what makes me fuck better."

Before I can stop her, she's dropped to her knees, both of her palms rubbing at the front of my pants.

I resist, backing away from her, but she follows. With a bottle in each hand, I can't exactly stop her from what she's

60

obviously intent on doing. She starts murmuring dirty words, and then she's drawing my zipper down and revealing my hot flesh to the cool air. Her mouth descends, and my head drops back against the wall, and just like that, she's in control. She's always had this way about her, the ability to control me with just a sexy twist of her lips. Lyra is the kind of girl that uses her sexuality to dominate people, especially men, and I've never minded it. Until now.

Lyra moves with measured precision; her oral skills have been well honed over the years, and it's a talent she only gets better at. Usually, she blows my mind in a matter of minutes, but today is different. Today, I'm distracted. Today, my thoughts are haunted by a certain tourist's wife that I can't get out of my head.

"Are you close?" Lyra groans as she works me up and down.

My eyelids flutter open as I realize her high-pitched tone is practically killing my chance at a release. I catch sight of Kerrigan's group of friends through the window; the laughter is almost audible from here, and it makes something inside me ache. I'll never be good enough for Kerrigan. I can't give her this life that she's used to, and even allowing myself to consider it is a useless undertaking.

"Cole?" Lyra pauses, forcing me to lock eyes with her. I can't speak, can't reply. The lone thought running through my mind is that I'll only ever be good enough for a girl like this. A girl who has a kink for fucking the help.

"Cole, baby?" She stands, recognizing that something is wrong. "Are you okay? Am I doing something wrong?"

"No, no. You're perfect." I fake a smile.

She shrugs out of the cover-up and starts to slip out of her bikini top. "Maybe you need a cowgirl to—"

"No, not right now. I have a group to take care of—"

"There's always a group around — *come on*, it never stopped you before. I'll make it quick." Her tone shifts from whiny to flirty.

"There's something about this group, though. Something I can't put my finger on."

"Really? I find them dull. They're literally the least interesting group of people I've ever spent time with."

"You're not looking hard enough, then."

"Oh, please." She waves me off, pouting again.

"They act like friends, but it's just that — an act. None of them trusts any of the others, and I want to figure out why," I say.

"The secrets of rich people, *so* fascinating." She rolls her eyes and wraps her cover-up around her waist.

At that moment, the film crew walks by the window, close enough that if they glanced in, they would definitely see us. I grunt under my breath, "Fuck those ghost-hunting guys."

Lyra follows my sightline out the window. "Those guys? They're the most interesting thing here." She tilts her head as she speaks, anger bubbling to life in her. "Wait, is that why you couldn't finish? Because you were distracted with the tourists out the fucking window?"

"I work on tips. If I don't cater to them, I don't make enough cash to get through the winter. You really are spoiled. Jesus, Kerrigan was right. It doesn't look good on you."

Lyra's temper flares before she spins and stalks out of the kitchen. I follow her, champagne bottles in hand, as we both head back to the group.

The crack of a slamming door carries across the yard, and everyone's attention diverts to Kip and Kerrigan's villa.

"Jesus, those two are going to kill each other. So much marriage drama this week. Don't they know how silly they look with all the bickering? I don't know how you do it," Lyra grumbles.

"Seems like a normal amount of marriage bullshit to me."

She turns then, flashing me an accusatory glare. "You want to fuck her, don't you?"

"Who?" I stiffen.

"*Kerrigan.*" She says it like a curse word.

"What's it to you if I want to get my kicks fucking the tourists' wives?"

She flinches. "Don't make me fuck a married guy to get back at you."

I laugh. "We never dated, Lyra. Stop acting like my ex. It *really* doesn't look good on you."

"*You* look good on me." She slides her shorts down her legs, revealing a tiny strip of bikini fabric at her hip.

"Lyra . . ." I protest, but she's already turned on me. She flashes a devilish grin before she plants both of her palms on my chest and pushes me back into the room we just vacated. Without asking, she slides both bottles out of my hands and sets them on the side table.

"You wanna get your kicks with a tourist's wife this week? I'm game as long as you let me play too." She puffs out her lower lip and then plucks the string of her bikini top and pulls until it drops to her feet. She stands bare in front of me, intent on us happening, and because she's so familiar, like a cozy blanket or a best friend, I let her have her way. I love her in a way, and I know she'd lose it and make a scene if I denied her. So I take one for the team. It's not sweet or romantic, more frenzied and quick. Lyra's touch is demanding and needy. Normally, whatever vibe she shows up with, I'm game for. But this is a new intensity I'm not used to. She's a new woman, or maybe I'm a new man.

Kerrigan is here, and I can't deny that it's changed me. The one who got away has found herself right in my lap this week, and all I can think about is making this week last as long as I can. Maybe even forever.

CHAPTER ELEVEN: RYLEIGH

Winding my way along the shore path is difficult under the best circumstances, but this night-time stroll adds another level of risk. I've walked this rocky path a few times in the nights since we arrived at Stonecliffe, unable to sleep and with only myself to blame. I'm regretting taking Kerrigan up on her offer of an island getaway, and if I'm honest with myself, the more the days creep by, the more my regret deepens. The energy when everyone is together is off. Maybe I should have expected that, but I didn't. I expected a nice vacation. At this rate, I would have had more fun spending the afternoon at IKEA with Daniel.

"Shit!" I hear her voice before I see her.

My heartbeat triples when a human shape pops up from behind a slab of granite.

"Oh my God, you scared me," I hiss, hand to heart, as I come to a stop at Lyra's shoulder. "What are you doing out here?"

Lyra is wiping off her phone, her frown apparent even in the limited moonlight. "I was just leaving Cole's place. What are *you* doing here?"

I don't like the way she seems to be accusing me of something. "Out for a late-night walk."

"Is that so?" She tilts her head at me, assessing my features like she's just seeing them for the first time. "Why are you *really* here?"

"Excuse me?" I straighten my spine. "I told you. I couldn't sleep, so I went for a walk."

"I heard you the first time. I just don't believe you." She fingers the hem of my Old Navy T-shirt with a smirk. "I think Cole was right. I think there's more to all of you than you let on." She grins like a Cheshire cat. "Ryleigh, the poor little Midwestern girl with a secret, hanging out with these wealthy assholes. You're so clearly out of your league here. You don't belong — *one of these things is not like the others*," she sing-songs with a giggle, and it's then I realize she must be drunk.

"Sounds like you and Cole were having a lot of fun tonight," I comment.

"Mm, we were. So, tell me, Ryleigh." A drunken smirk spreads across her face. "How many rich dicks did you have to suck to get here?"

"You're insane." My blood boils, and all I can think about is taking a rock to this woman's head and crushing her skull until she shuts up.

"Little girls like you are parasites . . . just thirsty little social-climbing parasites. But guess what? Your game only works on the ones dumb enough to let you latch on to them. You're a guest here. If I want you gone, you'll be gone before anyone even has a chance to miss you."

"Nice, really mature." I move around her on the path.

"I know you're hiding something," she calls to my back. "And I will find out!"

I don't reply, only adding more steel to my spine as I walk away. Lyra has a lot of opinions about me, but I have a few about her that have me wondering what her deal is. Why does she hang out here when she could be any other fabulous place? Why is she so willing to accept the scraps Cole throws her way? She's a girl who knows what she wants, and what she wants is definitely something here. Or someone.

I have a feeling everyone on this island has a secret, and it would be in my best interests to find out what it is before she discovers mine.

CHAPTER TWELVE: KERRIGAN

"I don't trust her," I admit.

"Who?" Ryleigh asks. She's been distracted this morning, and I'm trying to temper my annoyance.

I frown, taking in her hunched shoulders and red-rimmed eyes. "Are you tired? Didn't you sleep well last night?"

"I was up late," Ryleigh says. For some reason, I don't believe her. "And Daniel snores like a jet engine, so there's that," she adds as an afterthought. "You don't trust Mika?" I look at our friend. She's set up with the masseuse on the other side of the pool, while Ryleigh and I get pedicures and manicures. "Why?"

"I don't know . . ." I finally whisper. "I'm just picking up on something between her and Kip. Like they have a secret."

"Hm," Ryleigh murmurs. "I never picked up on that."

"Well, there's a lot you don't see, Ryleigh." I can't help the cutting tone that laces my words.

"Okay," she says, eyes suddenly on me. "Sorry."

I adjust the sunglasses on the bridge of my nose. "No, I'm sorry I'm being short. Kip and I were fighting last night, and I guess I didn't get much sleep."

Silence hangs between us, and I notice for the first time that Ryleigh never really adds much to the conversation, just listens. Always listening. My dad told me countless times as a kid to listen when people tell you who they are, but Ryleigh doesn't really tell me anything. *Ever.*

"But I'm confused," Ryleigh finally says. "What does that have to do with not trusting Mika?"

"I caught them arguing last night. That's what Kip and I were fighting about." I press my lips together, finally breathing the next words to life. "I think they're having an affair."

"What?!" Ryleigh nearly chokes on her tongue.

I shrug. "A woman just knows these things. It's a feeling. You'll understand when you're married someday. I've spent nearly a decade with this man, I can tell when something is off."

"There could have been a million reasons they were arguing. Mika was probably pissed there isn't Veuve on tap or the shellfish was too *shellfishy* or something."

"Wouldn't she talk to Cole about that, then?" I appreciate that Ryleigh is trying to give Mika and my husband the benefit of the doubt, but not everyone deserves it. "They were whispering heatedly when I came around the corner of the main house. Thankfully, they didn't see me, because then Kip yelled something I couldn't hear and Mika walked off, but not before she threw him the middle finger."

"Oh." Ryleigh scrunches her eyebrows.

"I think they're up to something right under my nose."

"Maybe it's business," Ryleigh offers weakly.

"Kip tells me everything about his business. We practically run it together. He would've told me if something was wrong. Mika too. It's not that. I know it's not that. Please don't insult me by telling me I don't know my husband."

Ryleigh balks, twisting the tiny umbrella in her grapefruit paloma before setting it down next to her chair.

"Lyra saw them fighting too. I'm not making it up."

"I ran into Lyra last night too. She seemed drunk off her rocker. She was kind of a mess," Ryleigh intimates.

"You saw her? Late last night?" I shift uncomfortably.

"Yeah. I saw her on the shore path."

"The one that leads to Cole's cottage?" I ask.

"Yeah, is there another one?" Ryleigh answers.

"Sure. The other side of the island has a path that leads to some old fishing huts. It's a mess, though — lots of rusted fishing equipment and abandoned buildings. I should talk to Cole about getting that side of the island cleaned up. It's a health hazard." My mind tangles with thoughts of Cole then. "I know it's crazy, but sometimes I think about getting back at Kip by having my own affair just to show him how it feels." Ryleigh doesn't say anything. "Hooking up with the caretaker would really get back at him, don't you think? I mean, I wouldn't do it — not after last time — but I like my little revenge fantasy." A dreamy smile turns my lips.

"I don't know if that's the healthiest of the options . . ."

"What? Revenge is good for the soul," I laugh.

"As good as chicken soup, huh?" Ryleigh giggles.

"Absolutely."

"Morning, ladies." Kip's voice filters on the breeze as he places a hand on my shoulder. "How hard is it to get some grapefruit juice around here? Did you ladies take the last of it for morning cocktails?" He's teasing, but something in his tone still makes me uncomfortable. "So, how's it going out here?"

"Good!" I do my best to cultivate positivity that I don't feel. "I was thinking we should go to one of the little islands nearby for a picnic tomorrow. What do you think?"

"I think—" Kip drops down into the lounger beside me — "the secluded islands are dangerous. The weather report is warning about a thunderstorm coming with gale force winds and hail."

"Ha." I roll my eyes. "The weatherman's always wrong anyway. Let's plan it, and we can always do a rain check if the weather doesn't look favorable."

"Well, you're welcome to do what you want, but I think I'm going to stick close to home base tomorrow." Kip is distracted by his phone.

"You've been sticking close to home base every day." I pout. "Work, work, work."

"Babe, you know the investors are breathing down my neck with this project. Stop acting like a needy child, would you?"

"A needy child?" Emotions form a painful ball in my throat.

"You see me working — all the phone calls and angry text messages I'm handling — it's getting to me, all right? Can you step outside of your spoiled little universe for a minute and cut me some slack?"

"For how long, though? How long am I supposed to keep cutting you slack for being an absolute asshole?"

"Jesus, Kerrigan. You know the vote for the sale of the island is coming up. If this deal falls through, we're all toast. Every one of us. Something's gonna give soon. I just need a little more time to make this work."

I can't look him in the eye. Not after everything. I know he's not wrong, but that doesn't make him right either. The truth is, I've felt the gulf dividing us grow wider with each passing day.

"Whew! I feel like a million bucks!" Mika adjusts the belt on her spa robe as she approaches us. Cole managed to find a masseuse to come to Stonecliffe at the last minute. So far, Mika and Stavros are the only ones to take advantage. "Fill me in. What drama did I miss while I was getting all relaxed over there?"

I can't bring myself to look at her.

"No drama yet." Ryleigh finally addresses Mika. "You got any?"

Mika grins and then settles into the lounger beside Ryleigh. "As a matter of fact, I do."

"Well, spill the tea. Stop keeping us in suspense!" Stavros appears in his own spa robe, ready for his massage.

"Well, I've been trying to figure out what the deal is with the caretaker. So hot, so mysterious. I just know he has a story." I balk when I realize she's talking about Cole. "So, I did some digging."

"Famous last words," Kip grunts.

"Hush." Mika waves him off. "I'm very good at reading people, and this guy gives me a low-key criminal vibe. A girl should always follow her instincts about these things, y'know." She looks like she's enjoying telling us what she found way too much. "You'll never guess. Did you know a girl went missing here last summer?"

"What?" Ryleigh's voice rises with alarm.

"Yep." Mika nods as if she's excited to be the bearer of this bad news. "I found an article about it on Stonecliffe. She worked part-time on Mackinac for the summer. According to the true crime forums, some of the locals suspected she was dating the caretaker of Stonecliffe Island. That would be Cole, right?"

I shrug, disliking the way she seems to be addressing this question to me.

"The police suspected foul play from the start, but they never found a shred of evidence. Her body was found in the lake after the spring thaw."

"Maybe she's a ghost." Stavros grins. "We should have a seance and ask how she died. There must be a Ouija board somewhere on this creepy island, right?"

"Honey!" Mika giggles and swats at his shoulder. "Maybe the paranormal team knows a little bit about it, though. I think I'll have a talk with them after all."

"Great. The next thing you know, Mika will be featured on Netflix, showcasing the ghosts of Stonecliffe to the world. We'll never get another booking again." Kip's sarcasm doesn't go unnoticed by Mika. She refuses to answer him, and it only adds fuel to the flames in my mind.

"Maybe Stonecliffe will make a killing in rentals then. Imagine all the ghost hunters — you'd be booked up for years!" Stavros's enthusiasm is equal parts annoying and contagious.

"Well, that may be true, but I don't want to be here for it. Our parents bought this place to be a refuge for us, not a circus," I finally say. "Honestly, I'm starting to feel sick. I

71

don't think I'm up for a massage today." I push off the lounger and turn toward our villa.

"You want me to get you anything, babe?" Kip calls over his shoulder.

I pretend not to hear him, instead turning to call back to the group, "I'll arrange for Cole to take us by boat to one of the other islands for a picnic tomorrow to make up for me bailing today. Later, kids!"

Once I reach our villa, I continue walking, making my way in the direction of Cole's cottage with a dozen questions on my mind. I just hope I'm ready for the answers.

CHAPTER THIRTEEN: RYLEIGH

"He is such an asshole," Mika mutters to Kip's retreating back.

I've had it up to my eyeballs with Kip's shit-talk. Even if it is true, why would I care? I finally muster the will to reply. "What makes you say that?"

"So many things. You haven't known them as long as I have. He can't be trusted, just know that." Mika clucks her tongue and then swipes the paloma from my hand and takes a sip from the side. "Mm, this is good. The grapefruit juice is so refreshing and summery — I'd never think to use it, but it's great."

Kip and Kerrigan drink grapefruit juice like other people drink water. If Cole weren't able to get it, I have no doubt they'd overnight a shipment to Stonecliffe without a second thought.

"Where is Cole with more alcohol?" Mika calls out. "I don't want to remember any of this trip."

I don't reply, distracted as I check my phone notifications for the hundredth time today.

"Let's get out while we still can!" Mika giggles and takes another long swallow of my cocktail before passing it back to me. She shakes her head, eyes still lingering on Kip's diminishing figure in the distance. "He treats his wife like garbage. You can see that, right? Kerrigan is off-her-rocker crazy, but even still, she's way too nice for him." Mika shakes her head and looks out to the blue lake beyond. "She could dump him tomorrow, and even that would be too kind."

"She said they're trying to have a baby," I croak lamely.

"A baby." She waves her hand at me. "They have to have sex for that to happen."

"How do you know they aren't?"

"You're her best friend, you should know — Kerrigan is an open book with a little bubbly. She told me all about their bedroom issues the last time we went shopping together in the city. She said they hadn't been together in months, and that was a few months ago now." She shrugs. "But who knows, maybe they're back at it like teenagers." Mika stands from her lounger and then muses, "Wouldn't that be crazy? Kip and Kerrigan with a baby. What a nightmare." She winks at me. "For the sake of all of us, I hope they never have sex again."

I fake a laugh with her, but all I want to do is cry. I went from driving up north expecting a relaxing getaway to living in a nightmare high school drama. Accusations and lies come and go like the current among this crew, and all I can think about is that if I don't escape this so-called circle of friends soon, I'll become one of them.

"Why don't you tell her the truth?" I finally venture to ask Mika.

"Tell her what? That she chained herself to the wrong man?" Mika waves me off. "I'm not any better at marriage than she is. I just know I wouldn't like being ignored and treated like dirt by my beloved husband." Mika's gaze lingers on the vibrant blue water and expansive bridge in the distance. "The truth is, I can't afford to tell Kerrigan the truth about anything. She's my best customer. Who do you think she calls when she needs a dress for a charity gala or gallery opening? Kerrigan Lange does *not* wear off-the-rack, darling. It's designer draping and hand-sewn beading only for that one. She's spoiled, but she pays my bills." Mika shrugs. "Our friendship is long but shallow, I suppose." She turns, nailing me with curious eyes. "What about you?"

"What about me?" I feel my defenses rise.

"Why don't you tell her she could do better than that piece of shit she married?"

"Oh." I struggle for the right words. "I don't really feel comfortable saying something so personal."

"Well, I guess that makes both of us shallow friends then, doesn't it?" She tips her champagne flute in a toast to me.

I try to fake a smile, but it falters. I can't think about why her words have hit a sore spot in me right now. All I can think about is how observant Mika Morales is. So observant that I'm starting to feel like I'm walking around with a secret painted on my chest for all to see.

CHAPTER FOURTEEN: COLE

"Those swells look wild." Kerrigan's smile is bright, her cheeks wind-burned a shade of pink that makes her look as youthful as ever.

I walk through the seafoam left by the waves and up the sand to her. "Island life looks good on you. You should stay awhile."

She doesn't move when I drag my fingertip along her temple and tuck a windblown lock of hair behind her ear.

"I wish." Her eyelids flutter closed a beat before she licks her lips and says, "But I don't think I'm a full-time islander kind of girl."

"No?" A flirty grin sweeps across my face. "I think we could change that."

"Yeah?" She seems a little breathless, and I like that I have this effect on her.

"Absolutely. We should find out."

She slow-blinks as if she's trying to process my words. I want her to stay, and I want her to know it.

She clears her throat and then switches topics. "I was thinking, with that big storm coming, maybe we should evacuate."

I laugh at her suggestion. "Didn't peg you for such a worrywart. Is that what the city's done to you?"

"Me? I'm not worried. I worry about everyone else," she corrects, but she's also blushing, so I know my words have gotten to her. "It's just . . . I don't want to be stranded if the electricity goes out or something."

"You wouldn't be stranded, Ker—" I hold her elbows and give her a jostle — "you'd have me here."

She laughs. "Comforting."

"Isn't it, though?" I offer. "You know there are always a few big storms a year. It's nothing we haven't weathered before. The high winds make the surfing superior." I swipe the pad of my thumb across her cheek. "'Tis the season. Wanna try it?"

Kerrigan laughs like a child, and I'm glad to be the one who's elicited the sweet noise from her lips. "No, I'm still traumatized from the last time you tried to get me up on a surfboard when we were thirteen."

"Oh yeah." I grin. "I forgot about that." I drop down onto the sand, yanking the zip on my wet suit and pulling it down my torso. "If you're really worried about it, the estate has designated storm shelters and emergency supplies and shit in the basement of the big house. Most storms only last an hour or two anyway, and if it's really bad, we hide out in the shelter and play euchre till dawn." Most locals grow up playing the card game around here. "Not a bad night, all considering."

"Really? That sounds like a pretty shitty night in paradise. And I'm terrible at euchre."

"Hm, so the city stole your sense of adventure too, I see."

"And you're still a shithead, I see," she giggles.

"At your service." I kick a spray of sand at her leg. "The catamaran is out for servicing this week anyway. Evacuating everyone would be pretty difficult. I don't think you'll find any vacant hotels either, especially not on Mackinac."

"I guess I didn't think about where we would go. Maybe we should just head home."

"Don't be dramatic. You'd be driving headfirst into the storm anyway. Look at those swells. The storm is already brewing. Can't you feel it in the air? It's about to get angry out there. Just sit back and enjoy the ride, baby."

"Please, my entire life is a ride. Between business and the gallery and Kip — try being married to Kip and then talk to me." A laugh tinged with bitterness fills the space between us. "Wanna butter me up?"

"Um, yeah?" I laugh. "Who says I'm not already?"

"I meant with sunscreen. Still got a dirty mind, huh?"

"Wouldn't be myself without it."

"Amen." She teases and then tosses the bottle of sunscreen in my lap. I catch it and then turn to squirt a pile of it onto her creamy skin. I rub it in slowly, taking my time with her. I like touching her again. In fact, *I love it*. I forgot how good this woman makes me feel just being in her presence.

"I wish Kip wouldn't have come this week."

And there it is. The elephant on the island that's been swallowing up all the air since she arrived.

"He thought about skipping the reading — how insane is that? But his father was adamant that everyone be present or else Stonecliffe Island would go to probate court, and who knows how a judge would have disbursed the shares." She wrings her hands as she speaks. "I'm sorry I'm complaining. It's just a weird feeling when life doesn't turn out quite like you planned."

I choose my next words carefully. "Things seem . . . heated between the two of you."

"He's a dickhead." She shrugs.

Silence lingers as I rub the sunscreen into her pink flesh. "I'm trying to be patient," she continues softly. "I know he's overworked. I feel for him. He's doing whatever it takes to keep the business afloat. He wants to bring the firm into the modern era, so he went all in on this crypto hedge fund that he swears is a sure bet. He says it'll make us rich beyond our wildest dreams, but he didn't account for the financial regulators breathing down his neck. It's risky — everything about it is risky — and Kip has made enemies. It's been almost impossible keeping the investors at bay. It's ridiculous. The Lange family name affords us so much status and prestige and access in Chicago, but there's almost no working cash. My husband got access to his trust fund when he turned forty last year and sank it all into the hedge fund. We have so little liquid cash . . . this get-rich-quick scheme needs to pay off soon." She pauses, almost talking to herself as much as me, it seems. "I'm afraid of what might happen if it doesn't."

"He sounds like quite the risk-taker," I offer. The more she's upset with him, the better my chances of spending time with her are. Kerrigan and I are the same age, thirty-six, and our birthdays are only a week apart in July. As kids we often shared birthday parties if her family was on the island that week. Even though Kip is just five years older, it feels like a decade or more separates them because he acts so superior to everyone else.

"He's borrowed money from a lot of important and well-connected people in the global financial market. He's been under so much stress, honestly, I don't blame him for having an affair. Mika is busty and gorgeous and glamorous and so free-spirited. She's more successful in her fashion business than I could ever hope to be with my gallery."

"Whoa, whoa, whoa. You think Mika and Kip are having an affair?" Not much can shock me, but Kerrigan just has. "I figured something was going on, but not between them."

"Oh?" She turns, catching my eye. "Who did you think?"

"Uh . . ." My mind moves through all the possibilities I've considered in the days before now. I knew Kip was up to something, and I knew Kerrigan caught Mika and Kip mid-argument, but everything about the two of them seems too obvious. I have a feeling they'd be a little more cautious about hiding their affair if that's what it is. "I wasn't sure what was going on. I just got a strange feeling, I guess."

"I've been ignored for so long. It's weird, living in a house with someone without actually being with them. We're like ships passing in the night."

"Sounds fun," I grunt.

"It's not." Kerrigan leans into my shoulder with a playful smile. "But I'd like to have some."

79

"Fun?" I trail a fingertip through the sand between us. "How long has it been?"

She pauses so long I raise my head. "What if I said since the last time I was on this island?"

"I'd say that's a shame. I'd also offer to change that."

"Yeah?" she breathes, and all I can think about is pressing my lips to hers. Would she push me away or lean in? I'm dying to find out. "I had an . . . *intimate entanglement* once with a man at the athletic club. It was brief, but it was the best sex of my life. Wild and raw and life-changing. But I felt so much guilt afterward, I confessed everything to Kip. I thought I was lucky to have such an understanding and open-minded husband then. Now, I'm not so sure. Our marriage has been a struggle, but I thought that was normal. Fast-forward ten years and I'm battling all this regret and resentment that nothing about him or us has changed since then." She twists her hands in her lap, pausing to look at the giant rock that's perched on her left ring finger. "*Vows*. What do they really mean anyway?"

"Whatever you want them to mean. You don't have to have the marriage everyone else has. There's nothing wrong with making your own way."

"Yeah." Her warm gaze lingers a long moment on mine. "I've never let myself wonder what it might have been like if I'd stayed here — stayed on the island for good." She gnashes her teeth.

"Does he know about us?" I finally ask.

"No. Why would he? We don't talk about our exes. We don't talk about anything. That's basically the problem." She's trailing her fingertips along my forearm, and I don't think she even realizes she's doing it. I like it, though. I like being with her. We share another long moment before Kerrigan finally breaks the silence. "This week has me wondering about a lot of things." Kerrigan finally breaks the silence.

My heart is clamoring behind my ribcage, and before I can overthink it, I lean in, grazing our lips together in the barest of touches. "Same."

Kerrigan wraps her arms around my neck, fingertips weaving into my hair as she leans deeper into our kiss. I'm hesitant, afraid to come on too strong and send her packing when I've only just found her again. Kerrigan shifts her body to face me fully, and on instinct, I grip her thighs and pull her onto my lap. She locks her legs around my waist and makes soft little mewling noises as our tongues dance together.

"Well, well, well. Look what we have here." Stavros clicks his tongue as he walks up the beach toward us.

"Shit," Kerrigan grits out. She shoots off my lap, standing up and pushing her hands through her hair before she addresses Stavros. "Hi. I was just leaving."

"Didn't look like that from here." Stavros grins and plops down in the sand next to me. "Shame on you two, having fun without including the rest of the group."

I don't say anything, annoyance still throbbing through my veins at the interruption.

"Oh, I forgot to ask—" Kerrigan spins just before she reaches the shore path — "can you take us to one of the deserted islands for a picnic tomorrow before the storm comes in? Maybe the staff could prepare a lunch for us. Some wine and cheese and cold cuts, at least."

Jesus. This woman went from worrying about the storm to demanding the staff make a picnic for her and her friends. "At your service, *Miss*."

I tip my imaginary hat in her direction. She rolls her eyes and then turns and takes off down the path away from us.

"That one's a firecracker," Stavros laughs.

"Always has been." I watch her as she retreats. "The tourists' wives are as hot as they are entitled. It's a law of nature, I'm sure of it."

Stavros's laugh bounces off the limestone cliff that rises behind us.

"She knows there's no goddamn staff. The caterers only drop off prepared food. They don't even stay for dinner service. I'll be the bastard preparing this little picnic in paradise tomorrow."

"Oh, she knows it, bro." Stavros watches Kerrigan then looks back at me. "But that holier-than-thou attitude is a bit of a turn-on, isn't it?"

I let out a laugh. "Truer words were never spoken, and I don't know what to do about it."

"Not a damn thing, my friend. Not if you know what's good for you. Firecrackers are fun to play with, but bring 'em to bed and you will get burned." Stavros looks out to the lake as he continues. "She's testing your limits, brother. It's up to you what you let her get away with."

I let his words sink in. He's not wrong. Lyra's father said if anything fishy happens this summer, I'm out on my ass for good — history or not. My father may have spent his life caring for the tourists on this jagged slab of rock in Lake Michigan, but someone else holds the deed to this land. The Mayer family isn't the land-owning sort. The amount of social capital and liquid cash required to buy an estate like this will never be within reach for people like me — people chained to their family tree, held back by a rural education and an abundance of generational trauma. Destined to be the help, never the owner.

The truth is, without Lyra's friendship and her father's generosity, I would have been out on my ass long before now. If I lose this job, the judge will consider my probation violated, and I'll have to subject myself to the whims of the legal system again. I've considered all my options, and none of them are great. I've spent so much of my free time catering to Lyra's spoiled demands anyway, why not make it official and put a ring on it?

Life with Lyra would be wild, spontaneous, chaotic, and possibly a hellscape — but at least there would be no question marks about my future. Then again, Lyra's father would probably write her out of the will if she married a loser like me. Girls like her run off to the city and marry up, and then have half a dozen babies for the nanny to take care of. But not Lyra. Lyra wants no part of traditional married life, which is the one reason I think we might actually be a good fit for each other.

Being with Lyra would be an odd mix of pleasure and punishment, like my own kinky purgatory with a penthouse view.

On the other hand, leaving the island — the only place I've ever called home — feels unimaginable. My personal history feels as deeply entwined with this slab of rock as the roots of the birch trees that line its shores. I've known most of the crew at the Pink Pony since kindergarten, but maybe it's just that deeply rooted history that keeps me locked in place, forever frozen by the fear of the unknown. Most of the people who grow up here claim to love the island life but blame the boredom that comes with rural isolation for their addictions and vices.

I've learned there are two kinds of people that come out of this life — the ones who stay and the ones who go, and just like oil and water, they rarely mix.

I've never wanted to be one of the leavers, but maybe Kerrigan will change that.

Maybe I want her to. Maybe with her, the vices will dissolve into the one thing I've been looking for: love.

CHAPTER FIFTEEN: KERRIGAN

"Oh Captain, my Captain!" Stavros steps onto the deck of the old Chris-Craft and claps Cole on the shoulder. "Got any booze on this fair barge?"

"Oh please. It's ten in the morning. I'm still feeling last night's palomas." Mika adjusts the colorful tote on her shoulder as she sits on one of the bench seats. "How can you even think about drinking?"

"It runs in my veins, lovely." Stavros plops down next to her. "Is that the problem with you lot today? Everyone's nursing hangovers? You wouldn't last an hour on a fishing boat in the Mediterranean."

"Nor would we want to," I mumble, pulling my sun hat lower to block the head-splitting rays of sunshine.

"I've got ingredients for pineapple mimosas, per Mika's request." Cole interrupts the tension. "Everything is below deck if you want it now, but we're only about ten minutes from Grand Manitou Island, and then we can get a proper mixing station set up."

"Sounds perfect, Cole. Thanks," Kip gruffs, remaining glued to his phone. "No need to booze before we even leave shore."

"Speak for yourself," Stavros grunts, but he doesn't move. "I'm starting to think it would have been more fun if the boys had stayed home today. Whatcha think, Daniel?"

"Huh?" Daniel lifts his head from the handwritten scribbles that cover his spiral-bound notebook.

"You getting lots of good inspiration for that little book you're writing?" Kip's eyes are boring into Daniel.

Ryleigh leaps to her friend's defense. "This is Daniel's third book. His previous two self-published releases were critically acclaimed." Ryleigh defends her friend.

"Isn't critical acclaim just another way to say commercial flop?" Kip is consumed in his phone again, and I think for the first time that I've never met someone with such a strong sense of indifference toward other people.

"Can you try not to be an asshole every once in a while?" I hiss at my husband as I consider Cole. The broad stretch of his shoulders under the crisp white cotton of his tee is simple but alluring. Kip wears collared shirts and well-pressed chinos and deck shoes, while Cole exudes such easy charm in his sandals and cargo shorts. He's everything that Kip never was. It hits me then that maybe I was drawn to Kip Lange because he was everything Cole Mayer wasn't. I thought the grass would be greener if I married a boy from the city, but instead, it withered and died a slow death.

I left a piece of myself here on this island. I have regrets about kissing Cole last night. I never meant for anything to happen between us this week, but then again, I never meant for Kip to hibernate in our villa with his laptop all week either. He's left me feeling like the lone life preserver trying to save this sinking marriage.

"I told you I didn't want to do this." Kip finally looks up from his phone with a grunt. "Jesus Christ, there's a storm coming. We'll be lucky if we make it back to Stonecliffe in one piece in this rusted piece of shit."

"It's fine," Cole interjects. "We have a few hours before things get intense. This old boat doesn't look like much, but she's just right for short trips around the bay. I wouldn't take it into open water or to the big island or anything."

"Comforting," Daniel mutters, still scratching away on his pad.

"Whew, there's a low-key vicious vibe on this boat. I stand corrected. All of you could probably teach a thing or two to those crusty old Mediterranean sailors," Stavros chuckles.

"Amen!" Mika claps.

"I thought the streets of Athens were rough, and being an immigrant in Chicago is no treat, but this week with you crew might beat them all." Stavros winks at Ryleigh, but she only averts her eyes.

"I see now why you and Daniel can't live together," I direct to Ryleigh. "All that snoring makes you cranky."

"What snoring? I never snore," Daniel defends. "Rye's late-night sleepwalking is the real problem."

"I don't sleepwalk," Ryleigh insists.

"Then what has you up pacing the room like a zombie every night?"

Ryleigh clamps her mouth shut and shoots Daniel a look like he's just revealed her darkest secret. I can't help but wonder about all the unspoken words that seem to pass between them. What secrets do they have, and why does it seem like not even Daniel trusts his friend? "Wait!" I blurt. "Ryleigh said you snore all the time."

"She's delusional." Daniel seems genuinely angry.

"Excuse me." Mika stands, interrupting us. "I need to use the little girls' room. Don't kill them while I'm gone." She drops a kiss on Stavros's cheek before heading below deck.

"So, Stavros, what kind of work did your parents do once they got to Chicago?" Daniel's question takes everyone by surprise. He's shown exactly zero interest in any of us this week, so why all of a sudden is he so interested in Stavros? Daniel is quiet, and in my experience, you can never trust the quiet ones. Shy, reserved minds think before speaking and have a way of coming out on top in the last inning just like an underdog.

86

I don't know what Daniel is up to this week. Maybe he's just looking for a week-long retreat to relax and work on his book, but why does it feel like he's more aware than he lets on? Always *watching, waiting, writing*. It's unnerving, and for the first time, I'm wishing that when Ryleigh mentioned bringing him along, I would have found the words to decline. Why would anyone want to spend a week with people they've never met before? I crack a smile at the thought that none of us really knows one another like we think. We allow the sparkling parts of our personalities to bubble to the surface, while the dark secrets remain buried deep.

"Work?" Stavros's laugh cuts through my thoughts. "My dad refused to leave the motherland and is still fishing from his tiny village every day, and Mom did what she could to get by. She was a housekeeper for most of my growing-up years in Chicago's West Loop. When I was thirty-four and still hadn't been approved for a green card, I knew I'd have to take matters into my own hands." Stavros looks out to the horizon, fog clinging to the wide swath of green steel and cables that suspend the Mackinac Bridge. "I dodged immigration for years until I finally met Mika. I would have fucked anything for a green card at that point, but luckily, I didn't have to, because I met the most beautiful and funny woman in all of America at a fashion pop-up on Michigan Avenue."

"Always the charmer." Mika returns and settles next to Stavros again, and I wonder if she overheard the first part of that sentence. I cringe at the thought of being used for a green card, but maybe it's a dynamic that works for Mika. They certainly look more the fun-loving couple than Kip and me.

"Ugh, I'm suddenly not feeling well." Mika's face distorts, her pale-pink lips turned down as she rubs her tummy.

"Seasick?" Ryleigh asks, placing a hand on Mika's bare knee.

"I guess, but I never get seasick."

"The water is pretty choppy today." Ryleigh frowns with worry. How can she be nice to Mika after everything I've told her?

"Welcome to Grand Manitou," Cole announces as he idles the boat up to a run-down wooden dock. It's so weathered it looks like the original settlers to this area may have built it themselves.

"Doesn't look very grand from where I'm sitting." Kip looks up from his phone long enough to gripe.

"There's a waterfall on the other side of this island, right?" I perk up as the boat comes to a slow stop.

Cole loops a rope around an old piling on the starboard side and then opens the door and drops the small walking plank. "The waterfall is a beautiful hike if you're careful. There's also a small community of fishermen on the opposite side of the island. You can walk the entire shoreline in a few hours, but I wouldn't do it. The fishing crew that lives here full-time is a pretty grizzly sort. The guys live off-grid for a reason — ex-cons looking to stay off the radar—"

"What kind of place did you bring us to?" Mika interrupts.

"Sounds like a pretty salty bunch." Stavros drops a kiss on Mika's knuckles.

"Saltier than you're used to in Chicago," Cole confirms.

Ryleigh finally speaks up. "Are we safe here? Ryleigh finally speaks up. With, you know, the ex-con fishermen lurking around?"

"Oh yeah, the guys are mostly harmless. But that doesn't mean they don't love giving the tourists hell every chance they get."

"Please, have you driven through the south side of Chicago after dark? We'll be fine," I affirm as Cole helps me step off the boat and onto the dock. It sways with my first step, and my eyes widen. "Holy shit, this thing is a death-trap."

"Ker, the water is barely three feet right here. Worst-case scenario, you get those fancy sandals wet before I jump in and save you."

I scrunch my nose at Cole, and he only winks back at me. I like his attention, but having Kip so nearby is unsettling to say the least.

Daniel and Stavros are next off the boat and make a joke of the perilously swaying dock with every step. Daniel hits the sandy beach first, kicks off his shoes and, with his notebook in hand, heads off down the shore, picking his way around the little rocky inlets and tide pools.

"Is the waterfall this way?" Stavros points in the direction Daniel went.

Cole nods in response. "Keep to the shore. You can't miss it."

"Is that abandoned ghost town still along the shoreline too?" I ask, vaguely remembering a defunct white clapboard lighthouse and a few small buildings and fishing cottages scattered around it.

"Sure is. State finally condemned the lighthouse. Remember when we used to sneak in and climb the stairs to the top?"

"Yeah." I smile at the memory. It's comforting how well he knows me and our shared history.

"The ghost hunters asked me to bring them over here before the end of the week to do some filming, but I told them it wasn't a good idea with the storm," Cole confesses.

"So instead you brought us? Great, thanks!" I swat at him.

"Nah, I'd just rather bring you. Those guys have more than enough footage of the island. I wish they'd fuck off already."

"Well, that's no way to think of a paying client, now is it, Mayer?" Kip slaps Cole on the back as he walks off the dock. "Where's your sense of business acumen, *bro*?" My husband is mocking Cole, and I've never been so embarrassed over his general lack of manners than this week. Has my husband always been so arrogant and entitled, and I only overlooked it before now?

"Whaddya say we explore that ghost town, *Ker*?" Kip slings his arm around my shoulders and practically hauls me off alongside him. Annoyance heats my veins because he's just used the nickname Cole has always called me. It's ours. And now, it's Kip's too. I don't know why it bothers me like it does; I only know that everything about my husband is bothering me this week.

"Come on, Ryleigh. Let's go hunt for this waterfall and leave the lovebirds to themselves." Mika is still artfully dodging my husband. I can tell something is simmering between them, and I can't help but wonder if their history runs much deeper than I originally thought. Mika and Kip and I practically grew up together, though Mika and I only reconnected again a few years ago. Our fathers have done business together, and Mika and Kip usually argue more like brother and sister than friends. But something has changed between them that I still can't quite put words to.

"Enjoy the adventure! I'll have food and booze set up on the beach when you get back." Cole waves. I wish I were tucked under his arm at the moment, exploring this island barefoot with my flirty childhood sweetheart at my side. I know I'll find myself in trouble if I continue to compare Cole and Kip, but I can't help it.

"So what's up with that punk?" Kip huffs.

I bristle. "What do you mean?"

"He's pretty *fucking* into you, *Ker*."

"No, he's not. We're just old friends."

"Please, he has his own nickname for you. What else don't I know about you two? Is this like the last time?"

"Kip, Jesus. No. Of course it's not like last time. He called me that long before you even knew me."

Kip doesn't respond, but he does lock our hands together as we walk down the beach in the opposite direction to everyone else. I've never felt afraid of my husband, but he's so on edge with this business, a new sense of anxious desperation wafts off him. An old saying my father often repeated comes back to me then. Never trust people who *think* they're desperate — they'll do anything, including step on you, to make that feeling go away.

Kip's confident demeanor is one of the things I loved about him in the early days, but did I mistake confidence for arrogance? At what point did I find myself on a path that I no longer want to be on with this man? I can't even remember the last time I trusted him, if I ever did. I trusted his name to open doors and afford me access to Chicago's heaviest hitters, but did I ever really trust him with my heart?

"Now I'm glad I never let you come up here by yourself. I can't trust you not to run off and fuck the help at every opportunity," Kip mutters under his breath. "I thought we agreed on discretion. Could you be any more obvious this week? God, Kerrigan, I just need this deal to go through, and then you can do whatever the fuck you want. Just don't compromise the deal."

"Are you fucking kidding me?" I unlatch myself from him and put distance between us. "It's always about the deal with you. And it's not like you're being so discreet. *Ugh*. I didn't come to paradise to fight and reopen old wounds with you. If I would have known it would be like this . . ." I'm fuming but setting Kip off will only make matters worse. He has never hit me, but that doesn't mean I haven't seen him come right up to the line.

"Would have been a helluva lot more fun if I'd stayed home."

"For both of us," I spit. "Feels like I have a babysitter this week."

"Hardly knew I had to babysit you until now." Kip's face is turning a shade of crimson I only see when he's fighting to control his anger. He flexes his fists at his sides and sucks in a few deep breaths. "I know you fucked him."

"What?" I spin, anger throttling my veins as I take in my husband. He's a stranger, eyes wild and muscles straining with tension. "Are you fucking nuts?"

"Nope. I can see it in the way you look at him. He's been inside you. I can see it. Stop fucking lying."

"You know, I wish I would have fucked him. I should have let him fuck me all night long. He's younger than you, probably wild in bed. I bet it'd be worth it. It's not like you've been much fun these days."

"You're such a gold-digging bitch." He's seething, and I know I've hit my mark. "I'd divorce you if I didn't think it'd cost me so fucking much money."

"Right. And marry someone else? You think the next girl will put up with you fucking around all the time? You think the next gullible pop tart you marry will wash your clothes and make you dinner and let you stick your dick in other people? Make no mistake. I'll cut any bitch who tries."

"You're deranged."

"You haven't even seen the worst of me yet, *darling*." I wink just to throw him off his arrogant asshole game. "I took self-defense for years before I met you. I could make someone disappear in a second if I wanted to, especially around here. So many remote and unpopulated islands, finding a body would be almost impossible." A wry laugh falls from my lips. I'm enjoying the way Kip is squirming under my gaze. "It's not like you spent any time here as a kid — always fucking off at some stupid boarding school. I'm the one who knows every cliff and cave on these islands."

"Psycho—"

"With all the tourist and fishing boat traffic, it wouldn't even look suspicious seeing a boat docked at one of the uninhabited islands. A body floating in the water would look just like an accident . . . not foul play." I am in control here, and it's time my husband realizes it. Kip owes me after everything I've put up with. And considering all I know about him and his business . . . I've worked too hard for too long to get the life I dreamed of; I won't watch it slip through my fingers now.

"Kerrigan—"

"Why don't you send this message to your little tramp?" I rest a calm hand on my husband's cheek. "Fuck with me or my husband — and die."

CHAPTER SIXTEEN: RYLEIGH

"I can't go on," Mika complains in her thinly veiled New Jersey lilt for the hundredth time. "You're like a mountain goat over those rocks. I'm about to twist an ankle over here."

It's been over an hour since we departed the boat and almost as long since we split up from Stavros and Daniel, who walked inland to search for the abandoned village. Stavros is intent on finding a ghost this week, even as his wife suffers with seasickness.

"Slow down, would you, Ryleigh?" Mika's whine tears me from my thoughts.

"Sorry. Do you need help?" I hold a hand at her elbow to steady her. She's got one rhinestone designer sandal perched on a boulder as frothy white waves rush between the rocks below us.

"I think I need to go back."

I can tell she feels bad, and in truth, she's not even a little bit prepared to hike the rest of the way to wherever this waterfall is. "Do you want me to walk back with you? I'm happy to."

"No, no, don't you think about it. I'm still feeling off from the boat ride over. I think I'm just going to set up a blanket on the beach and watch the waves come in." She adjusts her sun hat and sends me a sparkling smile. "Are you sure you're not mad that I'm leaving you? If I didn't feel positively horrible, I wouldn't. 'No girl left behind' is my motto."

"You're fine, Mika," I say, smiling deeper when she blows me a kiss and then turns back the way we came.

"You know, I think it might be easier to walk in the water." She slips off her sandals and then weaves between two groups of boulders and drops into the surf. The water is only halfway up to her knees. "Oh, this is nice! The sand between my toes is like a luxury spa treatment." Her smile is wide as she waves at me. "Have fun at the waterfall!"

"See ya in a bit!" I call back and then continue picking my way along the rocky shoreline. I pause to listen every few yards for the sound of a waterfall, but it never comes. Within minutes of leaving Mika, I'm missing having a companion to distract me from my own swirling thoughts.

This week has been much harder than I imagined. It's been difficult to break the habit of checking my phone multiple times an hour for messages that never come. I wonder constantly what he's thinking, if he misses *us*, if he wishes we were back in the city together. I knew navigating this week would be a challenge, but I hate to confess I expected at least a few stolen text messages or phone calls in between work projects and Zoom meetings.

"Jesus, you look like you've seen a ghost. What's going on? Where's Mika?" Daniel's voice startles me from my inner world.

"Where did you come from?" My breaths come fast, adrenaline rushing through me.

"I split on Stavros. The abandoned village is a dump. Rusted fishing equipment everywhere, hardly the tourist trap I was expecting. Why do you look like that? Are you okay?"

"I'm fine." I push my hands through my hair and wipe my fingertips across my lips. "Is something on my face? What are you talking about?"

"You look sick, Rye." Daniel's eyes move up and down my form.

"I don't feel sick." I scowl at him.

"Huh. You look all sweaty." Daniel makes an *eww* face. "Where's Mika? Kill her already?"

I laugh. "She does whine a lot. Hopefully that was our first and last hike together. She nearly broke an ankle on the rocks back there, and she had the tiniest little sandals on. She and Stavros—" I shake my head with a smile — "two peas in a pod."

"Honestly, I don't know how you stand it. Are these the people you've been hanging out with since we got our own places? I can't leave you to your own devices, can I?"

"Shut up."

"Seriously though, Rye. These are the kind of people I like to pretend don't exist. They're so spoiled and entitled and out of touch with what's really going on in the world. If you can't talk about fashion designers or trust funds or luxury real estate, you are nothing to these people."

"They're not so bad. They've welcomed you, haven't they?"

"They've tolerated me. That's about the most I can say."

"Stop." I shoot my friend a glare. "They're nice. You're the one who's being judgmental now. Who have *you* been hanging out with? Where is this 'eat the rich' thing coming from?"

Daniel tuts. "I've never been more excited to get home to my shitty little apartment, that's all I'm saying."

"You seem stressed." I state the obvious. "Are you behind on your deadline?"

"No."

He's grumpy. While this might be normal for anyone else, it's unusual for Daniel. He's the most patient and kind human I've ever met. Whatever these people are bringing out in him isn't good.

"I think all the sunshine is going to your head. You're normally a little hermit, chained to your desk all day," I tease.

He shakes his head, not even my lame attempt at humor able to bring him back from his dark mood. "They create their own trouble, all of them. I can't stand it anymore. These people are the definition of *more money, more problems*, but . . . they're idiots. They're idiots on a good day and fucking ass-holes on their worst."

"Jeez." I squint against the sunshine and the negativity my friend is throwing my way. "Tell me how you really feel, why don't you? Did something happen that I don't know about?"

Tension bunches at Daniel's shoulders before he murmurs, "If I could get a flight off this island, I would in a heartbeat."

"There's only a few days left," I offer lamely.

Daniel doesn't reply, and we walk in silence for a few minutes. Without discussing it, we've both turned back the way I came, heading in the direction of the beach and the boat.

Daniel's next words carry a hard edge. "I can tell you want to be one of them."

"Me? That's not true." Irritation prickles at the back of my neck.

"I can tell, and I don't like it." Daniel won't look me in the eye. I hate that he thinks he can see through me like this, like I'm one of his simple-minded characters. "You're better than them, Rye."

"Daniel—"

"I mean it, Ryleigh." He uses my full name, something he does only when he wants me to know he's at his limit. "They have money. That's it. And it sounds like they don't have much of that, if you believe what they're saying this week."

"They're just driven. Motivated. So few people like to work, and even fewer are bold enough to achieve the kind of success they have. Over and over. I just want to . . . *learn* from them."

"Learn what? Learn how to ask Mommy and Daddy for more money? That's the only difference, Rye, I promise. I know it probably feels validating to be welcomed into their lives and to have friends who are so superficially successful, but from an ethical perspective—"

"Stop, Daniel. Jesus, stop it. You've aimed so much hate toward them all week. I can't even enjoy a few days in paradise because I'm worrying about you so much. Maybe you should ask yourself why you're so angry lately. Or why you hate successful people so much."

"You're ridiculous." Daniel stomps off ahead of me, weaving around boulders and trying to avoid the surf.

"Try some gratitude for once, hey?" I call at his back.

"Gratitude? I should have gratitude? For what? Being the third wheel? For finding exceedingly more creative ways to dodge sexual microaggressions all week?"

"What the fuck are you talking about?" I finally catch up to him, and he's breathing hard.

"Ugh." He grunts, then looks up to the sky. "Stavros tried to kiss me at that stupid abandoned village."

"What?!" I cry

"He was pushy about it too, like he expected me to *want* it. Disgusting."

"Oh God, Daniel." I gather him in my arms and hold him tightly. "I'm so sorry."

"It's okay," Daniel sighs. "I've dated asshats like him before — they're just looking for a fun time. Always trying to use people. He's hardly unique."

"The more I think about it, the more it makes sense." It finally sinks in that Stavros is exactly the lothario cad that he says he is. He has no airs about him; what you see is exactly what you get.

"My time would have been better spent at home finishing my piece or working on my book. And here I thought paradise would be so relaxing and give me some focused writing time. I can't hear my own thoughts above all the fucking drama and narcissism coming off these people."

I don't answer, trying to be mindful of Daniel's recent stress. I'm definitely starting to regret bringing him, and I'm getting sick of the fact that his first priority in paradise is to hit his deadlines. It's not as if a lot of Daniel's articles get sold, and as many times as he's submitted his novels to publishers and agents, he's never once been offered a deal. I love him and support his art, but frankly, I love paradise and am willing to do or witness anything to be here with all of them. I'm trying not to be resentful that Daniel apparently doesn't feel the same as we walk back along the beach.

"Hey, kids!" Stavros appears almost out of nowhere. "Where's Mika? I want to show her this cool cave I found."

"She went back to the boat a while ago," I say.

His eyebrows scrunch together. "Really? I just came from the boat and didn't see her."

"Maybe she took the long way back." I smile.

Stavros sends me a skeptical look. "What long way? It's all beach or thick woods, and trust me when I say Mika would not go near the woods — too many creepy crawly things for her."

I shrug. "Not sure, then."

Stavros's gaze swings to Daniel as if he might have the answer to Mika's whereabouts. Daniel doesn't say anything, suddenly seeming very interested in an outcropping of pink granite rock as he avoids our eyes. Stavros sighs, grumbles something I can't quite make out, then turns on his heel and heads around a group of boulders before disappearing from sight.

We wander with silent steps, and at one point, I even slip my shoes off and hold them as I walk in the waves. After twenty minutes of quiet strolling, we finally turn around the tip of another rocky outcropping, and the boat and dock come into view.

"What's wrong with Stavros?" I squint against the sunshine.

"Hopefully he threw himself off the boat," Daniel quips.

"No, look." I point in the distance as Stavros tears the pads off the boat benches. He's shouting something at Cole as Kip holds Kerrigan in his arms on the shore. "It looks like he's looking for something."

Daniel moves quickly and wordlessly. I follow him as we jog down the beach to reach everyone else.

"What's up?" I ask when we're near Kip and Kerrigan.

"Tell the truth — what happened on the walk between you and Mika?"

"Me and Mika? Nothing. We walked for a while and then she wanted to head back."

"Are you sure, Rye?" Kip eyeballs me.

Annoyance bubbles in my veins. "Of course I'm sure. The last time I saw her was right around that cluster of pink granite rocks." I point behind me on the beach. "What's with the third degree anyway?"

Stavros looks up then, visibly shaken. "She's gone."

CHAPTER SEVENTEEN: COLE

"You."

Kip's eyes shoot up as Stavros descends on him. *"Me* what?"

"This is your fault. I know you did this."

"What the fuck are you talking about?"

"You've been fighting. Mika told me what you said—"

"This has nothing to do with that." Kip's anger flares. "Jesus, Kerrigan, control your dramatic friends."

Stavros is seething, his jaw working back and forth as his fists clench. He looks like he's ready to pound Kip into the sand. His breathing is fast and shallow, and for the first time in a long time, I think I might be breaking up a fist fight today.

"Low-rent scum. We shouldn't have invited them, regardless of the will." Kip addresses Kerrigan. "It should have been just us this week." Kip looks around the group before stopping at me. "What about you? Where were you when Mika disappeared?"

"I was here almost the entire time! She never came back. I never saw her. I thought she was with all of you."

My stomach churns as I realize that unless Mika comes back safe and sound soon, I'll be out on my ass before the snowflakes fly.

"Bullshit," Stavros sputters.

"Maybe she went for a swim?" Daniel offers.

"Mika doesn't swim alone!" Stavros yells. "She would *never* go in without me."

"I'm sure she'll be back," I offer.

"Maybe she ran into one of those fishermen you were talking about." Ryleigh casts around the group with worry.

"Let's hope." I take my phone out of my pocket and check to see if I have service. I don't, not even a single bar of reception. I'm hoping this doesn't turn into a crisis, that it's just a case of tourists drunk on sun and drama, but if it's not and emergency services need to be called, the only option left is the satellite radio on the boat. I've never had to use it, so I don't even know if it's working, but for Mika's sake, I hope it is.

"Hey! Did you guys see this?" Daniel is standing on the bow of the boat, and he's holding something in his hand.

"That's Mika's scarf." Kerrigan's eyes round. "Why is it soaked in blood?"

Stavros rushes up the dock and onto the boat. He yanks the bloody scarf from Daniel's hand and inspects it. "Mika was wearing it this morning. She was wearing it when she walked off with Ryleigh down the beach. Where did you find this?"

Daniel points to a section of the boat bench. "There."

I move to where he's pointed and lift the pads on the bench, looking for any other clues to her whereabouts. I find only one.

"There's more blood."

"No." Stavros covers his mouth.

"Okay, nobody move." I back away from the group and step toward the captain's helm. "I think we need to call the police."

"What?" Kip grunts. "I'm sure she's fine. She probably had a bloody nose or something."

"But what if she didn't?" Ryleigh asks. "That's too much for a bloody nose."

Kip steps into my space. "I don't understand how her scarf got on the boat, covered in blood, and yet you didn't see anything."

"I wasn't here the whole time," I state calmly.

"Oh? Where were you, then?" Kip says.

I shake my head, my own anger bubbling to the surface. "I took a walk out to the point, picked some wild blueberries on the way, then came back to start setting up lunch. The last I saw her, she was walking down the beach with her." I point at Ryleigh.

"I-I don't know where she went. She just walked off by herself." Ryleigh stumbles over her words.

"Then we should split up and look for her. I think calling the police is a little premature." Kip lifts his phone in the air, searching for a signal. "Maybe we can call her." He frowns as he continues to search for reception. "There's no fucking service in this godforsaken place, though."

"Look!" Daniel yells, holding a large rock in his palm. "It's bloody — this . . . this looks like it was used to maim someone." Worry descends on him. "We should call the police."

"I already tried. The satellite phone isn't working, there's too much cloud cover to get a decent signal." I hit redial, confirming for him that the call won't go through. The damn thing has been on the fritz all summer, I should have replaced it before now. But as much as I'm concerned for Mika's safety, I'm just as concerned about having the wrong kind of attention from the police with another accident on my watch.

Kip huffs and continues to walk down the beach and away from us in search of cell reception.

"And we should all stay together," Daniel finishes, setting the bloodied rock on the edge of the dock.

"Maybe she just went to look for help because she's bleeding. She was having trouble on the rocks with her sandals. I bet she just cut herself and used the scarf to try to stop the bleeding." Ryleigh is hopeful.

"Darling, this is *Hermès*." Stavros stares back, as if that word should mean something. He sighs. "It's French silk. It probably costs more than you and your little boy toy's rent combined. She wouldn't use this even if it was her last resort." Stavros's eyes narrow in on Ryleigh. "Wait — *you*."

"Me?" she squeaks.

"You were with her last."

"No — I left her. I mean, she left me. She didn't want to walk anymore because she was struggling with the rocks."

"How do we know that's true? Mika was wearing this scarf when she left with you, and now here it is. How can we trust anything anyone says?" Stavros accuses.

"Daniel's right," I finally interject. "We shouldn't split up." I look out to the horizon and Stonecliffe Island in the distance. "Mika didn't just vanish like a ghost. Someone here knows more than they're letting on. One of us did this," I accuse. "No one can be trusted."

Kip returns. "Look, we still don't know that this isn't an accident. Kip has returned. It's doing us no good just sitting here." He pauses next to Ryleigh before frowning. "I think a few of us should go back to Stonecliffe and call for help, and a few should stay here in case she turns up."

"No, no." I shake my head. "Absolutely not. If I bring some of you back, whoever is responsible for this — if someone is — could escape."

"What, so everyone is a suspect now?" Kip descends on me. "What the fuck? You're just gonna strand us here while you save yourself? Hell, maybe it's you."

"What motive could I possibly have for hurting her? If anything, all of you are suspects."

"I don't think we should split up either," Kerrigan finally chimes in.

"Great. That's fucking great. You would side with *him*."

Kerrigan doesn't reply, but I see tears spring to her eyes. She retreats to the opposite side of the boat near Daniel and Ryleigh. "Can I sleep in your villa tonight? I'm not comfortable being alone with him." By *him*, I know she means her husband.

103

Stavros steps closer to me then tips his head. "Where is Lyra today? What is she up to? Why is she here, clinging to us like a pathetic shadow? She's sharing dinners and listening in on private conversations like she gives a shit, but we don't know anything about why she's really here. She never spends time on Stonecliffe, and the one time she isn't around, someone goes missing? Her dad was supposed to be a *silent* investor but Lyra's been in our business from the start."

"I don't know where Lyra is today, but I know she wouldn't give enough of a shit to do anything like this." I shrug.

Stavros's muscles are taut with tension, and he's looking more and more unhinged with each passing moment. "We should go to the police and report her missing."

"It hasn't been twenty-four hours."

"So?" Stavros looks close to tears now.

"The police won't investigate someone missing for less than twenty-four hours because most people turn up before then. Plus, we're water-locked with a storm coming for us — even if we call now, the investigation probably wouldn't start until after this storm blows through." I look out to the darkening clouds in the distance. "Once that bad boy hits shore, we won't be able to get off the island at all."

"You can call someone, right?" Kerrigan asks. "On the satellite phone?"

"Maybe. I can try. But even if I can get reception through the cloud cover, they're still gonna ask if it's been twenty-four hours." The truth is, I'm at a loss here. I'm not even trained in first aid.

"So, we should just sit and wait for her?" Kerrigan is beginning to lose it.

"We have to look. We have to do something." Stavros looks wild with desperation.

Kerrigan breaks down, shoulders shaking as she devolves into tears. I want to go to her, but Ryleigh and Daniel are doing that job right now, and my getting in the way of that would only attract more suspicion. I can't afford to add fuel to this fire, so whatever happens, I have to keep cool or this crew will go off the rails. The more erratic they get the more likely they are to call the police and I can't have that happening. Not now, not ever. What happens on Stonecliffe Island needs to stay on Stonecliffe Island. If it doesn't, I'll be the one to take the fall.

"Let's break up into groups and search for her." I scan the group.

"Breaking up into groups is what got us into this in the first place. What if someone else goes missing?" Ryleigh says.

"Well, we don't have a choice. Kip and I will search the woods, Stavros and Daniel, why don't you head south on the beach — keep a close eye on the rocks."

"I'm not going with him," Daniel spits.

I sigh. "Okay, Daniel and Kerrigan, head south on the beach. Ryleigh and Stavros head north to the waterfall, maybe there's something you missed on the walk back."

"Look at those swells," Kip comments, taking in the churning water. "The currents could have carried her who knows where by now."

"Really, man? Shut the fuck up, would you?" Anger flashes in Stavros's eyes.

"He's right though." Worry crushes Kerrigan's features. "I-I don't think we have time to search for her. We can't be here once the storm hits, the boat doesn't have any room for us to shelter and it's not like camping out in one of the abandoned fishing huts is an option. If we don't leave now, we might lose our chance."

Stavros's features knit together with pain. "We can't just leave her."

"And we can't stay either," Kip grits.

As if in reply, a boom of thunder shakes the ground beneath our feet. Lightning spiderwebs across the sky before another clap of thunder rattles through me.

"I think we should leave," Daniel chimes in.

"I think you should shut the fuck up, it's not your wife that's out there somewhere."

"Stavros—" Kip clasps a hand on his shoulder — "we can't lose anyone else either, man."

"He's right." Kerrigan's taking deep breaths now, like she's trying to avoid a full-blown panic attack. "I just want to go home — not the villa, but back to the city. I want the next flight out of this place."

"Well, great. I told you I didn't want to come in the first place. I wanted to tell the lawyer to fuck off and just meet us at my office, but you kept bitching and nagging." Kip's anger grows.

"We were supposed to be making a baby!" Kerrigan's shrill scream sends a shiver down my spine. "Everything is all a mess now." She flops down onto the bench and buries her face in her hands as she cries. Kip rolls his eyes and stalks off the boat and down the dock until he reaches the sand. He pauses once he's on the beach, thrusting both hands into his dark hair and letting out a guttural yell.

I turn, heading back into the captain's quarters. "I'm not taking any of you back to my island."

CHAPTER EIGHTEEN: RYLEIGH

"What the fuck are you writing?" Kip snaps, descending on Daniel. He's sitting at the helm of the boat, notebook in his lap. "Always listening. Always taking notes. What are you? A private *fucking* investigator?" He snatches Daniel's notebook from his hands and makes a show of flipping through it. "You could at least help us look for her." Kip pauses on a page and begins to read out loud. "*And then S leans in and kisses me so hard and so quick, I just want to throat-punch him and run all the way back to Chicago. I hate every one of these arrogant assholes, and I'm beginning to think R is turning into one of them. Surprised she'd let wealth come between a twenty-year friendship, but I guess you never really know someone.*" Kip closes the notebook and tosses it back at Daniel.

"Daniel?" I gasp. "How could you say that?"

He only shrugs, but his face turns a deep shade of crimson.

"You're the real asshole here, buddy. Glad everyone else finally sees it." Kip grins. "Maybe it was you."

"Maybe *what* was me?" Daniel's anger flares to life as thunder shakes the boat.

"Maybe you got rid of Mika so you can be with *S* — I think we all know who that is." He glances at Stavros, who's scanning up and down the beach like his wife might come walking through the trees at any moment.

"Or maybe it was Stavros," Daniel says in an eerily calm voice. "He *did* only marry her for a green card."

"Kinda hard to kill your wife when your tongue is down another man's throat," Stavros barks.

"Fuck you all," Kip hisses, throwing us the finger before walking away.

"Hey, don't go far!" Cole calls out. "In fact, maybe I should tie your hands behind your back or—"

"What the fuck? Now you want to tie us up?" Daniel turns to Cole with an accusing stare. "Who the hell are these people, Rye? What did you get me into?"

"Tying people up seems a little extreme, Cole." Kerrigan holds his gaze, pleading.

"Is it, though?" he asks, eyes holding hers steadily. "Maybe I should tie *you* up." He drags his fingers along the rope that holds the boat to one of the dock pilings. "Apparently you think Mika was fucking your douchebag husband. Maybe in a fit of rage, you pushed her overboard, and she hit her head and the current carried her off before we even got back to the boat. Maybe that's where the bloody rock came from and explains why her scarf is still here."

Ryleigh sobs with shock, tears surging down her cheeks.

Kerrigan smirks. "Nice try, but I was with Kip and Ryleigh."

"Were you, though? For the entire time?" Stavros chimes in.

"Yep. Right, *Ryleigh*?" Kerrigan asks as I try to control my tears. "*Ryleigh*?"

"I dunno — I-I don't remember." My mind races as I try to repeat the events of the day. I don't think I saw Kerrigan at all after we left the boat. I think she's lying right now, trying to make me her alibi even though we weren't together at all. My heart thuds and my skin burns and itches with anxiety. My breaths turn shallow. I can't think. I can't breathe. I suddenly wish I'd brought my anxiety medication, but I haven't needed it in months. Why would I need anxiety medication in paradise?

Violent intensity swirls in Kerrigan's dark irises.

I realize then that Cole is right — none of us can be trusted.

Kip is lingering off in the distance, one foot perched on the edge of a jagged rock as he thumbs through his phone. I look down at the silent screen in my palm. While I'm normally calm under pressure, this week has left me feeling vulnerable and eager to hear from the one person I haven't had contact with. Maybe he's just busy with work like he says. Or maybe, I think for the first time, I'm the one who's not getting the messages. Maybe as soon as I get back to the city, a barrage of texts will descend as my cell connects to a decent tower for the first time. I take a deep breath, attempting to control my racing mind as I watch Stavros try to drum up a group of us to create a search party. He's wiping at his eyes, and when he turns into the afternoon sun, the salty tear tracks sparkle on his bronzed skin.

"We can't really stay here all night, can we?" Kerrigan squints up at Stavros's worried face.

"I have blankets and mattress pads below deck, and I've slept on the beach before. It's not so bad after a few drinks." Cole looks dead serious.

"Are you kidding? We're all just going to sleep here on the beach, waiting for someone who clearly can't take care of themselves?" Kerrigan's face twists with annoyance. "I bet she just went to look for help and forgot to leave a note. Or—" her eyes cut across the group of us and land on Stavros — "maybe she's having a kinky vacation quickie with one of those fishermen Cole was talking about."

"Kerrigan!" I cover my mouth.

"What?" Kerrigan says. "Either that or she's dead — just look at all that blood on her scarf. Wherever she is, we can't help her now. We're fucking stuck until this storm passes."

I see Daniel's frown quirk into a quick smile before falling again. I gulp down the painful lump in my throat as Stavros blinks and a new swell of tears rushes down his cheeks.

"No, she's right," he says in a ragged voice. "This has to be foul play."

"Hey!" Kip is calling from down the beach. "Hey! Is this Mika's?"

He's jogging down the beach with something the shade of sand in his hand. He's breathing hard once he reaches the group of us posted by the dock.

"That's hers," Kerrigan gasps, and then turns into Daniel's shoulder and bursts into tears. Daniel remains frozen, and then one tentative hand pats her on the shoulder as she sobs.

"Where did you find it?" Stavros swipes the bloody straw hat from Kip's hands and then turns it over as if inspecting it for clues.

"It was wedged between the rocks a few hundred yards down the beach." Kip's eyes are wide with alarm, like he's rattled for the first time since Mika vanished.

"Was there anything else?" Stavros pleads. "Show me."

Kip blinks once, as if he's deciding how much he really wants to help, until he relents and shrugs for Stavros to follow him back down the beach.

"We should light a fire," Cole grunts. "Storm is supposed to hit about sunset. We're gonna want shelter and warmth before then."

"Are you kidding me? What fucking shelter?" Kerrigan spins, shooting daggers at him. "There's not enough room on this boat for all of us. I'm not sleeping here. I'll fucking swim back to Stonecliffe if I have to. You can't keep us hostage."

"You're the one that wanted to come to this fucking island so badly. And I can keep you here if the safety of someone in the group is in jeopardy."

Kerrigan huffs, turning back to the beach and stalking off toward the wooded shoreline.

"A lot of this shit is gonna be waterlogged and unusable," Cole mumbles to himself.

I cringe when I realize what's actually about to happen. We've suddenly found ourselves stranded on a deserted island with a storm descending. And Kerrigan is right — even with some blankets and mattress pads this boat just isn't big enough for all of us to sleep, and only the helm is covered, everyone else would be soaked to the bone and probably freeze once the wind and waves pick up.

Cole stalks off down the sand in the direction of Kerrigan before he calls back, "Search the shoreline for dry driftwood we can burn. There's a cliff that overhangs the beach about a hundred yards that way." He points in the opposite direction of Kip and Stavros. "We might be able to ride out the worst of the storm there. I just don't want to be forced into close quarters with you fools."

Daniel and I pick our way silently along the beach, scanning for dry firewood and not finding anything.

"Do you think she really just walked off?" Daniel finally murmurs.

"I-I don't know," I confess. Another clap of thunder shakes us before the sky overhead quickly turns a dark shade of navy. The wind swirls my hair in front of my face as the tops of the birches that line one side of the shore bend sideways.

"We're missing our window to leave," Daniel says through clenched teeth.

"But we can't leave Mika," I say but I know he's right — we can't be out here searching for someone during the storm. It's suddenly turned so dark anyway, I'm struggling to make out anything more than a few feet in front of us. I can hear the rest of the group near the dock, but all I can see are dark shadows and whitecaps surging the shore.

"Imagine if something happens to the boat, and after the storm calms, we're stranded because it's damaged." I hear Kip say from the dock.

"I can anchor the boat in deeper water and use the dinghy to get back—" Cole offers.

"No," Daniel says forcefully. "No separating. How do we know you won't just drive off and leave us here? You have the most access of all of us. Why should we trust you?"

Cole's gaze hardens on Daniel's.

"Whatever we do, we have to do now." The wind causes a chill to whip through me. "I'm freezing, and we need to figure out where we can stay the safest and the driest. Arguing isn't going to help."

Kerrigan finally wanders up with a few blond sticks of driftwood. "That's all I can find. This island is barren." She tosses them in the sand at our feet. Kip and Stavros join the group looking somber and worried, only a few sticks of kindling in their hands.

"We can't stay," Kip finally says. "We didn't find anything more than a few sticks for a fire. This island is a wasteland."

Cole doesn't answer, but his eyes swing around to land on each of us. "Is that what you want? To leave your friend here?"

None of us has the courage to say it aloud, but we all nod yes.

It doesn't feel like the right decision, but then, what if doing the right thing means losing everything? We can't risk all of our lives to save hers. The smartest move is to wait out the storm safely and then come back in the morning and form a search party.

"Fine." Cole doesn't say anything else, only turns back to the dock and heads to the captain's chair.

We all follow him, Stavros still clutching Mika's water-soaked sun hat. Kerrigan settles on the nearest bench, and Kip sits beside her, throwing an arm around her shoulders and hauling her to him. She tucks herself into the crook of his arm like they've done this a thousand times, and then she breaks down into uncontrollable tears. He whispers something into her hair, shushing and calming her as he strokes her long, dark strands. "We're gonna find her."

I swallow anxiously as I force my eyes to meet Daniel's. He's staring down at his phone, forehead wrinkled in concentration as he swipes through various screens.

"What are you looking for?" I finally ask, feeling on autopilot after all the chaos of the last few hours.

"Flights home."

I sigh, heart cracking in my chest. "I'm sorry, Daniel."

"Don't be. You couldn't have known these people are fucking nuts. Or could you?" He glances at me then skips back to his screen again.

"Good luck getting cell service," I quip.

"It's spotty but I won't stop trying until my ass is firmly in the seat of a plane. As soon as those clouds open up and the internet gods shine down on us again, I'll be the first one out of here."

"Shoulda gotten on Lyra's good side and left with her," I mumble.

"And make conversation with that walking STD?" Daniel laughs. "No thanks." A rolling wave rocks the boat, and I thrust a palm out, clutching at his elbow so we both don't go overboard.

"Dude, aim the bow of the boat into the waves. Don't you know how to drive?" Kip's anger reaches breaking point, and he stands, stalking into the captain's quarters. He shoves Cole away from the wheel. "Let me do it before you kill us all," Kip growls. "If you haven't already started."

"Fuck you!" Cole charges at Kip and shoves him hard enough against the wall of the captain's quarters that Kip howls and holds his shoulder.

"Fucking *lunatic.*"

"Just let him drive. He got us here safely, he'll get us back safely," Stavros begs, emotion covering his face.

"Did he, though?" Daniel inquires. "We *are* down one of us."

Daniel's words hang in the air as ominously as the swirling dark clouds that cast shadows over our heads.

"Maybe we should get out the Ouija board — we'd probably get straighter answers out of it than any of you," Kerrigan snarls.

"A Ouija board? What is this, a fucking game of *Clue*?" Kip grunts. The boat falls silent as Cole spends the next twenty minutes clutching at the wheel and fighting to stay out of the troughs that threaten to capsize our small craft. By the time we reach the dock at Stonecliffe, the wood is soaked and slick with waves crashing over the structure.

"Dear God, please grant me some Wi-Fi to get the hell off this island." Daniel holds his arm in the air, smartphone aimed for the clouds as he searches for a signal.

"No way," Cole grunts as he ties a knot in the anchor line and then drops the plank to allow us off.

"What do you mean?" Daniel snarls.

"No one is leaving, not until we get the police involved. I can't have another tragedy on my watch."

"Another tragedy?" Stavros asks.

"Oh, that's right. Mika said something about a woman who vanished." Kerrigan's eyes widen. "This has happened before."

"What do you mean?" Fear tightens Stavros's features.

"I don't think that's what this is about," Cole mutters.

"Why not? A girl went missing last summer. Now another one has gone missing. It's exactly the same," Kip counters. "I think it's *us* who need to think about calling the police on you. How do we know you're not going to bail on us in the middle of the night? You've done this before. You know what to expect, and that gives you the advantage — not us."

"Please. You have all the access that I don't. You can book a private flight off Stonecliffe as soon as the storm clears and leave me here to take the fall for the disappearance of the tourist's wife." Cole looks wild with anger now. "I have nowhere to go if I leave."

"Well, the fuck I'm staying like a sitting duck on this island with a murderer," Daniel gripes.

"Murderer?" A new voice appears from outside of our group. It's the director of the film crew, and they seem to be filming. "Thought the storm would make for perfect B-roll for the doc, but now we've stumbled into a murder?"

"No!" I speak up, my voice croaky with emotion. "We don't know what happened."

"We'll let the viewer be the judge of that." The director's eyes twinkle with the possibilities.

"After you edit the life out of it and paint us all as murderers," Kip says.

"Hardly," the director snaps. "But I do like to find the story behind the story."

"Rye, come with me, please. Hanging with these people only causes trouble." Daniel's arm is at my back.

"No, I . . . How would we . . . You can't even get a signal," I protest.

"Maybe there's a local with a four-seater plane or—"

"Good luck getting them out here in this," Cole gruffs. "And good luck to any of you who think you can make a go of it in these waters. The storm is only getting worse. It's practically a death wish."

"Cole's right," I breathe. "We have to do what's best for Mika. If anyone leaves before she's found . . ."

"You're crazy if you think I'm staying." Worry etches Daniel's features. "I won't risk my life for these people, Rye. I don't know why you are."

"It's crazy to leave now. We almost capsized getting back to Stonecliffe. Asking anyone to come get you now is a risk. Even riskier than staying, I think."

"It's a gamble I'm willing to take," Daniel says. "There's no telling how long we'll be stranded here after the storm, or if any of us will even make it out alive." His eyes skirt around the group. "How much food and fresh water do we have anyway? We're already down a boat. What next?" Daniel's shoulders slump, and he walks away from us, heading up the path to the main estate. I follow him silently, picking my way up the path, being careful to avoid rocks in the darkening evening. "People like that are so useless, they're better off dead."

My spine tingles with the vicious sentiment from my friend. I've never heard him talk like this, and for the first time, I wonder if he's always been this way or if he's turning into someone I don't really know anymore. My oldest friend is scaring me. Between what he's writing in his journal and the hatred he's spewing for my new friends, I can't help but wonder if I ever really knew him at all. As I reach the highest point of the shore path, Daniel and I part ways. He walks with his head down in the direction of our villa, and I veer away from him.

My mind wanders to the few survival statistics I've heard over the years. I think a person can live without water for around three days. That should give us enough time to find Mika somewhere on Grand Manitou Island. Unless . . . unless the unthinkable has happened and she's been washed out by the waves, unconscious and hurt, unable to save herself. Maybe that would explain the sun hat. I cringe, wondering if Mika simply fell into the water, or if the group is right and something much more sinister happened after I left her. But who would do it? Who would even have the motive?

A vicious yell jerks me from my thoughts. It's Kerrigan. I'd know that high-pitched tone anywhere. I hear more arguing and, on instinct, duck behind a giant lilac bush. My heart hammers as I try to ease closer with my ears open. I breathe quietly, moving a few green leaves out of my line of sight, and then I see them. Kip and Kerrigan.

I can't make out what they're arguing about, but Kip's face is contorted with rage. I lean closer, eager to decipher the insults they're throwing at each other.

And then I hear it, the one thing I wasn't ready to hear. *"I know it was you."*

CHAPTER NINETEEN: KERRIGAN

"Oh no," I moan as the bistro lights that are strung up under the pergola start to flicker.

"Well, there go the lights," Cole grunts.

It's funny, I couldn't get enough of him before today. But now . . . Now, I see that Cole in a crisis is not the man I thought he was. His calm, cool, collected demeanor evaporates into arrogance and smugness. I've never disliked him so much as I do in this moment. But can I trust him?

"How much juice you got with the back-up generators?" Kip directs to Cole.

"Enough for the night if we don't go crazy with it." Cole busies himself lighting the propane lamps that anchor the four corners of the pergola. "You got any signal with that StarLink thing you got?"

"Not yet, too much cloud cover, but I'll keep trying," Kip mumbles.

"I thought it was supposed to work anywhere," Cole retorts.

Kip huffs. "Well, it's not fucking magic. This is a pretty big storm." We all huddle near the outdoor kitchen under the covered part of the structure as the wind whips the trees. The rain hasn't started yet, but the sky darkens with shades of gray as claps of thunder rock the sky. Despite the dark and stormy surroundings, a fire roars in the outdoor fireplace and gives a false sense of cozy security.

"Looks like the waves are getting bigger," Daniel muses as frothy whitecaps dominate the shore below us. We all remain silent as we watch the storm gather strength. A vicious energy permeates the atmosphere and settles like firecrackers in my bloodstream.

"This storm will be a deadly one." Cole's voice is somber.

"If it isn't already." Kip's retort is biting and makes me flinch.

Ryleigh speaks up. "Shut up, would you? You're not help-ing." She levels a withering look at my husband for a moment before she tears herself away and the meek little hunch of her shoulders returns.

"What?" Kip shrugs. "I'm just saying, if she's still out there alive, she won't be for long."

"Ugh!" I slam my hand on the table with a howl. "You're positively un-*fucking*-bearable this week."

"Hate to break it to you, babe, but it's the company. These aren't my people, they're yours." Kip stalks off into the yard, headed for our villa. I follow him, too strung out on the pain of what we've become to stop myself. By the time we reach the front doors, I'm hot on his heels, and he knows it.

"Be a little more obvious, would you?" I spit.

"Obvious? *Please*." He cackles like a Disney villain. "I see the way you look at that caretaker."

"The caretaker?" I scoff. "At least I don't fuck people I do business with."

"Jealous, much?" His eyes twinkle. I hate that the twin-kling thing they do was one of the reasons I fell in love with him, and now he's using it against me, making me hate him. Making me want out of whatever this is.

"Jealous of a snobby socialite? *Hardly*."

"What?" His face twists with confusion.

"You're always on your phone, always texting, always talking to *her.*"

"You're paranoid," he says, unconcerned.

"We don't even have sex anymore! Don't you care? Don't you want to connect with me? Touch me again? Don't you want what we had?"

"What we had," he scoffs. "That ship set sail after your flirty little fling with the pool boy from the athletic club that almost cost us everything." Kip's tone is bitter. "Cost me fifty-thousand dollars to keep those dirty videos off the internet. Have all the fun you want, Kerrigan, but when it starts costing me money, I have a problem with it."

"No. This is not like that."

"The hell it isn't. If I wouldn't have bailed you out, God knows where we'd both be by now." We don't ever talk about this, don't talk about what it took to make things better between us . . . and now we're here. Off the rails again and fighting about who ran us into the ground this time.

"Just . . . please be aware. You're embarrassing me, that's all."

Kip rolls his eyes. "You're being absurd, and these kinds of accusations are what's damaging us. It has nothing to do with me being on my phone too much or not."

"Fine," I manage to say, then turn back to the doorway. Rain is pelting the windows now, and the wind is bending the trees so much outside it looks like a tropical storm is descending on the island. "I'm filing for divorce as soon as I get back to the city." A baby can't fix us. We're broken beyond repair, and this divorce will be the first clearheaded thought I've had in years.

"Good," my husband finally calls out. "Life will be easier without you. *And* cheaper." I turn, watching him open his laptop and plop down onto the chaise. "I wish you were the one missing, not Mika."

I don't know if he knows I've heard him. I think if he did, he wouldn't care. I hate him. I want him to pay. I want him to feel the hurt he's inflicted on me for so many wasted years.

Waves of rage pummel my system, but underneath is sadness. I can't afford sadness right now.

Rage is better than heartbreak.

Rage is better than being numb.

CHAPTER TWENTY: COLE

Morning, Babe! Sorry I bounced without saying bye yesterday. Daddy had a charity event he asked me to attend in his place last minute so I left before the sun was up. I should be back Friday if you want to hang out ;) How was your picnic with the tourists? Did you avoid the storm?

I wake to a morning text from Lyra. Swiping a palm over my face, I push out of bed as a feeling of resentment settles over me. As soon as she left, everything blew up. She's been hanging around this particular group of tourists more than any other before. It's got me wondering if dear old Daddy sent her to watch over me this summer. Or *them*.

"Untrustworthy bitch," I grunt as I make my way to the bathroom. Her leaving right before Mika vanished last night looks bad for her and for me. I should've known she wasn't to be trusted — a former addict can never be relied on. I can attest to this first hand. The first time we met, she left me to do a line of coke in the bathroom with another guy.

Hello, first red flag.

I decide to ignore her message and instead get dressed and head outside to survey the storm damage. It's bad, but not the worst I've seen. The worst damage is along the shore. The pathway that leads from my caretaker's cottage up to the main

121

estate is nearly washed out in some places. I kick a fallen birch branch off the path and groan, thinking not for the first time that I'm sick of serving the tourists all day, every day through the summer. I continue to walk and think about one of the guys I graduated with who's now settled in Santa Monica with a tech start-up and a bubbly blonde wife. Maybe after this summer, it's time I take a break. Lyra's father won't like that I'm not here to watch over and repair things during the off season, but I can't even begin to care what his needs are right now. At the moment, this island feels like it might be the end of me. If I don't get out now, I may never get a chance. And when I do leave, I won't look back. I won't ever have to think about any of these crazy fools again. It just pains my heart that it means leaving Kerrigan behind too. *Again.*

I pull the emergency satellite radio out of the pocket of my cargo shorts and switch it on. I wasn't able to get a signal on it last night or on the boat radio, but maybe now that the skies have cleared, I'll have a better chance. As soon as the radio is on, it connects to the satellite, and a computer-generated voice warns that another storm is scheduled to hit the islands later tonight. I cringe, realizing we'll hardly have a chance to organize a search party for Mika before the next storm descends. I dial the number to connect me to emergency services, and within a minute, I'm on the phone with someone.

"Hi, it's Cole Mayer on Stonecliffe. I need to report a missing person. One of the guests of the estate."

"Do you suspect she's been hurt?" comes the operator's reply, her voice crackling with the poor connection.

"Yes, there's blood. *A lot* of blood. We'll need someone out here to help us search for her. She disappeared on Grand Manitou yesterday."

"I'm sorry, sir. I'm afraid all emergency services are grounded until further notice." Her voice fades in and out, and I'm struggling to catch all of her words.

"What's that supposed to mean? We should just look for her ourselves?"

"I don't know, sir. I've logged your situation in the computer. We'll get someone out to you as soon as it's safe, but right now, we're backed up. There's a lot of damage to the marina. We couldn't get our boats off Mackinac right now if we wanted to."

"What about St. Ignace or Mackinaw City?" I ask.

"They're more backed up than we are," she replies.

"Shit," I breathe.

"I'm sorry, sir. Best of luck."

The line goes dead, and any hope I have of finding Mika fizzles with it.

I have to resist throwing the satellite phone on the ground in frustration. Instead, I shove it back into my cargo pocket and continue along the shore path as it leads down to the main dock on the island. Something is off; I can feel it the moment I approach. A few of the deck boards are splintered and broken, probably from the waves crashing the catamaran into it all night. The repair crew wasn't able to come from the mainland because of the storm, so now I've got a boat that already needed an engine rebuild that is now scraped and dented all along one side. It will take me at least an afternoon of repairs, but that's not even the worst of it. The boat now has a giant gash along the starboard side. A gash that I will not be able to repair myself. Stonecliffe is now down two boats, which leaves us officially stranded.

It's then I notice that something else is missing. The dinghy that's always attached to the back of the catamaran is gone. I pick my way along the dock as safely as I can to get a closer look. The waves must have carried it offshore, but it's still odd that it's not in my line of sight. It must have landed around the other edge of the island, if it hasn't been destroyed beyond recognition. I leave the dock and continue making my way along the shoreline, splitting from the path that leads to the guest villas. Puffy white clouds against a bright-blue sky lend a peaceful quality to the morning, a stark contrast to the dark thunder-clouds that ravaged the island all night.

A glimmer of light catches my eye among the boulders. I bend, freeing the item from among the jagged rocks. It's a single sandal, sparkling with rhinestones, and the most ostentatious thing I've ever seen. It, without a doubt, belongs to one of the tourists' wives, more junk left behind for me to clean up. This island was better off when it was a simple fishing cove.

Rich people ruin everything.

CHAPTER TWENTY-ONE: RYLEIGH

"This belong to anyone?" Cole tosses a sparkly thong sandal at our feet.

I recognize it instantly, covering my mouth as I whisper, "It's hers."

"*Whose?*" Cole's eyes land like a hawk on mine.

Tears rush down my cheeks as I realize last night wasn't a dream. Everything about it was a very real nightmare. "Kerrigan's. Her sandals match mine. We bought them together last summer."

"Wait? Where's Kerrigan?" Kip looks around the group. "I thought she was with you."

I shake my head. "I haven't seen her since we got back to the island last night."

"What the fuck do you mean? She left our villa last night. I assumed she was headed to yours." Kip approaches me with a violent stare. "Are you telling me Kerrigan is missing too?"

"I don't know," I squeak, shrinking from him. "We never saw her."

"Hold up. How do we know you didn't do something to her?" Cole advances on Kip, coming between the two of us.

In that moment, I'm thankful for Cole's intervention because I'm no longer sure I can trust Kip Lange.

Did he do this? *Did he do everything?* Or was it Cole? I went for a late-night walk last night because I couldn't sleep and saw him through his cabin window working on something at the table. It seems unlikely that he'd be calmly at work in his cabin if he'd just done something to Kerrigan, but I guess anything is possible.

"I knew we should've left," Daniel grits. I flinch, because he's probably right. "We should never have gotten wrapped up with these people."

"She has to be here. They have to be here. Maybe they're together — do you think? We have to find them." Stavros is visibly shaking, his voice cracking with emotion as he scans the waterline with the smallest pair of binoculars I've ever seen.

"Another storm is coming," Cole mutters almost apologetically.

My muscles tremor and shake with fear as I watch Stavros have an emotional breakdown. Kip's anger is spiraling with each passing moment, and Cole seems wary and suspicious as he watches all of us with a look of quiet disdain.

"We have to stay together. We're safer if we stay together, right?" Daniel looks genuinely concerned for a change.

"Are we?" I ask, unsure for the first time since Mika's disappearance.

"Where is Lyra?" Kip shoots the question to Cole.

"She left," Cole says.

"That's convenient." Daniel shakes his head.

"Okay, okay. Everyone stay calm. We have to think clearly about this—" Kip holds up his hands.

"You know, *you're* remarkably calm for a guy whose wife is missing," Stavros observes.

"Back at ya, bud," Kip gripes.

"At least I'm not a thief," Stavros shoots back.

"What the fuck are you talking about?" Kip's demeanor turns threatening.

"How about the fact that you never got her money back? She only wanted her investment back to float the business. You probably offed her to get rid of the headache. Now you never have to repay her, right?"

"That's between Mika and me." Kip advances on Stavros.

"Mika invested heavily in Kip's little crypto fund, and now she needs the returns ASAP to shore up the design business because one of the warehouses in Milan caught fire." Stavros slumps into one of the outdoor chairs. "Her father's *very* important friends are breathing down her neck for their money, but Kip won't pony up." Stavros shoves his hands into his hair. "Did you lose all the money? Be honest for once, would you?"

"It's staked — locked up in the market right now, just like I told her," Kip explains.

"I told her she was never gonna see that money again. What kind of fucking loser hustles friends at a Christmas party? A pathetic swindler, that's who." Stavros's eyes burn bright with anger. "Kip is shorting all of his investors. I'd tell you to get your money out now, but I'm sure it's already too late."

"Is that true?" I peer at Kip but he looks away.

"Regardless, we should still probably stay together. If we're all going to make it off this island, we have to watch out for one another," Kip says. "And we need to find Kerrigan." He gestures to Daniel and me. "You two search the cabins. I'll take the shore path. Cole, can you check your cabin? Stavros, can you check out the other side of the island?"

I nod as Kip turns in the direction of the cabins, shouting Kerrigan's name into the breeze.

Daniel turns away from the group, crushing his palm against his face. "Rye . . ." His gaze settles on mine. "When a wife goes missing, statistically . . . it's usually the husband."

"Hey—" Cole chirps, pointing at Daniel — "he's right. Kip and Kerrigan were always fighting. Lyra even recorded them on her phone."

I should help Kip search for Kerrigan but I'm bone tired. I can clearly see that he's hurting. Even under all the abrasive comments, he needs a support system right now. I wonder what Kerrigan would do. I imagine my friend putting aside her annoyances and nurturing him in the way a wife should.

"Maybe we're overlooking something," I muse, scanning the coastline in search of any previously missed detail. Daniel huffs, dubious. "You know, the theory of Occam's razor — the simplest explanation is the most likely one." I frown in thought. "Cole already found a sandal. There must be something else to help us figure out where Kerrigan went."

"Maybe Cole did it," Daniel accuses.

"What? Hey!" Cole thrusts his hands into the air. "Lyra is gone too. Maybe she's missing. We don't have proof that she really made it off the island. It's just better if we stay together."

"Think about it. We thought Mika was seasick," I say, thoughts percolating. "But she spends summers on a boat in the Mediterranean, and she was fine on the ride to the island. There's no reason for her to be seasick."

"Mika grew up on yachts," Stavros confirms. "Maybe it was something she ate." Our eyes swing to the only person who's been serving us food all week.

Cole stiffens. "So, what are you saying?"

"Maybe it was you. Maybe it was the both of you," Stavros says. "Maybe someone on your staff poisoned her. Maybe you're working with them to—"

"There is no staff, you spoiled fucks!" Cole stalks off, leaving Stavros, Daniel, and me alone under the sun-soaked pergola.

Daniel heads for the shoreline with a grunt, "I'm gonna look for Kerrigan while you guys stand here and fight like kids."

I follow him, mostly because he's the only one I trust on this island.

I think again how our paradise has turned into a prison. Now, it's every man for himself.

CHAPTER TWENTY-TWO: COLE

"This has to be an accident." My mind spins as I think about how I'm going to break this to Lyra's father. Two missing people in two days — nothing about this is good. I'm worried for both of them, but in truth, I'm worried for me just as much. We've spent the last few hours hunting all over this island for any sign of Kerrigan but she seems to have vanished into thin air. Somehow, I keep falling into the worst kind of trouble without even meaning to. If the police catch wind of a second missing person on the island, there's only one person they're going to suspect. *Me.*

Lyra's father will get rid of me without a second thought, because another missing person is just more bad press for Stonecliffe. It's hard to turn a profit with the tourists when their wives keep disappearing. No one wants to stay at a resort where the guests die.

Whatever happened this week will be the end of all of us if we can't get to the bottom of things soon.

I still wonder about Lyra, though. I sent her text messages yesterday to tell her about Mika, but none of them were delivered. I've been trying to call her on the satellite phone all morning but the call isn't connecting. The service here is so spotty, I can't depend on any of the normal methods of communication. I just wish there were a way I could confirm that Lyra actually got off the island. It's probably foolish of me to worry about her. She's always been independent to a fault, but with the way the last twenty-four hours have unraveled, I can't *not* think the worst. My mind is running wild with every possibility, and the one person I want to talk to — Kerrigan — has vanished on me.

Is there a chance she left on purpose? Maybe she couldn't handle the fighting with her husband so she left without telling any of us. Short of rowing herself to the mainland, I don't know how else she could escape, though. And even then, she would have at least told me, right? And then I think of how private Kerrigan has been over the years, only revealing things when it best suited her. No, I realize, she wouldn't tell me anything she didn't have to; she and I go way back, but that means little in the world she lives in.

"I know what you did." Kip's angry voice is suddenly at my side. "We all know."

"Know what?" I growl, thinking how much easier things would be if this tool would have been the one to disappear.

"Mika found out about the missing girl last summer. It's all over the internet." Kip's eyes are locked onto mine. "Just like the other tourist who had the 'unfortunate accident'. I know you were the main suspect, accused of negligence after all the alcohol and drugs you provided. Why haven't you put up a fence or a guardrail on the cliffside to prevent it from happening again? It's almost like you don't care. It's almost like you're inviting tragedy."

"You don't know what you're talking about — she jumped off a boat to swim and never resurfaced."

"She was high and broke her fucking neck and her parents tried to sue Stonecliffe. That's why Lyra's dad gave you the ultimatum about staying here, because he cleaned up your mess for you. Paid for the legal team that got you off, didn't he? Without him, you'd be homeless and bankrupt. And maybe even in jail."

Kip isn't wrong, and I hate him for it. Lyra's father was very clear on the terms of our agreement. Either he breaks my neck for ruining his business, or I work off the debt free of charge until he says otherwise. I can still hear his warning: *One mistake and you're dead.*

I thought my duties would be lawn-mowing and snow-plowing and maybe some landscaping or handyman work, but my first day on the job, it was clear no one else would be on the island. Meeting tourists at the boat dock, scheduling day trips, arranging deliveries and caterers and cleaning crews — all my responsibility.

Jon Caruso is sucking every last drop of work out of me this summer.

"And Kerrigan . . . Well, everyone here can tell you've been obsessed with her since we arrived."

"So you think I did something?" I snarl.

"Maybe you know what happened and you're covering it up so you don't get in more trouble. I get it, dude. But just tell me where she is so I can help her. I won't press charges, just let me help her."

"As if you can do anything for her." I walk away, but he follows.

"Okay. Whatever, man. I was hoping you would just come clean, but if you wanna do things the hard way—"

"Fuck you—"

Before I can finish, Kip is on me, launching a pathetic punch at my head before I lock a palm around his wrist and stop him.

"Look, I get why you're doing this. This is scary for all of us, but fighting doesn't help us find her sooner." I do my best to relax with adrenaline still shuttling through my bloodstream. I can understand why they're accusing me. I can even understand why the police always suspect me in times of foul play. I'm the first to admit that this looks very, very bad for me, and now with Lyra gone too, things look even worse. I don't know what happened to Mika and Kerrigan, but I know whatever it is, I need to look out for myself first, no matter what.

"I'm watching you, asshole. We're all watching you," Kip says, pulling his phone out of his pocket and checking it again for service. I wonder just who it is he's trying to talk to. Whatever the situation, it must be important because he's been glued to that thing all week. I follow a few steps behind him, eyeing his form as he walks ahead of me before I hear him mumble, "Fuck this vote — this is fucking impossible."

CHAPTER TWENTY-THREE: KIP

"This doesn't look good." I move in long strides in the direction of the villa Kerrigan and I are meant to be sharing. Until she *vanished*. "This doesn't look good at all."

My mind can't help but crawl over the many possibilities. Or *crimes*.

The entire purpose of this week away was to be present for the will reading and then work on closing the deal, and if I can't get all the signatures to sell this island soon, the entire fucking deal is underwater. This deal is my only shot at coming back from this fuck-up. Cole will be the most difficult — we already spoke on the phone about the possible sale of the island last year and he was adamant that he would not be selling his shares. I'd hoped a little more time would work in my favor with him, but nothing about this week has gone to plan, so asking him to sell now feels like the worst option. And it would have been easy just to tell Mika that she needed to sign over her share of the island if I'm going to get all of our investment money back from the crypto fund, but a confession like that could trigger financial regulators. I'd like to say that every deal I've made has been held to the highest ethical standard, but success in business often requires overlooking morals in favor of gains. Ultimately, I know if federal agents investigate, the more they dig, the more they won't like what they find.

And then a lifeline presented itself. If Kerrigan is missing, I'm the sole inheritor of her life insurance and the trust . . . That's just enough money to float the business and pay off the remaining debt. It really is the perfect plan — a windfall for me and the ideal way to pay off my investors. But it also makes me the prime suspect in my wife's disappearance.

And of course they think it's me. With the way Kerrigan and I have been fighting all week, it's not hard to imagine me pushing her off a cliff in a fit of rage and trying to play it off as an accident. God knows I've wanted to on a few occasions. Kerrigan has a way of getting under my skin like nobody else. Keeping my anger in check over the years has been difficult, to say the least, but not impossible. And sure, it might benefit me if I can stumble into a windfall to fix my problems — then I don't even have to worry about getting the last few signatures. But killing her? Do people really think I'm that guy?

Shoving a hand into my hair, I lean against the door of the villa and sigh. "Lyra's father is going to have thoughts about all of this."

"What does Lyra's father have to do with anything?" Ryleigh's voice rips me from my thoughts.

"Jeez, you scared me. Do you always make a habit of sneaking up on people like that?" My frown softens when I see the look of pained concern on her features. I need to be a little nicer if I'm going to get through this. "Lyra's father mentored me in business. He taught me everything I know, and he still advises me now with the crypto fund and the markets."

I don't add that even if I manage to get all the signatures I need on the deal, my shares will still funnel directly to Lyra's father because all the investments are underwater right now, including those of my biggest investor — *him*.

"Is that what's up with you this week?" She's looking me square in the eye now, as if she doesn't trust me either. Hell, I don't know if I trust myself anymore.

134

"That, and the fact that Kerrigan won't get off my ass about making a baby. I have way bigger issues to deal with. This is serious business. I don't think she understands that. It isn't something that Kerrigan getting her damn baby can fix."

Ryleigh is silent a long moment before she wipes at a watery eye. "She may never get a chance now."

And with that, Ryleigh turns, heading away from me and into the blinding sunshine. I've fucked up, I know I have, but sometimes it's too late to turn back. Sometimes the hole you've dug for yourself is so deep, it's better to just keep digging until you find the light on the other side. Sometimes, you have to commit to the sin and see it through to the end.

CHAPTER TWENTY-FOUR: RYLEIGH

"Kerrigan was right," I announce once I'm back at the pergola.

"About what?" Daniel asks.

"Kip. Maybe everything."

"What do you mean, *Kip*?" Daniel steps closer.

"He's an asshole. I know he's busy, but his shitty comments certainly aren't helping." My heart sinks deeper in my chest the more I think about it.

"I think he did it." Daniel practically reads my mind. "He has the means and the motive to get rid of both Kerrigan and Mika. I don't trust him. He's the only one who doesn't have an alibi, Rye. Think about it."

My thoughts linger on Daniel's words. "I think I misjudged him. Ugh, how did he fake it for so long with everyone?"

"Fake what? Being a good human? I'm pretty sure he wasn't fooling anyone." Daniel tips his head at me, eyes crawling over my face and making me uncomfortable. "Did he really fool you?"

I only shrug. "I like to think the best of people. Sometimes it backfires, I guess."

"I guess." Daniel is still watching me, as if I have something on my face. As if he can see right to the core of me.

"It could have been a fisherman too," I offer weakly.

"Really? For both of them?" Daniel is unconvinced. "This isn't some shitty low-budget horror movie. There isn't some guy out there with a fishing hook for a hand, stalking and killing us one by one."

"How do you know? I'm gonna take a walk and look for more clues." I wave Daniel off and head in the direction of the shore path.

The storm has washed out a lot of sections of the path, and I take my time carefully making my way along the hazards. Whitecaps crest and froth along the rocky shoreline, and for the first time, I think how easy it would be to hide a missing body on this island. Stonecliffe is so remote, plopped in the middle of Lake Michigan, it's the perfect hiding spot. And the lack of dependable emergency services adds another layer of protection for any criminal. I understand now why Cole warned us off the fishermen who call the remotest of these islands home. The very nature of living in a place like this lends itself to secrecy.

I move with measured steps along the rocks, searching for anything unusual that may have washed up. The path winds along granite and limestone boulders and descends down a small outcropping before turning sharply to the north. I follow the rocky outcropping and train my eyes to the horizon in the distance, hoping against hope a boat carrying both Kerrigan and Mika will pop up out of the blue.

And then something does enter my line of sight. The tiny, pitched roof of a fishing hut peeks over a pile of dark granite.

I stumble closer, eager to find anything that might indicate that Kerrigan has been here. The storm could have washed anything on shore. I struggle to remember what each of them was wearing yesterday before they vanished. I blink back tears when I think about my annoyance with Mika the last time I saw her. Where would we be if I'd stayed by her side instead of splitting up?

I look up to the horizon, squinting into the sunshine as I struggle to determine what exactly I'm seeing. It looks like a small fishing boat puttering in circles in the distance. I can't see anyone behind the wheel, but with the way the halos of sunshine are splintering across the water, it's hard to see much of anything. I spend another minute trying to discern a vessel identification number somewhere on the hull but give up on seeing anything from this distance. I wave for a moment, hoping to get the attention of whoever is captaining the boat. I give up when I realize it's just spinning tight circles in the water, almost like it's unmanned. Or like someone set the anchor and put the engine in gear and then disappeared. Or worse, is busy trying to dispose of something. Like a body.

A chill runs through me then when I look back at the fishing shack, noticing all the rusted fishing tools and processing equipment scattered around the area. Tangled fishing line, bobbers, buoys, and nets are strewn around the rocks, and I think for the first time since I've come to the island that maybe a weapon would do me well. I'm on edge. Something about the line between wealth and poverty here doesn't sit well with me. And according to Cole, an underlying animosity simmers between the locals and the tourists which only seems to ratchet up to fever pitch in times like these. Friends have turned foe, and I can't shake the feeling that the storm has only just begun.

Then, out of the clear blue sky, a clap of thunder shakes the atmosphere, and a dark cloud rolls overhead. The waves, still churning from last night, gather fury in response. And suddenly, I find myself perched precariously on a rock with violent surges of lake water frothing below me. The granite has turned slick, and in the span of a moment, my position has switched from safe to threatening. This entire island is hostile — the most savage and traitorous force of all this week. Our peaceful picnic yesterday turned into a missing person case, and my morning walk has quickly become life-threatening.

I turn, anxious to get back to the rest of the crew, as a spray of lake water swallows my form and leaves a slick mist everywhere I step. Another flash of lightning cracks through the air and splinters along a broken leaded-glass window. A figure darts into the shadows of the shack, and on instinct, I scream. Fear throttles my system and I choke down another yell. If this is one of the old, crusty fishermen Cole warned us about and I'm trespassing on his property, I don't want to wait around to find out what comes next.

Another flash of lightning blinds me for a moment, and then a glimmer of something shiny and gold among the rocks catches my eye. Waves crash methodically as the tiny golden object remains still under a few inches of water. I bend, eager to get my hands on what looks like a key or something similar, before a hollow thud cracks my skull and my vision blurs then fades to inky black.

CHAPTER TWENTY-FIVE: RYLEIGH

"Well, well, well — look what the storm washed up."

I blink once, twice trying to force my vision to clear. I can't be seeing what I'm seeing. There's no possible way.

"Surprised to see me?" Kerrigan looms over me, and it's not that seeing her is setting my mind reeling; it's how she looks. So utterly normal. Faded blue jeans and white tennis shoes on her feet, a raincoat buttoned to the throat on top, and a high ponytail that sways in the wind. Her face is clean and make-up free, her striking, natural features deceptive. She looks every part the typical tourist's wife . . . *except for her eyes*.

They're wide and wild, the pupils dilated and boring a hole into mine. I twist and turn, realizing that I'm tied at the wrists to a rusted fish processing table. It was obviously used to gut and fillet the day's catch, with rusted tubes that angle into a small hole in the metal for refuse.

"*Whaz goin' on?*" I slur, blinking as a wave of red trickles down my right eye. "I'm bleeding."

"Had to get your attention somehow." Kerrigan's smile is wide, almost unhinged. I've never seen this side of her, but I can't say I'm surprised she's got one. Maybe it was the lingering darkness that drew me to her, the sense that she lives her life on some unseen razor's edge of pleasure and pain.

Tangle with sinners and become one, I think.

It's then I notice that Kerrigan is twisting a rusted fishing knife in her hand. The blunt end of the handle is stained dark red, and it occurs to me it must be the weapon she hit me with. I try to take in my surroundings. I notice a fraying rope tied at my waist, and with a quick jerk of my arms, I can tell it's the same rope that's keeping me tied to the table.

"I know what you've been up to," Kerrigan coos, leaning in and dragging the tip of the knife along my lips. "*Tsk, tsk, tsk.*" She grins. "And I thought you were my friend."

"I am! I am your friend," I plead, tears mixing with blood on my cheeks.

"Really? You think so?" She frowns. "Well, what kind of friend fucks your husband?" Her eyes dart down my body, and she bites down on her bottom lip with her teeth. A crazed look comes over her, sending a chill through me. "Well, you can have him. He's a no-good piece of shit who lost all of our money anyway." She drags the tip of the knife down the hollow of my neck. One quick movement and she could puncture the delicate skin and end me. And something tells me she would enjoy every minute of it. "In fact, you're taking him off my hands just in time."

"I don't know what you're talking about, Kerrigan. I promise."

"Bullshit." She presses the knife tip into my collarbone until a sharp pinch threatens to break the skin. Kerrigan seems drunk on the power she's lording over me. "I know everything."

"What's everything? I don't know what you're talking about." I work my fingers back and forth, trying to prevent them from going numb.

"My husband and I have an open arrangement; it's the only reason he agreed to marry me. He was supposed to be discreet and respectful — don't ask, don't tell, and all that — and he was . . . until *you* happened."

141

"Me?" I croak, trying to work the frayed rope against the sharpest edge of the metal table leg.

"*You.*"

"Kerrigan, please, you're not making sense—"

"Liar," she seethes. "I admit, you had me fooled. So sweet and innocent, I thought for sure it was Mika who was fucking my husband at first. But the more time we spent together, I realized Mika is too brash for Kip. He likes a good, meek little housewife to control. Let me guess, nice dinners and show openings and rooftop cocktails . . . He spoils you with all of it, right?"

I remain silent, afraid that anything I say might set her off.

"I know about the ring, you little bitch." She digs the knife a millimeter deeper, and I wince. "Now he thinks he loves you, and he doesn't even want to try for a baby with me. It was our dream, and you destroyed it."

"No." I squeeze my eyes shut as I beg. "Please, Kerrigan, don't do this."

"Imagine my surprise when I found out you were the one he knocked up."

"Ker—"

"I saw the baby gift."

I don't answer her, because nothing I say can fix this.

"Remember when you gave me the key to check on your cat when you went to your parents' house for the weekend?" She raises an eyebrow like she's just revealed the cleverest thing. "I didn't think you had it in you to betray me." Kerrigan drags the point of the knife along my collarbone as she purrs, "*So excited to start our life together, baby.*" Kerrigan's mocking voice drips with disdain. "*Once work calms down, I'm initiating divorce proceedings, and we can start the next chapter of us.*" And that stupid little onesie from Kip's alma mater. It's the one I told him I wanted to buy for our baby someday. I'm the one who pointed it out to him. And you stole it. You stole everything."

Kerrigan is in front of me then, and both of her hands land on my knees to still the trembling. "Please, Kerrigan. Please don't do this."

142

"Don't do what, darling?" She drags the tip of the knife up my inner thigh and stops at my waist. Her eyes sparkle with rabid excitement. "Don't cut *my* baby out of your belly and leave you to bleed out in the sand like you deserve?"

CHAPTER TWENTY-SIX: COLE

"Stonecliffe is underwater. When are you going to admit that and give up the past already?" Kip advances, snarling.

"Only because you spoiled fuckers have run it into the ground," I grit out. "I heard you talking on the phone about drawing up the paperwork to sell — I know that's why you're here this week, to try and get my island out from under me. Is this what your father would want? For you to sell your share to the highest bidder?"

"You're half the man he was."

"And you're not even that," I shoot, anger boiling over. I cock my arm back, ready to lay Kip Lange out in the sand if that's what it takes to shut him up.

"Hey — hey! This isn't helping." Daniel attempts to wedge himself between us.

"Leave them be!" Stavros yells. "Men have to work out their differences physically."

"I'm not going to watch them destroy each other," Daniel says in a measured tone.

"Our fathers wanted us to raise our kids here — to preserve the land for future generations." My voice turns nostalgic in an attempt to calm Kip.

Kip eyeballs me. "And now everyone from the first generation is dead."

"Except Lyra's father," I remind him.

"And none of them could have predicted what the future holds. We live in a different world now. The future is digital, not in real estate. If we don't capitalize on that now, we lose out," Kip says.

"You mean *you* lose out," I correct him. "Oh, wait a minute. That's what this week has been about, hasn't it? That's why you made the trip up here. You need signatures from all of us to sell."

"Ownership is tricky under a land contract." Kip is visibly upset.

"It was meant to be tricky," I retort. "So some asshole couldn't come along and sell the oil rights to the highest bidder, which is *exactly* what you're trying to do."

"The market is booming right now. We have to make hay while the sun shines." Kip is trying to cultivate some patience, but it doesn't come naturally to him.

"I'll never sell," I announce.

"Color me shocked," Kip huffs. "Headline: *Local Boy Never Leaves the Shithole He Grew Up In*."

"Fuck you. My dad was gifted a share long ago in exchange for his stewardship of Stonecliffe. It's because he was the caretaker these last fifty years that this place has survived and made all of your families money."

"Stewardship," Kip scoffs. "You know if tourists keep dying, the guests don't rebook, right?"

"Those were accidents."

"Accidents have a cost too. And what about Mika and Kerrigan? Were those just accidents too?"

I narrow my eyes, trying to put together the missing pieces. He's definitely accusing me of foul play, but he's got way more motivation to make one of those women disappear than I do.

"You need to sign over your share, Cole. There isn't a future for you at Stonecliffe. There isn't a future here for any of us. Hasn't this week proven that?"

I shake my head, still trying to figure out what Kip is up to. "Wait a minute — was this your plan all along? Create a few convenient accidents to blackmail everyone else into signing over their shares to you?"

Kip's jaw clenches. "You're holding us hostage with your stupid games. Everyone could use the money from the sale of this island, Cole. Every. One. Of. Us."

He pushes me in the chest, causing me to stumble and nearly fall. Instead, I catch myself and charge back at him, fist drawn before I pummel him with all my force in the cheekbone. I can hear the sickening crack, but it doesn't slow Kip — he's on me, and we're both rolling on the ground, fighting for the upper hand.

"Guys!" Daniel bellows. "Stop it already!"

"This is business!" Kip yells as he throws another punch.

"There's more history than you know," I direct at Daniel. "Stay out of it. This dumb asshole has had it out for me for years."

"Business has been bad since that girl vanished last summer, Cole." Kip is trying to out-yell me. "It was the headline in every local paper and morning news show for weeks, and again when her body was found that spring."

"It was an accident!" I say again. "Stop trying to make money off everything you see."

"It's not me who wants to sell!" Kip cries. "Lyra's dad found a developer for the place. It's the only way to get out from under this rock."

"Who wants out from under it? You're the only one who seems so damn concerned about unloading it."

"The profitability of the estate is gone. You used this place as your own personal drug den, while the rest of us went off to the city to turn what we had into millions. And yet here you are," Kip sneers, "like a fossil frozen in time. It's not like you just became a loser, right? You were born one, just like your dad and his dad before him. Just like everyone born here."

146

"And yet here *you* are—" I grin — "begging for my slice of the pie."

Kip's face contorts with anger. "You're better off dead, low-life local."

"You still need me."

"I just need your signature. I have a lot of ways of getting it."

A flash of lightning cracks the sky open, followed by a rumble of thunder that feels like it vibrates right through me. Waves swallow the shoreline of Grand Manitou Island in the distance — where just yesterday we were moored has now become a violent tumult of water and sand.

"How the fuck are we gonna get off this island?" Daniel's eyes are round with fear.

"Mother Nature, what a fucking beauty." There's a hint of a grin on Stavros's lips, the first time I've seen him almost smile since Mika disappeared.

"Yeah," says Daniel. "A real beautiful fucking nightmare."

CHAPTER TWENTY-SEVEN: RYLEIGH

"I'll make sure to hide any identifying parts of you well — wouldn't want your family to have to identify a piece of you at the morgue." Kerrigan's sneer turns amused. "I think I'll keep your tongue though, just for a little memento." She's glowing with ruthless glee. "So heartbreaking for them. I'll make sure to send my condolences when it hits the news that you're missing."

I clamp my teeth together to prevent sticking my foot in my mouth and making Kerrigan even angrier. The knife is still hovering within inches of my neck as she makes slow circles around me. She knows what she's doing, I'll give her that. No one will ever find me here. The location is too remote, and I'll likely be fish food before authorities even make it to the island to search for me. I spot a familiar boat anchored near a large outcropping of boulders. It's Cole's dinghy; usually it's attached to the catamaran, but now here it is, exactly where it shouldn't be. I realize then it must be the boat Kerrigan used last night to vanish, and it's probably the one she'll use to get away after killing me. And worse, Kerrigan knows this island like the back of her hand — she grew up on these rocks and in this bay. She could make my death look like an accident and get away free and clear. I'm sure she'd spin a story that I slipped and fell on a rusted piece of fishing equipment.

And then it hits me.

Maybe Kerrigan did something to Mika.

I hate thinking that about someone I once trusted, but the woman standing before me now is clearly unhinged. And the only chance I have of surviving is to keep her talking. If I can keep her talking long enough, I might even be able to untangle my wrists from the rope that binds them.

I yelp when I snag my skin on a rusted piece of metal. I can feel blood trickling down my wrist and pooling in the divots of skin between my fingers. "I'm bleeding."

"Here, baby." She throws a colorful scarf I've seen before at me. It's *my* scarf. "Recognize it? Thank you for letting me borrow it. I left the torn part with Mika's body." She winks. "It's the perfect crime, you see?"

I sob then, realizing she's thought of everything, right down to framing me for Mika's death, even if I do manage to escape this island.

"My dad had to put one of our dogs down when I was a kid. Mickey was kicked by a horse on the main island and was paralyzed and suffering. I didn't understand what it felt like to take a life — until now. Life-and-death decisions, playing God . . . it's intoxicating, Rye."

I shiver when she uses that nickname. It's so personal, so intimate. It's ours, and now she's using the familiarity of it against me. Killed by one of my closest friends. Daniel was right all along, and it pains me now that I didn't heed his warnings.

"I didn't think I'd ever sell my share of the island. It's always been my home away from home. I wanted to raise my kids here someday. I wanted the white picket fence with an island view." She circles me again, smile turning to a frown. "And then you happened." She looks so dejected, I think she might actually start to cry. "And then the business went bad, and Mika and Cole didn't want to sell. And then when Kip's

149

dad left you shares . . . You can't imagine how that pissed Kip off. You know that generation, old-school hippies wanting to live off the land and stuff. So naive. It's hard to make money off a pretty rock in the middle of nowhere," she sneers. "And now you have a slice of the pie. You're sleeping with my husband, and you own a part of my financial future. You just inherited a piece of my paradise. And let me guess. You're not ready to sell?"

I don't answer. I just need to keep her talking. I know she's not looking for my input here anyway. She's rambling, as if she's had a psychotic break. Her mood is swinging from frenzied and violent to eerily calm and collected. It's unnerving, and even more unsettling is the fact that if she tries to kill me with that rusted knife, I'll likely die a slow death, bleeding out into the sand while she cackles above me.

"I have to get rid of you. You know that, right?" She slides the pad of her thumb along my cheekbone and then along my hairline with the loving tenderness of a mother. "Kip and I are starting over." She places a tender palm on her belly. "I just found out we're having a baby. Did he tell you?" Her eyes sparkle with the revelation. "Our dream for a family is coming true. I can't have you ruining that. You understand, right?"

"Do you think he won't find out? You think he won't search for me?" I decide to play into her darkest fears. Maybe Kerrigan unhinged is my best chance of escape. If she slips up, maybe she'll leave me an opportunity to gain the upper hand.

A gust of wind jerks the old table up off its foundations, rattling and scraping my damp skin as it does. Kerrigan doesn't seem to notice that the table rocks with every powerful gust. If just one or two more strong currents of wind hit the shore, I might be able to wiggle the rope out from under the old, rusted legs. Kerrigan squats at my side, wiping some of the blood off my cheek before licking the cherry-red smear from the pad of her thumb.

"Mm . . . I love the taste of your fear."

"Sicko," I spit just as another gust of wind rocks the table and lifts the leg enough for me to wrench the rope beneath and out from under it.

Kerrigan shoots up without noticing that I've suddenly managed to free myself. She walks toward the old fishing shack, the bowed roof heaving in the wind before fat drops of rain open up on us. Rain and blood smear my cheeks and ruin my vision, but I keep my eyes on her back, my legs twitching with the anticipation of making a run for it. I don't think I have it in me to take a life to save my own, so my only other option is to run.

Run or die.

It's now or never.

And I choose now.

CHAPTER TWENTY-EIGHT: KIP

"Kerrigan is gone."

"What?" I'm sure I've misheard Ryleigh. Certain my brain garbled her words once they left her lips on their journey to my ears.

"She's just gone." Ryleigh twists her hands into knots as she looks anywhere but at the group of us under the pergola.

"What are you talking about?" Cole approaches, scanning her up and down. It's then I notice that she's bleeding. Like tears, her temple bleeds in streaks down one side of her face and into the neckline of her T-shirt.

"I found something." Ryleigh backs away from Cole and moves to Daniel's side. She turns, addressing him directly. "I found her."

"Her?" Stavros plants a hand on her shoulder and spins her body to face him. "Who? Who did you find?"

"I was at an abandoned fishing hut on the other side of the island. There was a fishing boat out in the bay, just spinning in circles, and I thought it was weird. So I started searching for anything out of place, and I found . . . I found . . ." She wipes at tears that are streaming down her cheeks. "*Her.* She hit me. I bent to pick something up in one of the tide pools, and she hit me over the head and knocked me out. I woke up tied to this old, rusted fishing table—"

"I know where that is," Cole interrupts. "You actually saw her? Is she still there?"

"I-I don't know." Ryleigh shakes her head, then presses a palm to her temple and winces. "I saw Cole's dinghy. I think she took it. I think something bad happened. I-I have the worst feeling."

"You just said she tied you up." Stavros squints. "What's the true story, Ryleigh?"

"I-I think she did, but it feels like a nightmare. I don't remember why, but she kept threatening to . . . to . . ." Ryleigh clutches at her midsection and nearly doubles over with pain. "She threatened to take everything from me."

Stavros's eyes glaze over with violent intensity. "That's it. I don't know what the fuck is going on here, but I think every single one of you is lying. I don't know why, but I think it's you who's to blame for my missing wife." He points at me. "And she's gone fucking nuts."

"Fuck you," I bark.

"Think about it. You have the most motive, and now your wife has conveniently vanished. I call bullshit on your story. I think you're a liar and a thief, maybe even a murderer." Stavros pokes an accusatory finger into my chest. "You have a way of falling ass-backward into a pile of shit and coming out smelling like roses. It's time there were some consequences for you. That's why Mika wouldn't sell her shares. You did everything you could to bully her into it, but you're not getting your way this time, maybe never again," he spits. "I hope you lose it all."

I shake my head, trying to keep my anger in check because I know this looks bad for me. Ryleigh is practically falling apart, shoulders shaking as she sobs. A piece of me wants to comfort her. But she has Daniel, her oldest friend, keeper of all the secrets in that stupid little notebook of his. I don't trust either of them, I realize, and while I may have the most to lose, they have the most to gain by telling the secrets that I know are between them. God only knows what kinds of lies are contained within that little notebook that could implicate me. I see the way he looks at her, like they have an unspoken language that no one else shares. And the way he's looking at her right now raises the hackles at the back of my neck.

Daniel knows.

"So did you or did you not see her, Ryleigh?" Stavros focuses on her shaking form.

"I-I'm not sure." She rubs her forehead, confusion crossing her features.

"I'm gonna try calling the police." Cole stalks away, phone in hand. A moment later, he turns to us and announces, "It's ringing."

"This is it," I breathe. "Whatever happens next is out of our hands."

"It always was," Daniel grunts.

"We had a chance before," I say to myself more than anything.

"We never had a chance." Daniel glares. "I'm starting to think everyone in your orbit gets burned sooner or later."

I ignore him, shoving a hand through my hair as I think about the calls I'll have to make to get myself out of this one. I can't go back to Chicago with a missing wife. The business will never recover. *I'll* never recover.

"Ryleigh is gonna take me to the fishing shacks to search for any sign of her or Mika," Stavros informs us.

"I'll come with you." Daniel follows them across the lawn. They turn a corner around a stand of evergreens and then disappear from sight.

I drop down onto the nearest sofa, and it takes everything in me not to break down. For the first time in months, my body wants to give up the fight. I can't rectify this; there's no fixing this situation. I have to let it unfold how it's meant to, have to let it play out. I take a deep breath and finally let out the conflicting emotions — my life, my future, my business, my wife, my everything is tied up in the next few moments, and I don't have control over any of it. This is the end; I can feel it in the marrow of my bones. I drop my head in my hands, finally accepting defeat.

* * *

The next time I look up, uniformed officers are approaching me.

I wince, feeling the loss of my life as I know it in every vein.

"Do you know where Cole Mayer was last night?" the youngest officer asks.

I blink, allowing my mind to catch up as I stare up at the policewoman hovering over me. *Cole. Cole.* They want to know more about Cole. Of course they do.

"No," is all I muster.

"And if we bring you into the station, we're not going to find anything suspicious, right?"

"Find anything?" I feel drunk, my vision hazy.

"If we take your fingerprints, I mean." A policewoman is scratching notes onto her spiral-bound pad.

"Nope," I finally say.

"We know Cole Mayer has had some trouble the last few years. You have any reason to suspect him in the disappearance of your wife?"

"Cole?" I repeat.

"Yes, Cole Mayer. The caretaker. Do you suspect him in any foul play this week?"

"Foul play? No, I don't think so," I mumble.

"Well, he's got a past that makes me think that if we bring him into the station and run his fingerprints against the ones at the fishing shack, we might find all the answers we need."

"Fingerprints?" I ask again, trying to shake the adrenaline-induced fog from my brain.

"Listen, this isn't our first rodeo with this guy. We'll take him in for further interviews and do all the due diligence. But there've been enough strange happenings on this island

155

to suspect more than just a string of coincidental accidents, don't you think?"

"Yeah." I nod, mind moving quickly to connect the pieces. What I hear them saying is that I'm not the main suspect. They're looking to nail Cole for this, not me. "I know what you mean."

"Good. So, did you see anything strange last night? Anything that might make you think that your wife would want to disappear or someone would want to hurt her?"

I shake my head. "Not a thing."

"That's what I figured." She scratches a few more notes on her notepad and then closes it and tucks it into her pocket. "I want you to know that this case is of the utmost importance to our department. We're aware of the implications a story like this can have on the local economy. Especially after last summer . . . Well, you can best believe we're handling it as quickly and discreetly as we can."

My thoughts turn to the five-million-dollar life insurance policy we took out last year. I imagine it tucked between car insurance and mortgage paperwork in my file cabinet. It's enough to start over with the business. It's enough to start a new life.

"We're going to take Mr. Mayer to the main station in Mackinaw City — more resources to process him," another officer from the sheriff's department informs the woman who's been talking to me.

"Sounds good." The officer flips the page on her notepad and looks at me. "We'll just need your contact information before you go back to the city."

"That's it? We can leave?"

"Sure. This is local business. It'll get handled locally. We'll let you know if we have any more questions. State police are on their way, and the Coast Guard is assisting from the air. I'll have the investigator in charge of the case give you a call when we know more."

"But my wife — you just expect me to leave her here?"

"Listen, Mr. Lange, we understand how worried you must be, but we've got a pretty good handle on what we're dealing with here. This isn't the first time Mr. Mayer has been involved when a woman has gone missing. Now, we can take you into the station and interrogate you for the next twelve hours, but wouldn't you rather be here helping the search team find your wife? Or maybe you need to go back to the city to handle some work stuff before you come back — whatever you need to do."

"Whatever I need to do . . ." I repeat, mind humming with how easy this has been, considering the circumstances. "I can't imagine leaving her here."

"Trust me, our search and rescue team will find her if she's out there."

"*If?* Of course she's out there," I retort. "Fuck, go on vacation for a week and lose my wife."

"Vacation? I thought you were here for a will reading?"

"Well, sure, that was the first hour. Kill me for hoping for some rest and relaxation the rest of the week," I groan.

"Right. Well, I'm sure I don't have to tell you this, but sometimes people don't want to be found, Mr. Lange. We'll do our best for you. With Mr. Caruso offering up extra resources, I have all the confidence we will find your wife and her friend soon."

"Jon offered up extra resources?" I ask, referring to Lyra's father. The silent partner in this island venture. The puppet master of Stonecliffe.

"Yes, in exchange for absolute discretion. After that last girl disappeared—"

"I have to make a phone call. Excuse me," I interrupt. "Thank you for all of your work on this."

Before they've even turned away, I'm dialing Jon Caruso's private line with one question repeating in my mind. How the hell did he know there's been another disappearance on the island?

"Jon," I say as soon as the line picks up. "I need a heli-copter off Stonecliffe." I decide not to push his buttons and ask the *how* question just yet.

"I can't charter something big enough to get you all off in one trip," he replies evenly, the timbre of his voice sounding a million miles away. He's probably drinking champagne on a yacht somewhere far removed from the hellish circumstances unfolding at Stonecliffe this week.

"I don't care about everyone. Besides, we're down a few bodies. Apparently you've already heard," I say.

Jon only huffs. "I might be able to call in a favor and get a helicopter off the ground. I'll see what I can do."

And then the line goes dead.

I shove my phone into my pocket and then spin, eager to get back to the villa and pack up my things and get off this island.

"Hey, are you okay?" Ryleigh's voice shakes me from my muddled thoughts.

"Oh, Ryleigh. Hey. Glad I ran into you, actually. I've got a helicopter on the way with room for one more if you want to come with me."

"What? You're leaving?" Her eyes are wide with shock.

"My staying isn't going to find her faster. There's an entire team searching for both of them. Hell, even the Coast Guard has boats out searching the bay—"

"Stop. I can't even think about what they might find." She crumples into a ball of tears, and for the first time since everything unraveled, I drop my guard and pull her close.

"They'll find her, Rye. They'll find both of them. I know it." She's so upset she can't speak, sobs racking her body as she trembles and shakes. "Did the emergency techs check out your injuries?"

"Y-yes," she stammers, spinning the ring I gave her around her finger with worry.

"I think you should come back to Chicago with me. You've been through more than anyone else here. I'll get you an appointment with my doctor in the city to make sure everything is okay. At least think about it." She nods, hiccups, and then lets me guide her to her villa. "You just pack up, and I'll let Daniel know."

"Wait. I can't leave Daniel." She hiccups again.

"You have to. There isn't enough room for another, not with our luggage too."

"But—"

"You or nobody, Rye. That's it," I insist.

"I-I—"

"Pack up your stuff, Rye. Okay? Just listen to me on this." I place my palms on her shoulders and guide her to the villa.

"I think . . . I think I need a doctor," she says, hands hovering at her stomach like she might be sick. Mika and Kerrigan are gone, and now we have to move on. Search and rescue teams will find them safe and sound, I have to believe that. I won't be able to live with myself if they aren't.

"I'll meet you back here in ten minutes, okay? We'll walk over to the airstrip together. I promise everything will be fine," I assure her. "Rye . . ." I hesitate before asking the question that's been nagging at me since she stumbled up to us this morning. "Did you do this?"

"D-do what?" she stammers.

"Take care of our problems?" I ask under my breath.

"W-what are you asking?"

"You know, the investments, the insurance . . ." I mutter. "When I told you a few weeks ago that Mika threatened to call the feds . . . At first, I thought Kerrigan might have . . . Well—" I shove a hand through my hair — "I don't know what I thought, but now that she's gone, I just need to know. Rye, did you—"

"Really?" she utters, an incredulous look crossing her face.

"I know. It's just—" I swallow.

"Maybe it was you," she interrupts me.

"What?" Anger bubbles to life in my bloodstream.

"The thing is . . ." Ryleigh works her ring in quick circles. "I saw Cole last night. It couldn't have been him."

CHAPTER TWENTY-NINE: RYLEIGH

Nine months later

Raindrops smear bloody rivers down the windowpane, distorting the halo of red brake lights from the street outside. I settle into the antique rocking chair, and my eyelids flutter closed as I look forward to a few moments of shut-eye while the baby sleeps. I've only been someone's mother for five days, and yet I'm so exhausted it feels like it's been a lifetime. Grateful for the cozy home we've managed to carve out of the chaos this last year, I'm just nodding off with a tired smile on my face when a soft thump jolts me fully awake.

The hairs on the back of my neck don't even have time to rise before I'm on my feet and shuttling back into the baby's nursery. I've been constantly anxious with the fear of losing her these last five days, even more so since we were released from the hospital. The care and feeding of a newborn life have consumed me, left my nerves on edge and my anxiety running at full speed. I try not to resent the tiny life we've brought into this world, but I'm so tired, I'm already dreaming of the days when full nights of sleep are not just a luxury but the norm.

I slip my hand along the tiny, swaddled bundle of baby that's nestled among dancing ducks and hopping bunnies. After reading a half-dozen motherhood books, I was able to quell most of my fears about bringing her home, but there's still one fear I can't shake. Her sudden loss of breath as she peacefully sleeps, me unaware in the next room over. So far, being a mother feels like a hangover that won't end. I'm constantly bleary-eyed and unaware of exactly what time of day it is, every loud noise causing my adrenaline to skyrocket. I find myself checking on her dozens of times at night, and now, just like with every other check before, she's fine. She's alive, and the tiny puffs of milk breath soothe my anxiety-ridden heart.

Turning, I slip out of the nursery and chalk it up to a neighbor next door or a car backfiring outside. But just when I'm about to settle into the rocking chair and allow the rain to lull me into a state of semi-peaceful sleep, another thump followed by three loud knocks jolts me again. I'm on edge, and who could blame me after the year we've had? But I remind myself that the past is in the past as I head for the front door of our West Loop brownstone. Nothing seems amiss when I peer through the fish-eye peephole. The street is quiet. The cold rain drenches the sidewalk and street beyond my focus, and it isn't until I hear a van fire up down the street that I realize we must have gotten a delivery.

Twisting the dead bolt, I move slowly as I open the door. Two snow-white boxes are waiting for me. I smile, about to bend, when I catch my husband coming down the street at a jog. He's rain-drenched, and I'm grateful he's here to bring the boxes in for me. After an emergency cesarean, the surgeon instructed me not to bend or lift anything, and I've been begrudgingly trying to follow orders while still keeping the house tidy and taking care of a newborn.

"What's this?" He's on the step now, ducking under the awning and planting a chaste kiss on my cheek.

"Just delivered. How was work?" I hum, enjoying his presence after the last eight hours with only a fussy newborn and a grouchy cat to fill the silence.

"Great. How's the baby?" He always calls her *the baby*. I try to tell myself he's adjusting to parenthood just like I am, but it annoys me every time he refrains from using her name. It's as if he doesn't expect her to be around long, like she's only a temporary house guest and not our daughter.

"She's been fussy today. I finally got her to sleep. She's milk drunk and happy at the moment."

He bends, stacking the boxes and gesturing me into the house. He follows me in, and then deposits the boxes by the side table. He kisses me on the forehead, then hangs the leather satchel I bought him for his last birthday on the hook in the foyer and moves off into the kitchen. I hear him making a drink and pathetically wish I could have one too. I'm breastfeeding, though, and having a drink now would require me to pump my milk for the next feeding. But I don't have enough of a stock built up in the freezer to supplement until the alcohol is out of my system.

"Who are the packages from, babe?"

"I'm not sure." I settle into my rocking chair and slide the stack of boxes to my feet. I place the first in my lap, wondering who is left that hasn't sent a baby gift yet. Slipping my fingers through the loops of the baby-pink bow, I unwrap the first and open it quickly. Wrapped in pillows of tissue paper, I find a pitch-black onesie with a tiny Halloween skull on the front. I frown, thinking how odd this gift is considering it's only May and nowhere near October 31. Was it delivered to the wrong address? I hold the onesie up to inspect it closer, and I shudder when I realize it looks like real bloodstains are painted on the skull.

"Another onesie?" He's at my side then. The smell of smoky, expensive scotch wafting from his glass is overpowering.

"It's bloody," I whisper as fear bubbles in my veins.

"What?" He snatches the onesie from my hand, inspecting it closer. "Maybe it's a defect from the printer."

"Or maybe it's not."

"Really? You think someone sent this as a threat?" he asks.

I'm silent a long beat. "What if it's about last summer?"

He balks, always shrugging off my worst fears. I used to love it when he brought me down to earth, calming my anxiety with a quick turn of phrase, but I've come to hate it. "What about the other box?"

I lift it into my lap and unwrap the pale-pink bow, cautious as I lift off the lid of the box. Peeling back the top layer of tissue paper, I catch sight of the contents, and an overwhelming sense of dread spirals through my system.

Tucked inside the box is a black-as-tar bouquet of roses. I lift them out of the box, thinking they look more like a funeral arrangement than a new baby gift. It's then I discover that the base of the bouquet isn't nestled into a vase but wrapped with a luxurious and colorful silk scarf.

Tucked into the folds of the scarf is a small note card addressed to me. I open it swiftly, and then tears leak from my eyes as I read the note.

Congratulations on your new baby.
Murder looks good on you, Mommy.

"Someone knows."

"Babe—" Kip lifts something from between the petals — "what is this?"

I snap my hands over my mouth. "I haven't seen that since . . . since Stonecliffe."

"What is it?" Kip frowns.

"A fillet knife." I take it from him and turn it over in my palms. "No one else knows . . ."

"Knows what?" Kip grunts then digs in the box for anything else. "What's this doing in here?" I glance up to find him opening a copy of the *Chicago Tribune*. His eyes narrow before he thrusts it my way. "Read the headline."

I can barely breathe, my vision tunneling as I read the words over and over.

LOCAL DESIGNER WAKES UP FROM COMA

I swipe the paper from him and scan the article. "*The head of Chicago-based fashion label Mika Morales* . . . I knew it," I spit. "I knew she wasn't dead," I huff and continue reading.

> . . . *Mika Morales was found by local fishermen and had no memory of who she was or what happened until just last week, when she was able to identify her devoted husband, Stavros Costas. At her side for the last nine months in a cognitive therapy center, her husband expressed overwhelming gratitude to the nurses and doctors at Lakeshore Psychiatric for the excellent care that has given her the chance at a full recovery. While Ms. Morales is able to identify her husband, she still cannot remember what happened at Stonecliffe Island last summer that caused her to sustain such a severe brain injury. The investigation remains ongoing.*

"Well, she's alive. That's good news." Kip takes another sip of his scotch and turns to gaze out the window.

I slip the silky scarf through my fingers and play with the fringe at one corner. The sharp *ting* of metal hitting the glossy wood floor echoes through the afternoon silence. I bend to find a simple gold and diamond ring at my feet. It must have been nestled in the folds of expensive silk. I scoop it into my hand and turn it over a moment before a bone-deep chill of awareness climbs through me. I know this ring.

I tuck everything quickly back into the box and then slide the wedding band into the pocket of my sweatpants.

"So what do we do now?"

"I don't know." I make a show of folding the newspaper and putting it back into the box it came in. "I do know one thing."

Kip looks over his shoulder at me. "Oh yeah? What's that?"

"I'm going to Lakeshore Psychiatric tomorrow."

CHAPTER THIRTY: RYLEIGH

"Stavros?" I utter as I adjust the baby carrier on my arm the next morning.

The man hunched over the hospital bed turns slowly, wide, haunted eyes taking in me and then the baby carrier before he turns back to the bed. "What do you want?"

I frown. "I saw the newspaper. I came to . . ." I look around the dark room, curtains closed with only the smallest sliver of daylight cutting through the shadows. I thrust out the small vase of lilies that I picked up in the hospital gift shop downstairs two minutes ago. "I came to say hello."

"Took you long enough, didn't it?" He doesn't move to take the lilies or even look me in the eye when he talks. In fact, he looks like a shell of the man I knew last summer. His skin is pale and waxy, missing the sparkling bronze luster he wore so well at Stonecliffe. He looks like he's been wasting away inside this hospital beside Mika for all of the last nine months. While I was giving life, they were languishing in the shadows of a hospital room.

"Should I open the curtains and let some light in or . . . ?" I'm wholly uncomfortable and wondering if here is the last place I should be. But I had to know for sure; I had to see for myself.

"Don't." Stavros rushes to stop me. "The light gives her migraines."

"Oh." I set the baby carrier on the floor at my feet and take in Mika for the first time. She sleeps peacefully in the bed, her arms folded across her torso like she's just been laid to rest. While her skin has always been a near-alabaster shade, her sunken cheekbones are the sallow hue of dirty concrete. She looks bedridden with sickness and like she hasn't breathed fresh air in years. It's funny how a vibrant life can fade to fumes in the blink of an eye.

"So, I guess congratulations are in order." Stavros glances down at my baby. "You and Kip, huh? Can't say I'm surprised."

I struggle to find the words to reply, his offhand comment leaving me stunned. "We had a small ceremony on the beach right before the baby was born—"

"You know how they found her?" Stavros wipes his hands over his face before folding into himself. "In the hull of an old fishing boat. Spinning circles in the bay and left to die. The boat had a slow leak. Investigators think it was punctured on purpose, because when the fisherman found her, the hull was filling with water and she was in shock. She would have died within hours if it hadn't been for him."

Chills erupt on my skin. "D-did you say the boat was spinning circles in the water?"

Stavros nods. "They think she was locked in, and when the storm tore out the dock, the boat was set adrift. Thankfully, it caught on something underwater and started doing circles — that's what made the fisherman investigate. And he found her . . . he found her nearly dead."

"Who do you think did it?"

Stavros glances up at me, accusation brimming in his blue eyes. "*You.*"

"Me?" I nearly choke.

"Or your husband. Maybe Cole. My opinion changes on the daily." Stavros pushes a hand through his overgrown hair. "Investigators are pretty sure Cole knows more than he's letting on."

"Cole?"

Stavros only shrugs. "He doesn't have motive, but there's no evidence to point to anything else." He glances back at his wife, love and anguish warring on his face. "You know, the night before she woke up, the doctors spoke to me about donating her organs — making the decision to donate the pieces of her that keep her alive, make her heart beat, make her *her*. How could I decide something like that? I told them I would never take her choice away from her, and thank God I didn't because she woke up the very next morning."

"That's incredible." I wipe away tears.

"Want to know what's more incredible, *Rye*?" Stavros holds my gaze for the first time since I arrived.

"What?" I ask.

"Mika woke up while I was listening to the podcast — she woke up to *her* voice."

"What? Whose voice?" I breathe.

Stavros raises an eyebrow. "Oh." A dark grin climbs across his face. "You don't know, do you?"

"Know what?"

Stavros huffs, then turns back to his wife. "At first, I thought your husband was behind it — thought maybe he was slow-feeding clues to the public just to torment me — but I don't think that's it."

My hands begin to tremble as it dawns on me who might have been behind that morbid baby gift.

"I-I'm so glad Mika isn't dead . . ." I wince at my choice of words. "I mean, I'm so glad she's going to be okay."

"She's not out of the woods yet." He shakes his head. "Whatever happened at Stonecliffe left a mark. She doesn't even know her own name."

"Sh-she doesn't?" A knot of emotion forms in my chest.

Stavros shakes his head and then clears his throat. "Thanks for stopping by, Ryleigh. I think it's time you leave now, though."

I cringe, realizing that no part of him wants me near his wife. What does he think? I'm going to poison her while she sleeps? I sigh, lifting the baby carrier and making my way to the door. "I'm glad you're doing well. Really."

Stavros doesn't reply, only grunts from beside the bed. I take it as my sign to leave.

Walking down the hallway, I rock the baby carrier against my hip and consider what this means. While Stavros may not have wanted me here, my visit wasn't wasted. Now at least I know for sure that Mika remembers nothing and was definitely not the one behind the macabre skull onesie.

"Well, hello there," are the first words I hear as the elevator doors slide open. From the moment I set eyes on the designer heels, I know who's standing in front of me.

"Lyra, hi." I don't bother to hide the cold tone in my voice.

"I heard you had a little rugrat now." She steps through the doors, making sure to brush my shoulder as she passes me. "Up to no good again, I assume?" She's brimming with disdain, arms crossed as she waits for me to reply.

"I came to see Mika, I-I didn't even know she was alive—" I think of how much Kip has kept from me over the months in an effort to protect me and make my pregnancy as stress-free as possible.

"No offense, but you and Kip cut out pretty quickly after they took Cole into custody."

"They took Cole into custody?"

"Yeah, you knew that." She leans forward. "You and that piece-of-shit husband really haven't talked to anyone since everything went down up there?"

I shake my head, heart rattling in my ribcage as I think about the damage done to everyone else's lives after last summer. "Kip didn't want me to stress out and lose the baby, so he—"

"He ignored everyone," she interrupts. "Your doting new husband treated everyone else like the asshole, when in real life it's him. Honestly, I'm starting to think it's you too. I'm surprised Stavros even let you see her."

I glower at her. "I was only there a few minutes before he kicked me out."

168

Lyra's grin widens. "Can you blame him?"

"I mean, I don't know when I ever gave Stavros a reason to hate me."

"Are you kidding? You were pregnant with your best friend's husband's baby and then tried to kill his wife and make it look like an accident. I'm pretty sure he has every right to hate you. You're lucky you're not in jail right now. Instead, poor Cole is doing your time for you."

"Doing my time? What are you talking about?"

"Ha," she laughs, "you really don't know shit, do you?" Her eyes do that villainous sparkling thing again, and it sends a chill along my nerves. "Kip's an even bigger douchebag than I thought." She latches on to my elbow and pulls me away from the elevator doors. "The short version goes like this: Cole was found guilty of gross negligence and involuntary manslaughter after the cops pinned enough circumstantial evidence on him. But the judge was an old family friend and knows Cole would never do anything like what they were saying, trying to sabotage the sale of Stonecliffe to save himself by neglecting it to the point of a fatality. He was responsible for clearing out all that old hazardous fishing equipment on the other side of the island where . . . well, where they found Kerrigan's blood all over . . . *everything*. And because everyone who was on the island knows there's no way Cole could have done what they're saying he did . . . Well, basically the only one left with motive is you. Or Kip." She smiles sweetly, as if she's just wished me a happy birthday. "And of course, you were the last one to see Mika on the rocks that day on Grand Manitou, so that seems like a dead giveaway." She waves her hand in the air with a half-shrug.

"Are you kidding?" I ask.

"Nope. I have the footage."

"Footage? What footage?"

"From the night Kerrigan disappeared. I found the tape from the CCTV camera that shows *someone* throwing something in the dumpster . . . someone small wearing shorts with a long ponytail. It shows you."

"Me? No, I don't think I—"

"The cops didn't think it was anything either, and they say they searched the dumpster and everything else on the island looking for evidence, but . . . You know what doesn't add up for me? When I slowed down the security footage, I found the weirdest thing in the first few frames. Whoever is in that video isn't alone. I know it. It looks like a second person walks into the frame half a step, and then the person with the ponytail — someone that looks a lot like you—"

"It's not me—"

"It looks like you. You run into the frame like you're scared of something or someone." She nails me with a look. "Who are you working with, Ryleigh?"

"I-I'm not—"

"I know you did something. And now an innocent man sits in jail accused of something he didn't do. You know he was beaten by inmates last month?" She dabs at her eyes, showing emotion for the first time during this little run-in. "You'd think there'd be some evidence that could prove he wasn't responsible for Kerrigan's death. No body, no crime, right?" She bends her head, swiping away more tears, and I start to think she actually loves him. I didn't know she had it in her.

"S-so," I stutter, "will you be in Chicago long?"

Lyra sniffs. "Long enough to make you uncomfortable." She leans in, looming close enough to me that I instinctually block the baby carrier from her. "It kills me that Kip got his way, even after everything."

"What are you talking about?" I back away.

"He doesn't owe Mika money now. Think about it: she can't sue him to get her money back if she doesn't even know her own name. She'll never be healthy enough to work again. It's only a matter of time before the design house goes under. Stavros was determined to get revenge for the longest time. You're lucky I talked him off the ledge. I told him to bring it to civil court, but he could hardly think straight, he was so worried about Mika." She clucks her tongue and shakes her

170

head. "While you and Kip were playing house, the rest of us were cleaning up the aftermath." Lyra folds her arms, and that villainous glint returns to her eyes. "Your little family is safe and sound." She smiles, glancing down at my daughter's peacefully sleeping body. *"For now."*

CHAPTER THIRTY-ONE: KIP

"So, what's next for Lange Investment Group?" Jon Caruso swallows the rest of his Old Fashioned and sets the tumbler on the table between us.

"Sky's the limit, Jon. I really feel that in my bones with this next opportunity." I sip my grapefruit paloma and smile.

"I can tell, son." Jon taps the thick manila folder at his side. "I'll have my lawyer process the wire by the end of business today. I appreciate your loyalty on this one."

"Happy to do what I can." I smile earnestly at the old man. He's over seventy and still shaking hands and sealing deals like he's forty years younger. "I'm just sorry the stuff with Cole—"

"Speak no more of it. All worked out for the best, as far as I'm concerned." His smile drops. "Got top dollar for the land, just glad developers were willing to work around that run-down little shithole that Cole owns. Bastard wouldn't even sign it over from jail, when he could've used the money for a decent team of lawyers. Who goes at a criminal negligence case like that with public defenders? Glad he finally changed his mind."

I shake my head, feeling the first twinge of guilt for Cole Mayer since finding out he'd been sentenced to serve time.

"I'll tell you who," Jon continues, "a fool."

I blink, trying to force away the thought that Jon actually might enjoy something about this.

"I was definitely surprised to learn about you and Ryleigh, of all people." Jon shakes the ice cubes in his glass and avoids making eye contact.

"Of all people?"

"Well, sure. After Kerrigan's father had that letter sent—"

I stiffen.

"What letter?" I reply on instinct.

Jon and I have never discussed this before, and all I can think is that if he knows that I knew about this letter all along — even *before* Kerrigan knew — well, that's enough prior knowledge to tie me to a situation that I *do not* want to be associated with.

"The letter about Ryleigh." His shrewd gaze locks with mine. I don't say anything.

Jon is a good man — I've never lied to him. Until now.

He watches me with a stony stare. Ironically, it's his instincts that I've admired most about him over the years, but now, it's those same instincts that seem to be telling him that I'm lying through my teeth to him — a man that has been a second father to me.

"Forgive me, son—" Jon clears his throat — "I guess I just assumed you knew."

"'Fraid I don't." I cross my arms and lean back in my chair. "Care to level with me?"

He only shakes his head, jaw set firmly. He looks like Lyra with that stubborn glint in his eye. "Guess it's not my business to say."

"With all due respect, this goes deeper than business, Jon. This is my family."

He nods, then pushes a palm over his forehead. "Your father wanted Ryleigh to have a piece of Stonecliffe for a reason."

"I know. She was shocked."

Jon grimaces. "She shouldn't have been." He pauses. "She's blood."

173

I frown and lean forward.

He continues. "Kerrigan's father met Ryleigh's mother on the road — nine months later, she was born. He was in her life for a while when work brought him to port, but her mom decided having no dad was healthier than a deadbeat who passed through town only once or twice a year. He still sent money, though, and when he wrote up his will, he made sure to set aside just enough shares of Stonecliffe for Ryleigh by way of your father. They were best friends all those years — your father knew about Ryleigh from the beginning. I only found out when I received that letter, the same one he wrote for Kerrigan before he died, explaining that she had a sister. A copy of that same letter was sent to me when your father's will was read."

"I don't think my wife got that letter." I shift through my memory, trying to recall if Kerrigan ever mentioned it. Had she? I'd been so wrapped up in keeping the fund afloat, I hadn't been listening to her like I probably should have been.

"I know she got the letter," he states. "The lawyer called me asking if I knew her mailing address. He left the letter behind in Chicago accidentally when he read the will on the island and needed a way to get it to her. By the time I returned his call a few days later to tell him I didn't know her address up there, he informed me she'd had someone pick it up at his office. In person."

"Really?" I ask.

Jon shrugs. Now I'm worried. There was so much left unsaid between Kerrigan and me that summer. I'd known for months that Ryleigh and Kerrigan were sisters, just one of the secrets I kept close as I waited for Kerrigan to get her letter. I assumed once she received the information about her father's other family, she'd come to me in a flurry of emotion and I could explain that I had it all figured out. I'd already set the plan in motion to secure our future and make sure the newest member of the family wouldn't upset the existing financial balance.

A chill runs through me as I realize Kerrigan was playing her own game all along.

"Are you sure someone picked up the letter after the will was read?" I finally utter.

"Sure am. In fact, it was the day the Cubs beat the Tigers seven to four. Second-to-last Friday in September last year. I have season tickets. I remember every game the Cubs win. I'm getting old, but I still gotta helluva head for numbers." He taps his temple with a grin. "So, tell me — how's that new baby doing? Keeping you up all night crying?"

I gulp away the baseball bat in my throat and offer a simple, "Good." I'm thankful for the topic change. "Ryleigh is great with the late-night feedings and stuff. I don't have to worry about anything." I swirl the ice cubes in my glass as I think back on how everything played out.

"She's a good one, always struck me as so sweet."

"Hm." I'm a little uncomfortable with the way he's talking about my wife. "She's a little rattled over a weird baby gift that showed up, though."

"Oh yeah?" Jon's eyes are scanning the room now, checking out the faces and only half tuned in to what I'm saying.

"I'm sure it's nothing," I mutter. "Probably some crazy person who heard about the case in the newspaper or one of Cole's supporters on social media." I cringe inwardly, wondering if Jon realizes just how big this case is — the missing-women headlines went viral and whipped the internet sleuths into a feeding frenzy.

"The small-town disappearance of wealthy tourist's wives sells a lot of papers."

"It's just too bad that people took sides," I grumble.

"They always do." Jon raps his knuckles on the table. "You trust your wife?"

His question catches me off guard. "Of course."

He frowns. "You trust her more than the last one?"

I ponder his words. Jon doesn't say anything unless there's a reason for it. I'm just struggling to understand what he's getting at with this. "Sure, Ryleigh is sweet."

He works his hands back and forth and then shrugs. "Hope you know what you're doing this time. I've handled things as best I can, but we're not untouchable here. The stakes are as high as they've ever been, you understand?"

"I do." I nod, feeling distressed the more this conversation continues. I look down at the new engraved cufflinks Ryleigh bought me for my birthday a few weeks ago. They must have cost a small fortune. I've never limited Ryleigh's access to my bank accounts, the ones she knows about anyway.

"You look good. You get a trainer?" Jon winks.

"Yeah, been spending more time in the gym. I've been trying to take it easy, enjoy the baby and work less."

"Well, money looks good on you." Jon stands from the table, tosses two one-hundred-dollar bills down to cover lunch and then pats me on the shoulder. "Money makes life a little easier for the family, right?"

I feel the weight of his hand like a branding iron. I owe a lot of my success to this man. I've looked up to him for as long as I've been building my own business. But why am I getting the feeling that he's leaving me with more than just the weight of his mentorship on my shoulders?

My muscles start to tremble with anxiety as Jon turns and walks out of the restaurant. I feel like I'm about to crumble. The polished shell I've spent so much time constructing is about to crack and fissure under the pressure. I feel like a fake and a fraud, and I feel like Jon can see right through me. He's given me a gift and saved Lange Investment Group from almost certain destruction. Now it's all on me to keep the ship afloat. *Again.*

My phone buzzes with an incoming text.

Mika remembers nothing, but Lyra suspects something.

Adrenaline spikes in my bloodstream.

My phone buzzes with an incoming call. "Hi."

"We're safe, right? Tell me we're safe," is the first thing I hear.

"Rye—"

"I can't stop thinking this is all going to come back on us somehow. I can't stop reading all the news articles and true crime forums about the case. I avoided all of it for so long.

I just couldn't think about anything but the pregnancy and the baby, but... You never told me . . . Well—" I can hear her voice cracking — "there's a lot you didn't tell me."

"I wanted to protect you. And the baby. This is a light at the end of this tunnel, babe. We just need this last deposit to come through, and then we're free and clear, whatever happens to Cole or Mika or . . ." I can't say her name. I've never been able to say her name.

"Stop, Kip — please. You can't make this go away by ignoring it. She's dead. Kerrigan is dead. And someone else almost died." She lets out a racked sob. "I feel so bad that we didn't reach out or help them or—"

I can't hear anything else she's saying because there's still so much she doesn't know. Including the fact that my first wife is probably *not* dead. "We did everything we could, Rye. I swear we did."

"Then why won't Daniel talk to me?" More tears. I imagine most of this is emotions from her fluctuating hormones; one of the nurses warned me that my wife might not be my own again for a while. I didn't think much of it then, but now, it's starting to make me wonder.

Can I trust my new wife?

"We're safe as long as we never go back, right? If we stay out of Michigan and keep a low profile—"

"Rye, listen, I promise there's no way this can blow back on us. We didn't do anything. There's no evidence to find that implicates us in any crime."

"I know, but . . . Cole—"

"Cole found himself on the wrong radar long before we knew him," I remind her.

"You said—" she hiccups softly — "you said he couldn't have done it. You said you saw him that night."

"Yeah?" I clear my throat, trying not to recall that night. I've spent hours trying to forget the moments before my last wife went missing, the awful things we said to each other still playing on a loop.

"That means he was framed, Kip. He's rotting in jail for a crime he didn't commit." *Shit*. The guilt is getting to her. I never should have let her go to the hospital, but the truth was, I was just as curious as Ryleigh about what Mika remembered.

In fact, I've been curious about a lot of things. Who was the last person to see Kerrigan alive? I know Ryleigh claims to have stumbled on a gruesome scene and the shock of it affected her memories of that night, but is that the truth? The fact remains that I did see Cole that night, and I did see Kerrigan — who seemed completely fine, if angry, when she stalked out of our villa after our fight.

The person I did not see that night was Ryleigh. Or even Daniel, for that matter. And where is Stavros in all of this? He has more motivation than any of us to take care of his wife in the hope of a big payout. He admitted that he married her for citizenship; what else would he use her for?

"Okay, it's fine. Everything is fine. You're right, Kip. Lyra can suspect all she wants, but the case is closed, right?"

"Mika's case isn't closed," I note.

"Well, it's a cold case, at least. She lived. What's to investigate?"

I sigh, registering the defiant lilt in my wife's voice.

"Honestly, everyone got what they deserved — even Mika. She tried to ruin you and the business and *us*." I can hear her boots clacking on the pavement as she walks down the sidewalk. "Something had to give, right? I hate that anyone was hurt, but sometimes the end justifies the means. Karma is a bitch, y'know?"

"Rye, what are you talking about?"

"Protecting you, that's what I'm talking about." I hear the *beep-beep* of the car doors automatically unlocking. "We have our whole lives to make up for what happened to Cole."

"Rye," I repeat. "Did you . . . Is this you?"

"Me?" She chuckles. "I love you. I would do anything to protect us. *Always*."

My mind swirls as I keep thinking, *Do I trust my second wife more than the first one?*

"Something had to give," she chimes.

"Yeah, but—"

"You're always so good at showing me how much you love me," she interrupts. "I wanted to do what I could to return the favor. I love you, and I would go to hell and back to prove it."

"Rye . . ." I gulp. "What are you capable of?"

My wife laughs softly. "With love, anything is possible, silly."

CHAPTER THIRTY-TWO: COLE

"Visitor for Mayer," the intercom blurts as the security door buzzes open.

I wait patiently at the steel table, tapping my fingers as I wonder who might be about to walk into the visiting area.

What happens next floors me.

A woman wrapped in a dark navy trench coat and black heeled boots approaches with a distinct limp. A wide-brimmed hat sits low on her head, and her hair is a shade of platinum I've never seen in real life. She sits down across from me, only a pane of safety glass separating us.

"Well?" I finally ask.

And it's when she looks up that I know exactly what I'm dealing with.

"Hey, Captain." My heart clenches like a fist behind my ribcage.

I shake my head, unable to help the bitter smile that climbs up my cheeks. "Ker—"

"Kandi Carson, true crime investigator. Thanks for taking this meeting with me."

I can't tear myself from her gaze. Everything about her is foreign, from the clothing to the limp to the voice

— everything but her eyes. She could never hide her eyes from me.

"How are you?" The smallest smile pulls at her lips.

I shake my head with a chuckle. "Fine. You?"

She clears her throat and lowers her voice. "I'm sorry I didn't come before now. I couldn't risk—"

"Risk what? Getting me out of jail? It's been nearly a year, Ker—"

"*Kandi*," she corrects.

"Whatever," I snap, growing more disgusted with the woman sitting across from me as it sets in that she is alive. She is here. There was never a murder to begin with. "What do you want?"

"Your help," she answers honestly.

"Hardly," I huff.

"I have proof." She straightens her back.

"Of what?" I ask, enjoying the way she's squirming. I'm the one in handcuffs, and yet I hold the power.

"That Ryleigh is deranged, psychotic. That she tried to kill us — all of us."

I shake my head, thinking it's she who sounds psychotic. "Where did you go?"

She frowns, breaking eye contact with me for the first time since she sat down. "The only place I could. I had to escape. After Ryleigh nearly beat me to death, I was afraid to go back, afraid to face Kip. Afraid he and Ryleigh were trying to kill me."

I assess her, thinking about the limp she walked in with and realizing she does look like a woman who's been fighting for her life.

"Where did you go, Kerrigan?" I say her full name for the first time, and it feels good. It also causes rage to bubble and churn inside me because whatever she's done has landed me here — doing time for no crime at all.

"Shut up," she hisses. "I used your boat to get to one of the other islands that night. I was just so sick of everything. I was happy alone for a while. I was waiting for the search team to find me camped out in one of the old fishing shacks, but when they didn't, I just felt so free . . ." Her voice softens. "Until I didn't."

"What does that mean?"

"Let's just say I received some new facts in the form of a letter that changed the game. I realize now that true happiness is getting revenge on Ryleigh for stealing my husband, my money, my life." A coldness comes over her. "I've been sending anonymous notes to the state police, trying to piece it together for them — Ryleigh tried to kill us all, and it didn't work. The worst it did was land you here, and I want to fix that. I want the right person to be punished for what happened at Stonecliffe last summer."

I sigh. "Why now?"

"Because . . ." She reaches out a hand and touches the glass and then thinks better of it. "I was pregnant, and I didn't even know it. I lost the baby after Ryleigh beat the shit out of me. A few days later, I started bleeding and clotting, and I just knew. I knew there was one more thing she stole from me. The thing I wanted the most." She opens her trench coat and lifts her plain white T-shirt to show the line of a scar cut across her torso. "She took everything from me." She blinks away fresh tears as she trails a fingertip across the glossy, pale-pink scar. "Even you."

"Why did you wait? Why didn't you come forward when prosecutors were trying to nail me to the cross for your and Mika's disappearance?"

"Because I didn't know! I didn't know you'd even been arrested. I've been living off-grid all these months as I try to piece together what happened that night and the next day. I don't know how I got to that side of the island, I don't know if Ryleigh found me or left me there. I don't know so much still, but the one thing I remember is her cutting me with a rusted fishing knife. I remember every excruciating second." She reaches across the table again, this time making contact with my hand and squeezing. "The first memory I have after the storm is of her. *Ryleigh.*"

I nod, taking in everything she's telling me. "And then you managed to row yourself to another island in my dinghy without bleeding out? Forgive me for saying so, but that sounds like bullshit."

"I promise, Cole, it's true. And I'll do whatever it takes to make this right." She squeezes one more time. "Do you believe me?"

I shake my head.

"I'll prove it to you." Her eyes sparkle. "I've got a secret weapon."

"Oh?"

Her smile twists gleefully. "Lyra."

CHAPTER THIRTY-THREE: RYLEIGH

"Thank you again for hosting that Mommy and Me group last week. You've been so indispensable since Jason was diagnosed. I don't know what I would do without you — seriously." My newest mom friend leans in for a half-hug as she jostles a sleeping baby in her other arm.

"Any time, I loved doing it." I air-kiss her.

"And your donation to the Children's Literacy Fund was so generous."

"Don't mention it." I wave her off. "I hope you have a great rest of the week. Call if you need a sitter or anything."

"Back at ya, Mama! Let's plan a playdate for next weekend," she calls as she trots down the steps.

"Sounds like a plan." I wave at her retreating back. The sun shines blindingly as I take in the crisp spring air. It's been a few weeks since my run-in with Lyra at the hospital, and while I've texted Stavros a few times to ask how Mika is doing, he hasn't replied, and I haven't been to visit her again.

I did send the hugest vase of flowers money could buy to her room, though.

I turn back into the brownstone, allowing myself a tired smile as I think about getting in a nap while the baby sleeps.

Just as the door clicks closed behind me, a loud *knock-knock-knock* jolts me to attention.

I smile, opening the door wide a moment later. "Hello?"

My heart sinks at the sight.

"Mrs. Lange?" An investigator dressed in civilian clothes is holding a badge in my face.

"Yes?"

"Can my partner and I talk with you for a few moments?" A shorter man steps out from behind her and holds up his badge for me to read. I stare, unable to form words. I've been dosing myself with Xanax just to catch some sleep at night, I've been so racked with nightmares about this very moment. And now, in a case of déjà vu, the investigator steps into my home and says with a smile, "You're friends with Mika Morales, right?"

I can't find the words to answer her. My vision is tunneling as the edges fade to black. The hum of blood whooshing through my veins with every beat of my heart reaches a deafening decibel. I feel like I'm slipping into an alternate reality. Like Alice down the rabbit hole, I'm falling into something I'm not sure I can find my way out of. "I need Kip."

"Mr. Lange has already spoken with us this morning. We'd prefer to hear your side of the story alone if you don't mind, Mrs. Lange."

"Oh," is all I manage to utter. "My side of the story?"

Kip and I never discussed this. What is my side of the story? My mind splinters with possibilities, and suddenly, I've forgotten which is even the truth.

"If you don't mind." The woman pulls a small recording device out of her pocket. I can tell she's being purposefully vague with her questions in the hope that I'll reveal something to implicate myself or my husband. "I'd like to record this. I just can't keep up with handwriting all of those notes. Your husband had quite a lot to say this morning." She runs the pad of her thumb along the small notebook in her palm, and I notice dozens of pages of inky handwritten notes. Is that just from Kip's interview? What could he have possibly told them that would fill so many single-lined pages? Nothing. He would tell them nothing.

"Can I ask what exactly you'd like to know more about?" I smile politely.

"Last summer. We'd like to hear your version of the events last summer at Stonecliffe Island."

"It's been so long." I swallow. "I don't remember much, unfortunately. Mommy brain is real." I push a hand through my hair, making a point of looking as tired as I feel.

"You know withholding information or lying to us about anything pertaining to the case could be considered obstruction of justice. Best case, you get some jail time. Worst case, they take away your daughter while you fight the case, and if you do win . . . Well, it will take you even longer to get your daughter out of the foster care system. Sounds like a lot of trouble for a busy woman like you, so let's just cut to the truth of the matter, okay?"

I swallow the fear tightening my throat. "Sure."

"Okay, so your husband mentioned that you saw Kerrigan Lange the night or morning of her disappearance—"

"No—" I shake my head, but the investigator continues to speak over me.

"Can you tell us in what condition you saw her? Was she well? Was she coherent?"

"I didn't see her!" I snap, annoyed.

"You didn't?" The woman scratches more on her notepad.

"No. I hit my head. I was confused and unfocused. Looking back, I think I had a concussion."

"Are you sure about that? Did emergency responders assess you for a concussion?" the man behind her asks.

"Yes. I mean, I don't know. I don't really remember. Honestly, I'd just found out I was pregnant, and with all the chaos and the storm — it was a nightmare week. I think my brain has blocked everything out."

"Blocked everything out?" The woman looks dubious.

I nod, scared to say anything else in case I implicate myself. I'm not even sure if what took place was a crime, but I know these investigators seem hungry to lay the blame on someone who was there that week.

"Have you spoken with Cole Mayer since that week?"

My eyes widen, surprised by the question. "No."

"But you know he's in jail, right?" The man has moved beyond his partner now, glancing over my shoulder and into my home.

"I heard that, yes."

"And have you spoken to Mika Morales at all?" His tone turns cold.

"I'm not sure how I could — she's been in a coma."

"Right. Well, we pulled the visitor logs and found some interesting names on the list."

"Oh?" I smile.

"Says you were there just the other week," the female officer chimes in, referencing a note from her spiral-bound pad.

"I was, but I didn't talk to Mika. She was sleeping. I only spoke to her husband, who wasn't very welcoming."

"I can't say I blame him," the man huffs.

"Really?" I ask him directly.

"Well, sure. His wife lay in a coma for nearly nine months without a visit from you or your husband. In fact, based on what we know so far, it looks like you and your husband escaped Stonecliffe as quickly as possible . . . almost like you were running from something. Or maybe you didn't want to be caught?"

"That's not what happened."

"Or should I say, future husband. He was your best friend's husband at that time, right? Is that why you haven't talked to your former friend, Daniel Feeney, since then? Was he upset about your betrayal?" The man's eyes twinkle back at me as if he's just caught me in my first lie.

"Betrayal? No. No! Kip wanted to make sure the baby was safe, so—"

"Exactly. So, did Kerrigan find out about the affair? Maybe in a fit of rage, you hit her or—"

"No. No, my mind is foggy, but she was so violent—"

"So, you *did* see her?" The woman scribbles more on her pad.

"No. I don't know. In the few days leading up to . . . what happened, she was so erratic, talking about how much she and Kip were fighting and how she wished she'd ended up with someone like Cole. She seemed a little unhinged."

"We heard about all the fighting. In fact, that's the one fact that keeps coming up. It's funny nobody seems to remember much about that week, but everyone remembers the fighting between Kerrigan and her husband — *your husband* now." The man's disingenuous smile causes chills to skitter down my arms. "And what would you say if I told you new evidence has come to light?"

"Oh?"

"Evidence that might prove that your friend Cole was wrongfully convicted." The woman's tone is calm and measured, as if she's gauging my reaction.

"He's not my friend—" I'm quick to reply and then clamp my mouth shut with instant regret.

"Well," the woman hums, "I guess that makes it easier to sleep at night."

"Excuse me?" I frown, anger stirring to life inside me. "I don't think there's anything else I can tell you. If you don't mind, the baby should be getting up from her nap anytime, and I need to be ready to feed her."

"Ah, yes. The newest little Lange." The man scans the kitchen and sitting area behind me with his hardened gaze before he tips his hat and plasters a fake grin on his face. "Well, thank you for your time. We'll be in touch if we have any more questions." He smiles and then turns, taking his time as he descends my front steps.

"Thanks," I mutter, forcing a tight smile.

The female officer takes a few more notes in her notepad and then tips her eyes up to meet mine. "Listen, we know there was foul play on Stonecliffe last summer."

I remain silent, staring back at this woman who may hold my fate in her hands.

She looks away and then back at me as if she's deciding whether to tell me more. She bites down on her lip and then flips to a fresh page in her notepad and writes something down before tearing the page out and folding it in half. She hands it to me discreetly, nods once, and then dips her head and turns to leave. Terror threatens to choke me.

I close the door swiftly, locking the dead bolt behind me, and then lean against the wood to unfold the note.

Beneath the Surface is all it says.

"What is this?" I wonder.

My first instinct is to call my husband, but something stops me. Can I trust him? The truth is, I'm not sure who I can trust, but I know the notes in that notepad were extensive, to say the least. I wonder then if they've talked to Lyra or Daniel, or are Kip and I the sole suspects? I grit my teeth, realizing that of course we're the main suspects — the villain in any story always has the most to lose.

But who really had the most to lose at Stonecliffe that week? Was it Kip, with his failing business deals and inflated life insurance policies? Was it Mika or Stavros, in an effort to get revenge after they lost their savings in the hedge fund? Or was it Cole? Desperate to avoid another accident, maybe he covered things up or changed his story to absolve himself of wrongdoing.

I suddenly wish we would have stayed in touch with everyone.

I sit in the rocking chair by the front window and begin my online search. By the time my husband returns home that evening, I'm knee-deep in a mix of facts, assumptions, and useless internet speculation.

"Evening." Kip kicks off his leather loafers and collapses onto the sofa across from me.

"Why didn't you tell me investigators came to question you? I could have used a heads-up."

"Sorry, I didn't have time."

I raise my eyebrows. "That's it? You didn't have time?"

He shrugs, pushing a palm over his face with a sigh. "It's not like we have anything more to tell them. We've done this before."

"Except now, apparently, there's new evidence."

"There is?" He sits up a little straighter. "Like what?"

"They didn't tell you?" I frown, trying to discern what is fact and what is meant to intimidate us.

"They didn't tell me a thing. Just asked the same old shit, wanted to know if I'd been to visit Mika or anything."

"That's it? They didn't mention anything else?"

"Nope." He shakes his head. I hate that the thought pops into my mind that I'm not sure I can trust this man like I thought.

"Do the words *Beneath the Surface* mean anything to you?"

CHAPTER THIRTY-FOUR: RYLEIGH

By the time the clock above the kitchen sink reads three thirty in the morning, I find what it is I've been looking for.

I finally know what *Beneath the Surface* means.

The True Crime Junkie forum I stumbled on over an hour ago has proven to be my most abundant resource for all things related to the "Mystery at Stonecliffe Manor," as the junkies commonly refer to it. Most of the facts aren't facts at all, just grandiose assumptions and circumstantial pieces of information presented as evidence. In fact, everything is evidence to these up-all-night internet sleuths.

And just as I was about to exit the screen and finally try to get some sleep, I came across it.

Six months ago, a participant on the forum posted a link to a podcast called *Beneath the Surface*. At first look, it seemed like any other true crime podcast, until I discovered the host: *Anonymous*.

The lack of any identifying name at all raises my hackles as I scroll through the main podcast page. So far, there are only six episodes available, and the release schedule seems to be on the first day of every month. True Crime Junkies live for the moment the podcast is available for streaming. They spend roughly fifty minutes listening to new evidence about the cases at Stonecliffe Manor and Island, and then they spend the next three weeks coming up with a wild array of possibilities. All of them are focused on what happened to Kerrigan Lange and if the events surrounding Mika Morales' accident are related.

By the time I've finished the first episode, I can see why the internet is buzzing. There are enough new details nobody else would know unless . . . unless they were there. And there's one more thing that nobody knows . . . the host's voice is familiar. *Too* familiar. I can tell that whoever Anonymous is, they're trying to disguise their voice, and they're doing a pretty good job. It sounds like they're using some sort of computer-generated effect. But sometimes, just sometimes, I catch a certain lilt of a vowel or a clipped consonant that makes my blood run cold. This is someone I know, and if I had to bet, it's also the someone who's sending bloody baby gifts to my doorstep.

By the time sunshine splits through the windowpanes, I've binged the first five episodes with my heart in my throat. And in true crime fashion, the fifth episode ends with a cliffhanger that promises audio snippets of private conversations that link one of the Stonecliffe guests to the vanishing. I let the podcast app automatically start the most recent episode as low-grade anxiety begins to cause my limbs to tremble and shake. I'm sure I'm not ready for whatever is coming next, and Anonymous does not disappoint.

"There is a murderer on the loose . . . and worse? That murderer is now a mother."

I gasp as the first line of the podcast plays. I scroll back and listen again. The opening music begins, and I leap off the chair and run for the bathroom to empty my already-empty stomach. My insides seize up and burn as I realize what's going on here.

Beneath the Surface was constructed to be an elaborate true crime story.

A true crime story complete with a villain and a victim.

And in this story, *I am the villain.*

The Mommy Murderer.

The host teases about private conversations recorded on the island that week that help corroborate their baseless claims. I fast-forward a few seconds, anxious to hear exactly what conversations these are, and when I finally land on one, my blood runs cold. This isn't just one or two snippets, dozens of private conversations have been edited and cut together to show all of us in our worst light. Daniel complaining that my friends are spoiled narcissists, Stavros explaining that he only married his wife to gain American citizenship, even Kip and Kerrigan fighting and bickering over things I wasn't present for. It's almost as if every part of the island was bugged — the patio, the boat, the guest villas. *Everything.*

Whoever was there that week knew what they were doing, maybe even had this planned all along. I'm having a hard time believing any of this was just the film crew catching random conversations with their equipment all week. There's even a conversation between Kerrigan and me, but the mic sounds hidden or muffled. I can't quite tell what's being said until the last line. It's then a shiver of awareness radiates through me.

"*Ugh.* This week would be easier if you just weren't here."

I remember thinking it. Kerrigan was complaining about Kip again, and as she walked away, that thought ran through my mind — but did I really say it out loud?

I hadn't thought so, until now.

I can't tell Kip.

Whatever he might think about what I've just heard won't be good. He may even leave me, refuse to talk to me, prohibit me from seeing our baby . . . But then that would leave him the single parent, and as much as I love him, he's not a nurturer.

If my husband knew the secrets I kept, it would be the end of us.

CHAPTER THIRTY-FIVE: DANIEL

"Did you talk to them?" are the first words out of my former friend's mouth when I open the door.

"Excuse me?" I let the door hang open and then turn, hardly able to look Ryleigh in the eye.

She follows me in, baby carrier slung over one arm and enormous mom bag on the other. "You heard me."

"I did. My ears are working just fine, thank you. The part I wasn't clear on was the *them*."

She sighs, setting the baby carrier on the floor in my galley kitchen. "I'm sorry, I'm sorry. How have you been?"

I roll my eyes, settling down in my office chair and ignoring her.

"Well, some way to treat an old friend. And here I thought you'd always have my back."

"Friend?" I laugh. "We're not friends, Ryleigh. Did you have my back that day you left Stonecliffe? Were you there when investigators interviewed me and took my notebook? That was quite literally the worst week of my life, and you did not have my back then."

Ryleigh remains silent, staring the floor by my feet. "I was . . . having a baby."

"Don't we all know it," I grunt, distracted by the blinking cursor on my laptop screen.

"Please don't be mad at me," she whispers. "You're the only person I've ever been able to trust. I know how messed up things were that week." She sobs and wipes at her cheeks with her palms. "I just . . . I just didn't know what else to do and I was so afraid that I would lose the baby, and Kip thought it would be best—"

"Don't say his name. Please. It's hard enough seeing you after all this time." I hear my ragged emotions creeping into my voice. "It's been nine months, Rye. How could you just leave like that?"

"I-I didn't know if you . . ." She trails off, crying harder. "If you would even like me anymore after what I did."

I know instinctively what she means. Ryleigh and I have always had our own secret language. We know each other down to the marrow, and it's only been the last nine months that have made me realize how unhealthy that is.

"I don't like what you did, but I could never hate you, Rye. I hate them — I hate every last one of them. But I could never hate you." I spin in my chair, looking at her for the first time since I sat down. She looks tired to the bone and racked with anxiety. "Has he been good to you?"

Rye sniffs, wiping her eyes one last time. "He has. For the record, I didn't know Kip — *he* — was married when we first met." She's brimming with remorse. "I just kept seeing him at the athletic club, and sometimes he would linger and talk to me on his way out. He has this way of making you feel so special when he wants to. When he invited me out to dinner and then his apartment later, I had no idea that . . . that he wasn't single." Ryleigh wrings her fingers, face twisted with sadness. "I didn't know until Kerrigan invited me over for Bloody Marys at her townhouse one Sunday a few months later. By then, we were . . . My head and my heart were so wrapped up in him. It killed me when he walked out in pajamas and bare feet and a smile that morning. I thought at first maybe they'd just hooked up, until Kerrigan introduced him as her husband." She sniffs, and I can't help but wonder if it's for dramatic effect. "I've been drowning in his promises ever since."

A lump forms in my throat. "I can't get tangled up with those people again." I hold her gaze for a long moment. "I hope you can understand."

"I do. I just wanted to see if anyone has come around asking about what happened at Stonecliffe."

"No." I shake my head. "I don't have anything to tell them anyway."

Ryleigh's eyes cast across my small studio apartment, lingering on the window across the room that overlooks one of the L train stations. "Have you heard the podcast?"

My eyebrows shoot up. "Podcast?"

She pulls her phone out of her giant bag. "Listen."

She thrusts the phone at me, and it only takes me a few moments to understand what I'm hearing. "Is that who I think it is?"

She shrugs. "I was hoping to get your opinion."

I listen as the electronically altered female voice continues to speak. "It's got to be her."

Ryleigh nods, then drops down onto the threadbare IKEA sofa we bought together our freshman year of college. "I think she's trying to frame me."

I nearly choke on my tongue. "What? Why?"

"*Duh.* For revenge. I have everything she ever wanted." Rye glances down at the peacefully sleeping baby in the carrier.

"Sounds dark. You really think she's capable of that?"

"Who else would be?" Ryleigh's frown deepens before she digs around in her bag and pulls out something I know I've seen before.

"This came in the mail." She thrusts a colorful piece of fabric at me. "It's Mika's scarf — the bloody one we found on the boat that day."

I raise an eyebrow as I turn the scarf over in my hands. "It's probably not really—"

196

"That's not the only thing." I can see fear visibly cross her face before she opens her palm and reveals something else. "It came with this."

I lean in, plucking a small diamond-wrapped infinity band from her hand. "What's this?"

"Kerrigan's wedding ring."

"How can you be sure? Maybe it's a cheap replica meant to scare you," I offer.

"Because I remember. And there's a box of wedding day photos with *that ring* on her finger in my basement."

"Honestly, Rye, this could be anyone. A crazy internet sleuth or Lyra just being an asshole—"

Ryleigh shakes her head. "I don't think so."

"What's the alternative? If it's not a stranger or Lyra or Stavros, then who could it be? Your husband?"

Ryleigh's eyes widen with alarm before she shakes her head furiously. "I-I don't know, but . . . do you think the police really believe she's dead? Her body wasn't found — no body, no crime, right?"

I let her words linger for a beat because they're insane — absolutely, positively insane. But isn't that life?

"You know, repeating it doesn't make it truer."

She swats at my shoulder, and I feel the easiness that only comes with a decades-long friendship bloom between us again.

I gnaw on my bottom lip as I think about the thriller novel I've been working on. My new agent thinks it's good enough to get a publishing deal. It's this story that's been consuming me since I left Ryleigh and Stonecliffe. But the fact is, it draws on a lot of real-life events. I've already made a point of changing the names — but for those who were there that summer, it will be no surprise. The only thing I haven't been able to figure out with this story is the ending.

The ending is everything.

It's because I've been so focused on this book that I let distance build between Rye and me over the last nine months. And it's also because I'm trying to find a way to write it that doesn't implicate her. No matter how I plot the scenes, it's Ryleigh who remains the most likely culprit. She was the last person to see Mika. And in her own words, she was the last person to see Kerrigan. Of that, I'm clear — I have notes from the very morning that Ryleigh stumbled to the pergola and claimed Kerrigan had hit her. I also have written down that Ryleigh recanted those words within moments, as if she knew her confession implicated her in a crime. And for the last nine months, I haven't known which side of her story to believe.

When I started this book, it was intended as a work of fiction inspired by true events, but the more I dig, the more I find. The case against Cole was in full swing by the time I wrote the opening lines. And now?

Now, this story has turned from a fictional thriller to an unsolved true crime case.

For the first time ever, I look at my former friend and wonder if she has it in her to lie to me. To hurt someone. Maybe even kill. The truth is, I don't trust her. Not after she married her friend's husband and had his baby so soon after Kerrigan's mysterious disappearance.

And the other truth? The more I think about what happened at Stonecliffe last summer, the more I think I might be close to solving the crime that uprooted all our lives. And if I can get to the bottom of it, it just might pad my bank account to the tune of millions. I could have my choice of book deals, and my career would be set for life.

I've only got to prove it.

"Well, I'll let you know if anyone shows up." I stand, eager for her to make her exit. "I've got a deadline with the agent," I say by way of explanation.

"Sure, of course." She stands, smoothing her blouse and blinking away some unnamed emotion. "Hey, can I just . . ." She frowns, as if she's warring with herself. "I've been having these nightmares about that night. My memory is foggy, but I think . . . I think I saw Kerrigan that night. I think she knew I was pregnant, and she tried to . . . Sharon Tate me."

198

"*Sharon Tate* you?"

Rye nods, fresh tears rushing to her eyes. "Y'know." She makes a cutting motion across her abdomen. "I just keep waking up to nightmares of all of this blood and the realization that I'm miscarrying and bleeding out in the sand and . . ." Her shoulders are trembling as she succumbs to her tired tears. "I'm afraid it's me."

I don't reply, afraid of what she means to say exactly.

"I'm afraid I tried to kill her."

I can't wait to hear what might come out of her mouth next. But even if it is good for the book, I don't really want to be the keeper of these secrets. I resent her for trying to unload them on me — Ryleigh has always done this, treated me like her on-call therapist. I can't be her sounding board anymore, as much as a piece of me wants to.

"Everything will be okay, Rye. I promise," is all I can muster as I lean in to give her a quick hug.

She catches me in her embrace, tears wetting my shoulder already. "I'm scared."

I rub her back. "Chin up. I'm sure that husband of yours will find a way to make everything go away."

She pulls away, swiping at her tears before taking a deep breath. "What if he did it?"

I shake my head, unable to stand any more of her anxious speculations. Ryleigh is at the center of this. I don't know how, and I don't know why, but until I do, I need to keep my friends close and my enemies closer.

"Stop worrying." I press my hands to her cheeks and smooth the pads of my thumbs across her forehead. "You'll need Botox sooner." That gets her to crack a smile. I grin, glad that I still have that ability. "There's my girl." I look down at the sleeping baby in her carrier. "What's her name?"

Ryleigh's face crumples again. "Daniella."

"Oh." I wonder if I've heard her right.

"I named her after the most loyal and honest friend I've ever had." I can see her gulp down her pain. "I'm sorry I wasn't a good friend to you."

I can't bring myself to reply.

I pass the baby carrier to my friend and then watch silently as she retreats from my studio apartment without another word. I close the door before she's even hit the first stair. I know I should be the gentleman and offer to help her down with the baby, but I don't have it in me to lift a finger to help her. Not after everything. It's also no surprise to me that Ryleigh would attempt to lay the blame for last summer on Kerrigan. The more time I have away from that week, the more the veil has been lifted from my vision, and I can see the slow-simmering disdain and maybe even unabashed envy that Ryleigh had for the other woman. I didn't find Rye's lingering glances at Kip suspicious then because Kip Lange commands a room. Everyone pays attention in his presence, just how he likes it.

And anyway, Kip isn't quite the upstanding guy that he'd have people believe. The more tensions revealed themselves that week, the more I knew Kip Lange was the kind of guy that used his friends as stepping stones to achieve his goals. And the more I knew I had to cut my ties with my longest friend in favor of writing this story just to figure out what happened.

I'd pitched the story to my agent as a fictional cautionary tale of friendship and ambition. From the moment Ryleigh and I met, I'd always thought of her as the quintessential best friend in the fairy tale of my life, but now it seems I'm the only sane one in an insane world. What happened at Stonecliffe — correction, what's *been happening* at Stonecliffe for a lot of years — is a tale so tantalizing, even Hollywood has come to call. I've often searched for the documentary we signed off to film that week, but with only the director's name of Jeremy to go on, I haven't been successful.

Now, there's only one person left I can think to ask. Only one person left who may know what happened.

I have no choice. I have to go back to the scene of the crime.

CHAPTER THIRTY-SIX: DANIEL

"Dock's just around the tip of Stonecliffe. Should be there in less than five." The captain's monotone voice sets my teeth on edge.

"I've been here before," I remind him. I had to pay the man nearly three times his typical asking price to get him to bring me to Stonecliffe this morning just because I didn't arrange transportation with him in advance.

"Mind if I ask what brings you up here?"

I groan, closing my notepad stuffed with case notes and tucking it into my backpack. "I spent some time as a guest here last summer."

"Yeah?" he grunts.

"And—" I scramble to find something to appease his curiosity — "I think I left something behind."

"Hm," he hums, and then slows the old fishing boat. "You musta been one of the last guests before Stonecliffe was sold to developers." Just as the words leave his mouth, we come around the jagged eastern edge of the island, and a series of tall mining rigs dominate the shoreline.

"Wow, they didn't waste time selling the oil rights, did they?" I wince. What was once a pristine pebbled shoreline bookended by soaring limestone cliffs is now an industrial worksite. Every available space of flat coastline is dotted with construction equipment and tools to service the operation. A drilling rig sits perched over a hole in the limestone shoreline, the lake water held back by a temporary steel berm. Stonecliffe looks more like the set for a post-apocalyptic thriller than paradise.

"No one knew Stonecliffe sat square in the middle of one of the Great Lake's largest crude oil deposits. Well, *someone* knew," the boat captain comments.

Kip knew a helluva lot more than he let on. So why go to such great lengths to keep it all a secret? If he would have just told Mika that the payout for the sale of Stonecliffe would allow her to keep her design business afloat . . . Well, I like to think she probably would have gone for it. She doesn't have the option now, though.

"Biggest deposit ever found in North America. Newspapers said it could be worth up to a trillion dollars — can you believe that?" He shakes his head. "The mining company needed just the right place to set up some test drilling sites, and boy did they find it at Stonecliffe." He shoots a look at me before his gaze returns to the island he's speaking of. "Sure was a lucky few who made it off the island last summer — funny how tragedy has a way of working out for some."

"What do you mean?" I ask.

"Well, with two shareholders out of the picture, it sure made it easier to sell the island."

I remain silent, working over the words he's just said. It's not something I'd thought of before because I didn't know the details of what happened to this place after I left it.

In fact, I'd done everything in my power to bury the memories.

The fisherman interrupts my thoughts while he slows the boat and edges up close to the dock. "Wouldn't it have been easier to have someone go lookin' for whatever you left and then mail it to you 'nsteada comin' all the way up here?" The fisherman interrupts my thoughts while he slows the boat and edges up close to the dock.

"Some things a guy has to do on his own, I guess," I grumble, slinging my backpack over my shoulder and waiting as the old man secures the boat at the dock and opens the door for me to hop off.

"Just give a call to the marina in Mackinaw if you need a lift back to the mainland."

"Will do." I wave once and then walk off the dock and into the sand. Without thinking, I make my way down the path in the opposite direction of the villas. I pause, pulling my notebook out of my backpack, and then jot down the handful of things the fisherman said about the deposit of crude oil surrounding Stonecliffe. I make another note to do a little research on who exactly the shareholders of Stonecliffe Manor and Island were. I know for sure Kip, Kerrigan, Mika, Lyra . . . and Cole and Ryleigh to a lesser per cent — but is anyone else listed on the deed or in the trust?

A seagull squawks above me and pulls my attention up. Despite the industrial mining operation that's been set up, the natural beauty of this place still pervades every angle. Just as I pass a hedge of overgrown lilacs, a movement catches my eye.

"Lyra?" I say just loud enough that she whips around and scowls.

"Daniel?" She's barefoot and bronzed, long and lean legs rushing toward me with a curious look on her face. "What are you doing here?"

"I came because I couldn't stop thinking about what happened last summer," I admit, unwilling to reveal much more.

"That makes both of us."

"How long have you been staying here?" I tuck my notepad into my backpack.

Her brow furrows, eyes narrowed as if she's considering whether or not she can trust me. After a moment she nods at me to follow her into Cole's caretaker cottage.

The door is already open, and once we're inside, it takes my eyes a while to adjust to the darkness. The first thing I see is a whiteboard criss-crossed with dry-erase marker lines in the way a crime scene investigator would. Each of the lines ends at a large letter inside a circle.

"What is all this?"

"The story of the disappearances of Stonecliffe," comes a voice I never thought I'd hear again in person, "also known as the 'Mommy Murderer' case. At least, that's what listeners are calling it."

I spin, feeling stunned as I take in the woman who's just stepped from the shadows of the cottage. "Kerrigan."

"Nice to see you, Daniel. You can call me Kandi, true crime investigator."

"What are you doing here?" I manage.

"So rude," Kerrigan huffs. "Trying to get my friend out of jail, for starters. And maybe put another one in jail."

I don't respond because I don't really think she wants me to.

"I know she visited you. What did she tell you?" Kerrigan continues to approach me.

"Who?" I step away from her, backing toward the doorway.

"Ryleigh, of course." Kerrigan steps into the sunlight, and I see her fully for the first time. She looks wild, her skin sunburned and hair untamed. She's still beautiful, with a youthful, sun-kissed glow on her cheeks and little if any make-up — but something in her eyes tells me she's far from holding it together. "Tell me."

"There isn't anything to tell. And why do you think I talked to her? Ryleigh stopped talking to me a long time ago."

"Oh, save it. Lyra dropped an AirTag in her purse at the hospital. We've known her every move for weeks. Now, spill it."

"Why?" I growl.

Lyra laughs, gesturing to the whiteboard with a nod. "You see the evidence against her, right? Better to be on the right side of the law on this one, don't you think, Daniel? Otherwise . . . Well, she'll take you down with her."

I refuse to give them the satisfaction of a reply. Ryleigh betrayed me, but she's not evil. She doesn't have it in her to be — but both of these women set my teeth on edge.

"Mika remembers." Kerrigan is close now, so close I can see the chapped lips and freckles from the sun on her nose.

"Remembers what?" My heart pounds as I wait for her next words. This is why I came. This is what I've been waiting for.

"She remembers seeing that gaudy tie-dyed sweatshirt Ryleigh wore all week, for starters."

"So?" I say, remembering the sweatshirt clearly. It's the one she's been wearing to bed since we were teenagers.

"That ugly sweatshirt is the last thing she saw before she was knocked out," Lyra explains.

I raise my eyebrows. Is it possible that my closest friend did this? I can clearly remember that Ryleigh had that sweatshirt with her the day Mika vanished. I can even recall she had it tied around her waist as she walked down the shoreline with Mika at her side. I was hoping to come to Stonecliffe to prove her innocence, but instead, I seem to be confirming her involvement.

"So that's it, then?" Both women remain silent, waiting for me to continue. "You're just here building a case for revenge?"

"It's compelling evidence, Daniel." Lyra approaches. "You know it is."

I swallow. She's right.

"The truth has to come out," Kerrigan pleads. "Someone has to shine a light on the stupid botched investigation that wrongfully convicted Cole. She betrayed me. She betrayed you. All of us. What else is she capable of?"

"I know you don't want your best friend to go to jail — no one does, but someone else is serving time for it," Lyra says. "You know whatever happened that week was suspicious, but Cole didn't have anything to do with it."

"And anyway," Kerrigan adds, "where does it end with her? She can't be trusted. You know it's true."

I bite down on my bottom lip, mind buzzing with possibilities. "She's not my best friend."

Lyra glances at Kerrigan, and I swear I see the smallest hint of a smile pass between them.

Knowing what I know now, there's a chance Ryleigh ends up in jail. But maybe she deserves it. She's become one of them anyway, and the truth needs to see the light of day.

"Maybe I should just hand everything I know over to the police. I could tell them what you've been doing."

"Fine." Kerrigan cocks her head. "But did you consider that maybe they already know?"

I hadn't considered that, but maybe this is just a way for Kerrigan and Lyra to deter me from making good on my threat to reveal them. "So, why wouldn't they arrest her, then?"

"Because the court of public opinion matters more than the truth," Kerrigan replies.

"We need the internet on our side," Lyra says quietly. "Without online rage and demands for justice, the judge will never approve Cole's appeal, and the case against Ryleigh will be lost to time."

"And so will Cole." Kerrigan squints away tears.

"Why not just come forward? Cole is sitting in jail for your disappearance — you could clear his name and he could walk free tomorrow."

"So they can pin Mika's crime on me? No way, I need this process to unfold organically. What good does it do if the wrong person is still sitting in jail for Mika's accident — anyway, Cole is partially responsible. He's been running the island into the ground for years — this isn't the first time tourists have gotten hurt on his watch. He's a nice guy but he's irresponsible. It is what it is. He'll be out in due time anyway, we just have to let things play out."

I drag my gaze away from her and linger for several moments on the whiteboard behind her. "That's the plan, then?"

Lyra nods. "That's the series outline for the podcast — unpacking the evidence little by little in sixty-minute episodes. We record from the bedroom. It's a pretty solid set-up."

"Honestly, it doesn't seem like much. It's all circumstantial. It's compelling, but . . . there's no way to prove what happened to Mika was Ryleigh's fault, even if Mika remembered everything tomorrow—"

"She will." Kerrigan smiles. "And even if she doesn't, we're covered."

Lyra turns her mouth down and examines my face as if she's trying to determine whether she can trust me. "We have more."

"More what?" I huff.

Kerrigan grins. "I bought the film footage."

Lyra steps closer to Kerrigan with a glint in her eye. "If you saw it, Daniel . . . Well, let's just say there's a lot that went on that week that we didn't know about."

I can't breathe, my vision tunneling as I realize what this means.

"We're editing it in the back room, and once you see the footage of Kip and Ryleigh together . . . there won't be any question left in your mind."

"It's damning." Lyra's buzzing with excitement. "They sneaked off together multiple times, embracing and hugging and kissing and . . . if you saw it, you'd hate her."

"We're calling it *Mommy Murderer* when we pitch it to the streaming platforms," Kerrigan interjects. "If internet true crime forums are any indication . . . Well, I think we've got a hit on our hands."

"And then there's that CCTV footage." Lyra shakes her head. "Ryleigh is such an idiot, she didn't even think to cover her tracks that night."

"Why would Ryleigh do this, though? Why would she do that to Mika? I understand the evidence lines up, but the motivation doesn't." I cast my eyes over the whiteboard in search of the connection.

"You don't think so?" Kerrigan blazes with anger.

"I think someone's been trying to undermine the profitability of this island for a lot longer than just last summer." I scan the whiteboard, searching for some unseen angle that makes more sense than Ryleigh trying to kill Mika and Kerrigan in a fit of rage — or whatever these two are proposing.

"Ryleigh wanted everything I had. Don't you see that? Kip signed off on the sale without my signature, took off with my money, and married my best friend. Ryleigh is reaping the benefits of the life I worked for — she even has the baby I wanted. *My* baby."

Lyra interrupts. "Within hours of Cole being interrogated, I pulled security tapes from that night. I sent a copy to investigators, and they suppressed it. They suppressed it because it didn't support their case that Cole was the guy at fault."

"What's on the tape?" I'm afraid to ask, but I have to know.

"Ryleigh," Kerrigan breathes.

"Ryleigh what?" I'm getting annoyed.

"Ryleigh discarding something in the dumpster behind Cole's cabin that night. The time stamp lines up. It looks like towels or sheets or—"

"That proves nothing."

"Maybe the part where she disposes of the knife will convince you, then." Kerrigan smiles.

"So then, what's your motive?" I look back and forth at them.

"What do you mean?" Lyra tips her head. "Beyond getting Cole out of jail—"

"That's just it," I interrupt her. "You're both in love with him. Is that the angle? And as soon as Ryleigh is locked up, the two of you will turn on each other?"

"Hardly," Lyra grunts.

"Well, I don't believe for a second that you're doing this out of the kindness of your cold heart."

Lyra squints at me, as if she's deciding whether to tell me the truth. "Fine. Daddy cut me off. So I've been staying here at Cole's and working on the podcast. The episodes get hundreds of thousands of listens in the week it goes out. It's a phenomenon. Sponsors are making it worth it right now, but without the streaming deal . . . Well, there isn't much we can do beyond that."

"You expect me to believe you two haven't been working together to dupe the rest of us from the very beginning?" The truth is, I don't know what I believe, but I know the key to my safety is to keep them talking.

"Kerrigan didn't know I was here," Lyra jumps in.

"I was staying at one of the abandoned fishing huts on Grand Manitou when I rowed across the bay for a day trip, and imagine my shock when I found Cole's cabin inhabited." Kerrigan glances at Lyra with a soft smile. "It was so nice to see a familiar face. I'd been hiding out from every living soul for a month when we finally found each other."

Lyra giggles. "You scared the shit out of me at first, just like Daniel did."

"You've been jumpy lately." Kerrigan circles her arm around Lyra's waist and plants a soft kiss on her bare shoulder.

My eyebrows jump up as I detect some sort of unspoken chemistry passing between the two of them. They're distracted, and on instinct, my eyes travel the dark corners of the space in search of a weapon or something I could use in case things turn sour.

"You know, it's funny you came when you did," Lyra says intensely. "You took all those notes last summer, right?"

"Yeah, but the investigators—"

"Confiscated everything, I know." She bites down on her bottom lip. "But you were the most observant one there. Always watching and listening, taking notes . . . You must have seen more than the rest of us combined."

I shake my head, unsure of where this is leading.

"We think you should write a book about Stonecliffe." Kerrigan looks wild with anticipation. "You don't even have to pin it on your friend. Just write the story you witnessed and let readers decide."

"I-I don't think—"

"I know you're writing something." Lyra's eyes turn a shade darker. "With your words, the truth has a chance to see the light of day."

"I won't write anything that isn't true," I vow.

"Of course not." Lyra shakes her head.

"Ryleigh should pay for the consequences of her actions." Kerrigan cradles her tummy as a tear slips down her cheek. "She wanted what was mine so much, she almost killed me." She sobs harder. "I don't care if she goes to jail. I just want the world to know the evil she's capable of. She plays so sweet and innocent, but she's a monster, Daniel. She's a monster who almost ended my life."

I don't have words to reply. I push a palm over my face as I slump down into the threadbare chair that sits near the sole window in the room. The idea of exposing the corruption that money and greed breeds among these people is powerful.

Pulling my notepad and recorder out of my bag, I grind my teeth as I begin to transcribe what I've just been told. Every day, every moment, every word is branded in my memory.

"Use whatever you need." Kerrigan gestures with her hand to the whiteboard. "Any questions you have or any research you need, we're here for you."

I stare at her for a moment, not sure if I'm ready for what she's asking of me.

Kerrigan seems to take the hint that I'm on the edge of walking out on them, so she does it first. She and Lyra nod and pass me a small wave before they exit the cabin and shut the heavy wooden door behind them. It closes with a soft thud, the same sound I imagine Mika's head made when it connected with the rock that nearly cost her everything.

I don't know if Ryleigh is capable of murder, but it already feels like I lost my best friend to these people, as obsessed with their wealth and status as they are. Maybe now is my time to reap the rewards of this association.

I don't need revenge like Kerrigan and Lyra. All I need is vindication. I have a feeling that if I can just get to the heart of the truth, it will set all of us free.

CHAPTER THIRTY-SEVEN: RYLEIGH

Six months later

"Look at all these people lined up to read your book, and you still haven't let me read it," I gush, jostling baby Daniella in one arm as I gaze up at Daniel.

"You shouldn't read it. It's shit. You know it is," he huffs. "But it's the story the publisher wanted." Daniel looks stressed but shrugs and half smiles at me, pulling on the entry door of the bookstore.

The smell of books and a rush of soft *oohs* and *aahs* hits me.

"They're all here for you." I swell with pride.

"No, they're here because the bookstore bribed them with free cookies and coffee. Today is launch day. I promise you none of these people have read the story — you're all in the same boat."

"Is that supposed to make me feel better?"

Daniel shrugs. "It's practically fiction anyway."

"Not according to this." I lift a copy of the hardcover in my hand. "*Murder at Stonecliffe*. Inspired by true events."

"The publisher tried to classify it as true crime, but I fought them every step of the way," Daniel tells me again.

He's been saying this a lot lately, and he's developed some sort of nervous twitch where he pushes a palm over his head and sighs. I chalked it up to being anxious about the book launch, but maybe it's more.

Daniel and I have gotten closer than we've ever been the last few months. After I found out Mika was still alive and slowly remembering, Kip became more distant. More distracted. He spent more time at work than he did at home with me and Daniella, and so my trust in him faltered. In the last three months, I've spent more time with Daniel than I have with my own husband. If this continues, Daniella will grow up thinking Daniel is her dad.

The owner of the bookstore clears her throat and stands at the small podium placed at the front of the shop. "We are so lucky to have with us the author of the next great American true crime story — and probably the next *New York Times* bestseller." She winks at Daniel, and he smiles softly. If I know anything about my oldest friend, it's that he hates this. He hates everything about the attention being on him, so when he told me he'd been invited to do a reading for his new book launch, I was surprised when he agreed.

"Please give him a round of applause. The author of *Murder at Stonecliffe*, Daniel Feeney."

The small group of readers has swelled to nearly fifty as the last of the people lined up outside are ushered in. It's now standing room only as Daniel takes his spot behind the podium and waves awkwardly at the crowd.

"Thanks for coming," he starts off. "Writing this story was a journey that took a toll on me. When I say I bled every word onto the page, trust me . . ." I smile as my friend continues, thinking he really isn't very good at this public speaking thing.

"Excuse me." A deep voice interrupts Daniel's.

"We're having a private event tonight." The manager of the bookstore moves to the front door.

"Ma'am, this is official business." The man holds out a badge to the woman, and she balks. "We need to speak to Ryleigh Lange."

"Who?" she sputters, and my blood runs cold.

Why would they want to speak with me?

"Ryleigh Lange?" Another plainclothes investigator moves around the crowd of shocked readers toward me.

Tears pinch at my eyelids before they run down my cheeks. "Daniella—"

"I've got her." Daniel is there, and Daniella — because she's spent almost every day of the last ninety with him — leans into the comfort of his embrace.

"Ryleigh Lange. You're under arrest for the attempted murder of Kerrigan Lange and Mika Morales," the officer recites as they approach me.

"No — it wasn't me," I manage to sob.

"It never is." The officer is locking my wrists together as the readers watch on in horror. They came to a book signing, and now they're getting a real show.

"What evidence do you have?" Daniel barks at the officer nearest him.

"That'll all come out in court. Tonight, I'm just followin' orders," she grunts, and then pushes me through the crowd. My veins are vibrating with fear and anger, my muscles are taut and heavy, and everything in me wants to run to Daniella and take her in my arms far away from here.

But I can't.

Because I brought her into this mess, and now we'll both have to live with the consequences.

"Wait," I whisper as the officer escorts me out of the book-store, "it's you." She pauses when she reaches the back door of a dark sedan. "You're the one who told me about the podcast."

She nods, betraying with something that looks like sympathy. "I-I'm sorry it turned out this way, just . . ." She leans closer. "They'll go easier on you if you cooperate."

"Cooperate? I don't know anything."

"You have to stop saying that. Everyone says that, and nobody believes them."

"But it's true." I choke on a sob as she slides me into the back seat.

"Maybe it is, but that book in there says otherwise." She gestures back into the bookstore. Daniel is standing with Daniella in his arms, and it's as if my daughter has picked up on the tense energy, because now we've locked eyes and she's reaching out for me.

"The book isn't true! It says right on the cover, it's *inspired* by true events, not *actually* true events." The investigator hesitates as if she's warring with herself about what to believe. "You know she's still alive."

This gets her attention.

She squints. "*Who* is still alive?"

"Kerrigan — who do you think?" I snap. "You know, the woman I supposedly tried to murder is hiding out right now in a podcast studio somewhere shouting out her bullshit to the world."

The woman frowns, then finally shifts her gaze to her shiny black shoes. "I believe you, but the evidence says otherwise."

I grit my teeth, realizing now that words won't get me out of this situation. Nothing will. "They should search the IP address the podcast is sent from."

"It's from an anonymous network. We've searched Stonecliffe multiple times. A whole forensic evidence crew has gone over every rock and searched every cave — there was nothing to find, especially not an entire podcast set-up. It's pretty easy to podcast from just your phone though."

"Well, she did it, then." I breathe, a fresh wave of tears rushing down my cheeks. "She got away with it. She won."

"Don't say that. Don't give up yet, honey." She pats my knee. "Have a little faith."

She backs away and then gently closes the door of the cruiser. Daniella's tiny cries are blocked from my ears, and another sob racks my body. The investigator slides into the front seat, wraps the seat belt around her body, and clicks it into place. "I'm telling you, Kip doesn't have it in him to be a single parent. He didn't even want this baby to begin with. They're going to take my daughter. I'm telling you, he'll give her up for adoption or someone will report him for neglect. She'll be handed over to child protective services, and then . . . And then—" pain fists at my heart as I try to breathe — "I'll kill myself."

"Don't you say that. If they take her, then you'll fight." She holds my attention in the rear-view mirror. "You hear me? It's not over until the fat lady sings, and as far as I'm concerned, they've got a helluva lot to prove if they think they're going to keep you in jail for long. If you're telling the truth, the evidence will show it — you have to believe that, honey. It's just gonna take some time for it all to come out."

"No. No, I mean it." My limbs start to tremble and shake. "If they take my daughter, I'll kill myself."

She shakes her head. "You don't wanna say that."

"I mean it."

"If you say it again—" she looks away sharply — "I'll hafta add it to the arrest record. And when you start throwing words like that around, well, things take a different course that you might not be ready for. Now, as it stands, I'm gonna pretend I didn't hear that, but if you say it in front of my partner, then there's no going back."

The passenger door opens, and the other investigator slides into the front seat.

I sit up straight and say the next words as clearly as I can. "I'm going to kill myself."

CHAPTER THIRTY-EIGHT: RYLEIGH

"Time for your meds, Ryleigh." The nurse enters my room with a bright smile. She's always so cheery, the one ray of sunshine in this mental health wasteland.

"I don't need them," I groan. "They make me dizzy, like I'm swimming underwater when I walk."

"Ryleigh, please." Kip sighs, uncrossing his legs and shifting in the chair. "The doctor said the side effects would be temporary."

"Temporary for whom? Because it's my brain, Kip. *Mine.* It's been two weeks, and the side effects have only gotten worse. I'm telling you, I don't need them."

He leans in. "Rye—"

"Don't call me that." He knows better. I've told him a million times not to call me that name. It triggers old memories of the girl I used to be, of who we all were before that summer.

"Sorry, Ryleigh," he corrects. "You know what happens if you refuse to take them. You're under court-appointed psychiatric care, and if—"

"Stop it!" I snap. I thrust out my palm to the nurse, and she passes me a plastic cup with a small white pill in it.

"They're just enough to keep you from hurting yourself, dear. They're not the enemy."

"That's not what they're for." I swallow the pill down and then continue. "They're to keep me complacent while this bullshit case is built against me."

"Then you shouldn't have said what you said." Kip's anger suddenly spikes. He's been like this every time he's come to visit me since my arrest. Testy and on edge, and I can't help but worry about Daniella, if she's safe with him, if he tends to her every soft cry at night, or if he ignores her. "If you threaten to kill yourself to a cop, there are consequences."

"And yet your first wife walks free."

"We don't know that. There's no evidence—"

"Bullshit. You heard the podcast. You know it's her as well as I do. I know my friend's voice."

"I don't know how. It's a garbled, disguised voice. I don't hear anything familiar in it."

"Maybe that's because you never really listened to your wife."

"Rye—"

"Stop talking. These meds make me hate you even more than I already did." I know I'm being petty and mean now, but I can't help it. He hasn't been there for me or Daniella since she was born. I don't know what happened to the man I married on the beach of Lake Michigan that day before the birth of our daughter, but he hasn't been the same since.

"Jesus, if you want a divorce, just say so. But I promise you, baby—" Kip reaches a palm out to squeeze my knee — "I'm doing everything I can to make this right."

"It will never be right again," I say. "Have you talked to Daniel?" Kip only shakes his head. "I thought he'd be there for Daniella."

Kip nods. "The book release was big. Second week on the bestseller's list."

"They were talking about it on *Good Morning America* yesterday." I sniff, feeling the noose tighten around my neck. "I don't have a chance at getting out of here, do I?"

I catch Kip's grimace before his features turn stoic again. "I won't stop until the truth is out there, Ryleigh."

217

I blink away tears, forcing my mind to think about anything but the present moment. "I remembered something else about that night."

Kip leans in, clasping his hands together at the knees. "Yeah?"

"The night of the storm, I heard yelling. I thought it was the wind or maybe even those weird ghost hunters up at the manor, but now . . . now, I think it was Kerrigan." His eyes are locked with mine. "Fighting with someone."

"We know that already. Investigators think it was Cole—"

"I thought so too at first, but I just kept thinking there was something I was missing . . ."

Kip shakes his head as if he's not even sure he believes me anymore.

"But it wasn't Cole. I saw him that night in his cabin."

Kip raises his eyebrows.

"Not like that." I shake my head. "I was out walking because I couldn't sleep. I came across his cabin late — almost midnight, maybe — and he was there at his kitchen table, all the lights on, working on something."

"Did you tell investigators that?" Kip looks weary but hopeful.

"I didn't remember it until last night. Besides, what could it change? I don't think it's enough for the judge to grant him an appeal."

"He'll be out soon anyway."

"How do you know? Have you talked to him?"

"Of course not. But the sentence is public record. With good behavior, he'll be out in the next year, I bet."

I take in his words, thinking how wild it is that whatever happened that summer still haunts each of us.

"Did you hire the private investigator that we talked about?" I eye my husband with a mix of love and disdain. You would have thought he'd be there for me. But no. Only as much as he's been obligated to be and not a moment more.

"No. I've been so busy with work—"

"Too busy to get your wife out of jail?" I hate him now, truly.

"This is hardly jail," he huffs.

I want to call him every swear word in the book, but I bite my tongue. "We have to find out who is behind this. Who is trying to frame me. You believe me, right?"

"Yeah, of course. All hands on deck. I'll have Martha send an email to that PI agency."

"A call. Make a phone call. Please." My voice cracks on the last word. "Someone is trying to ruin our family."

"I know, I know." My husband's eyes cut away from mine. "I'm doing everything I can." His forehead wrinkles. "Rye — the thing is, they found a piece of your scarf with Mika. It came out in the book. Investigators held that evidence back from the public, but why was there a piece of your scarf with her body in the boat?"

His words catch me off guard. "I-I don't know."

I wasn't wearing a scarf that day; I know that much.

And then it hits me. I know who did this.

CHAPTER THIRTY-NINE: RYLEIGH

"I think he did it."

Daniel's eyes scrunch together as he ponders my words. "What did he do now?"

We both know who *he* is. *He* is always the topic of our conversation. *He* is the reason I'm here, I'm convinced of it. I just can't prove it.

"What *isn't* he doing is more the issue." I frown. "I've been asking him to hire a PI for a month. But since the moment I was arrested, it seems like he does things to hurt my case more than build it."

"You're not really thinking . . ."

"I don't know what I'm thinking," I confess. "Only that I don't believe him." I slide a manila envelope across the table to him. Daniel has been there for me from the beginning of this nightmare. If I trust anyone, it's him. But even now, after everything, I'm still struggling to trust anyone. He did write the book that got me arrested after all.

Well, sort of.

As soon as I could receive visitors in the psychiatric ward, Daniel was there.

I'm allowed up to three visitors a week and no more than one every twenty-four hours. Daniel visits me more than Kip does. It's Daniel who fills me in on the milestones I've missed in Daniella's life. It's Daniel who keeps me sane. Daniel who keeps me getting up every morning and fighting this case.

"What is this?" Daniel's shoulders tense, but he reaches for the folder anyway.

"Open it."

I wait as he does. His fingers slip under the seal and then he's pulling out the single photograph that changed everything.

"What . . . ?" Daniel breathes as a look of shock covers his face.

"I knew she was alive."

"Where did you get this photo?" is Daniel's first question.

"It arrived yesterday."

"That's—"

"My baby," I finish for him. "With *her*. That's Kip's favorite restaurant. The one he took me to when he proposed."

Daniel takes several moments to process what he's seeing before he slides the photo back into the folder. "Do you think he's been involved from the beginning?"

"I don't know. I've considered everything. A murder-for-hire plot, an insurance scam, a flex to get me to sign over my percentage of the island. I thought Kip would always take care of me, so I didn't mind signing over my portion of the estate. I thought, good riddance — that place holds only bad memories. But now, it feels like I was set up to take the fall for something, and I'm not even sure what yet."

"Maybe it wasn't premeditated. Maybe it was just a crime of opportunity. You should talk to your lawyer about what it means."

"I already did," I say. "He can't do anything with a single photo. Plus, they're not even convinced it is Kerrigan. The hair is all wrong, and the shot is from so far away . . ." I feel heat crawl up my throat. "He also informed me that Cole is appealing his verdict and just waiting on a date for the hearing."

"What does that mean for you?"

"It means I'm probably fucked, thanks to amateur internet sleuths."

Daniel dips his head and sighs. "I don't know if you want to hear this, but . . . I saw him."

"Saw who?" I frown.

"Cole. He's broken, Rye. You wouldn't even recognize him. He looks . . . strung out or something. I've never seen anyone change so much. He got bamboozled by those awful people — and the worst part, he doesn't even want revenge. He just wants to forget it all happened."

"When did you see him?" Tremors claim my body as my fear for the future ratchets up another notch.

"I talked to Stavros. Mika is doing well, by the way. They think she'll make a full recovery. She's already walking and . . . well . . ." Daniel's eyes fall to his feet. "I think she's gonna be okay."

I let his words sink in. "I'll take the fall for this if Kerrigan isn't found, Daniel. Mark my words, that's been the plan all along."

"Rye—"

"I don't trust anyone anymore — not my husband, not Stavros or Mika, not even you."

Daniel nods, eyes warm with empathy. He finally looks up. "Cole is the real victim of this story, Rye."

CHAPTER FORTY: DANIEL

"Why do you have that look in your eye?" Ryleigh regards me with a curious smile.

I bite down on my bottom lip. She knows me better than anyone. It was torture not sharing my story with her before the book released, but I have faith the real truth will come out in the end — the truth that exonerates her *and* Cole.

That's why I've been coming every other day. Because it's my fault she's here, so it's up to me to get her out. I spend all the hours of my day trying to make amends by looking for the shred of evidence that will prove her innocence. I couldn't live with myself if I didn't. I just haven't found it yet.

"Did the lawyer get his deposit this month?" I finally respond.

She nods. "Thank you."

"It's the least I can do." I've been splitting the profits from the book with Ryleigh to fund her meager defense team because Kip won't. He says he's running into liquidity problems, but I don't know if I believe him. When I submitted the finished book to the publisher, I didn't expect Ryleigh to actually suffer any consequences. It's really a work of fiction woven with true events. It's the reader who's left to consider what really may have happened in the in-between. "Also . . . I was sent the same photo."

"What?" Ryleigh's voice reaches a new octave. One of the guards raises an eyebrow, but I wave him off to indicate that I'm okay.

"Along with a bloody copy of *Murder at Stonecliffe*."

Ryleigh's mouth opens and closes with shock. "Why didn't you tell me?"

"I am now," I reply.

"Who do you think sent it?" she whispers.

I swallow, tingles erupting across my skin as I share with her what I know so far. "I gave it to investigators the same day it arrived." Anxiety swells in my chest. "It was Lyra."

"Lyra?" she says. "Why?"

I shrug. "They found her living with someone in Greece."

"Greece?!"

"They think Kip and Kerrigan might be there too."

"But . . . but that photo from Kip's favorite restaurant in the city . . ." I can see her brain working through all the new facts.

"Probably taken a few days before boarding the plane to Greece. Rye . . ." I press my lips together. "They have the baby with them."

"What?" She visibly crumbles, and all I want to do is reach across the table and hug her, but I can't. Any contact and that guard will be on us in a second. "They stole my baby?"

"It seems that way." I wring my hands and avert my eyes. "There's more. It looks like Kip defrauded his investors. They're living under new names."

"What? Like one big happy family?" she snarls.

"I guess. That female investigator who arrested you didn't even want to tell me that much. She's in your corner, Rye. A lot of us are. The true crime forums are split. Everyone has a team — Ryleigh or Kerrigan — but I think what really happened is getting lost in the mountain of assumptions." I hesitate, wondering how much to reveal right now. "And . . . there's another photo. Kip and Lyra's father, well, it seems like their business dealings go deeper than we may have realized."

"What are you talking about?"

"Same restaurant, a few weeks earlier, there's a photo of Kip and Jon Caruso together. They met to sign some paperwork. The forensics team was able to zoom in on the photo and identify the company letterhead." I watch my friend closely, wondering if even her lawyer knows this next part yet. "Jon Caruso had something to do with the accidents that happened that summer. They can't prove it yet, but there's a paper trail from Kip's hedge fund to a new LLC created after the sale of Stonecliffe. I don't know if what happened to Mika was an accident or something premeditated, but it seems obvious now that whatever happened to Kerrigan was a well-strategized plan to get the other shareholders to sign off on the sale."

"How? Are you sure?" Tears swim in her eyes as she regards me with an expression of fear and hope. I assume fear that it might be true, and hope that if it is, we might finally get some closure.

"I'm not sure of anything. What I am sure of is that Kip and Jon Caruso are invested in the company that is currently drilling on Stonecliffe Island."

CHAPTER FORTY-ONE: COLE

"How have you been?" Daniel clears his throat, eyes shifting around the visiting room. He hasn't looked me in the eye once. I'm not surprised. I suspect none of them would be able to — if they'd come to visit. In truth, I never expected to see any of them again.

Lyra has been the only one brave enough to submit herself to a full-body search just to see me for fifteen minutes. But she came.

Daniel squirms, still waiting for my answer. I kind of enjoy his discomfort. "Are you really asking me how I've been?"

Daniel's eyes meet mine finally. Sympathy simmers back at me.

"It's been about what you'd expect sitting in jail for the last several months. So, what brings you to my little corner of correctional paradise? Let me guess, you're planning to write a sequel and make a little more money off what happened?"

Daniel swallows. "Of course not."

"So?"

"I just . . . always felt bad."

"Spare me," I groan.

Daniel sighs. "I hope the book maybe helped you somehow."

"I haven't read it, but I doubt it." I watch him shrewdly. I know he didn't have anything to do with my being put away, but he sure as hell didn't come to my defense either. Without a single witness to show up for me and testify about what they saw that night, the state had an open-and-shut case of involuntary manslaughter. They claimed I killed Kerrigan in a crime of passion, a lover's quarrel gone wrong. They considered tacking on a charge for Mika's accident. Ultimately, there wasn't enough evidence, and it was decided that if Mika's family decided to pursue justice, it would need to be in civil court.

"My lawyer says I'll probably be out of here in under a week as long as my appeal is granted. Just because I was the last person to see Kerrigan alive does not make me responsible for her disappearance."

"That's good. I'm glad," Daniel murmurs. "It sounds like you have a good defense team."

"After I was found guilty, I knew the public defender's office couldn't help me. So, I hired this new guy out of Lansing — cost me all of my shares in Stonecliffe and then some. Remains to be seen if it was worth it, I guess."

"I went back to the island a while ago . . . it's not the same."

"In what way?" I imagine him picking around my home while I sat locked up in here.

"It's loud. Industrial. The shoreline is . . ." Daniel looks up at me as he searches for the right words. "Well, it's just not the same. It felt . . . sad."

I nod. "I was the last to sell. I was the final five per cent. I held out for months, but when the state offered me the plea deal — guilty with a sentence of not more than forty-eight months — I took it, fired my lawyer, and hired the best I could afford with the money I got from the sale of my shares in the island. It didn't go far, but hopefully, it's far enough. I'm sorry that Stonecliffe got sold to big oil, but I can't be too sorry when it cost me my freedom."

227

The guard calls over the intercom that half our time has passed.

"What are your plans, if — I mean *when* — you get out?"

I consider my answer carefully because I don't really want any of these assholes to know where my next stop is. "I haven't decided. Alaska. Oregon. Somewhere far away."

"That sounds great." The tense positivity in Daniel's tone makes my stomach churn. "Have you — do you speak to anyone other than Lyra? Anyone who was there that week?"

My answer is measured. "I have not."

"Kerrigan — she . . . do you . . ." He stumbles. "Have you heard anything about her?"

"I have not," I repeat.

"It seems . . ." He's struggling again. I'd kick him under the table if I thought it'd help him spit the words out sooner. "She's alive."

I stare blankly back at him, frown forming slowly before I begin. "Of course she's alive. Did you really believe for a fucking second she wasn't? She knows those islands as well as I do. She can captain a boat and drink any of the men at the Pink Pony under the table. I knew goddamn well she was just taking a break from that gilded cage of a life she hated so much. Once I realized Kip had already negotiated a deal to sell Stonecliffe . . . Well, it all made perfect fucking sense to me. You really thought it was an accident or some crime of passion committed by Ryleigh? I didn't know what to think when she stumbled up and said she'd just been in a fight with Kerrigan, but then she claimed she hadn't seen her at all and she'd just hit her head." I let a wry smile turn my lips. "Kerrigan thought she had the perfect crime on her hands. Sex and lies and revenge . . . but she forgot about the wild card. *Me*. I knew her well enough not to buy into it — I loved her enough to see the real her beneath all the expensive bullshit."

The intercom crackles to life and announces we have one minute remaining. "Make no mistake, I loved her. But if I ever see her again—" I lower my voice to just above a whisper — "I will kill her."

CHAPTER FORTY-TWO: RYLEIGH

Two months later . . .

"Welcome to the island of Paxos, Mr. and Mrs. Andino." The valet at our bed-and-breakfast opens the door of the cab. "On behalf of everyone at Ionian Bluff, we hope your journey to us was pleasant."

"Yes, very." I pass him a few euros before he wheels our luggage to the entrance.

"That layover in Zurich was a nightmare," Daniel says under his breath as we walk through the entrance. The receptionist standing behind a Cycladic blue-tile desk smiles brightly at us.

"Welcome, Mr. and Mrs. Andino. We have your accommodation ready for you." She smiles and asks to see identification as we get close. I pass her the new passport I used to get me out of America and through customs in Switzerland. The new identification Daniel was able to secure for us has worked perfectly — we are now Mr. and Mrs. Matthew and Erica Andino, tech entrepreneurs and world travelers. The story is that Matt made millions off Bitcoin and then reinvested it into international markets, and we've come to Paxos to spend the summer working and soaking up the Greek sun.

The reality is much darker.

Long gone are Ryleigh and Daniel and the tragedy they witnessed that summer at Stonecliffe. It's as if their lives have been wiped off the face of the planet, but that's the way it had to be. It took me months to really forgive Daniel for his part in the publication of our story — but he wore me down, visiting week after week at the psychiatric ward. He was even there to pick me up when I was released and the assault and attempted murder of Kerrigan Lange were expunged from my record.

He is the reason I walk free today.

After the three months I spent under constant psychiatric care and being force-fed medication, Daniel's thrown-together team of legal experts was able to prove without a doubt that Kerrigan was alive — and living here. In Greece.

With the help of the royalties from *Murder at Stonecliffe*, we were able to fund a trip for the investigator to travel to Greece and confirm by photo that Kip, Kerrigan, and Daniella are living here under new names. I didn't want to follow them here, but Daniel convinced me it was the only way because extradition from Greece for anything other than politically violent crimes is unheard of. And so, the same day I was released, Daniel presented me with my new name, new passport, new life, and a plan to get my baby back.

And that's when I knew that I could forgive him, because he ruined my life and then saved it by buying me a new one.

Daniel explained that he told the story as he did because he thought he had the truth and that it deserved to be shared. But that summer, we learned that the truth is as malleable as any lie. The truth is only a matter of perception. Daniel apologizes often for publishing the book and letting the chips fall where they may, but that's all water under the bridge as long as he can help me get my baby back.

Paxos, especially on the more remote sides of the island, suffers from an old workforce and not enough people to fulfill the needs of the ever-increasing numbers of tourists. Armed with the address of the cottage Kip and Kerrigan are staying, I plan to interview for a work position at the café they frequent in the mornings for coffee, eggs, and croissants. I know this because it's the same café they've visited most mornings since the investigator first confirmed their presence here a week ago.

"Step one of the plan starts now, huh?" Daniel looks up at me with empathetic eyes after we're checked in to our shared room.

"I guess so. We didn't come this far to only come this far." We've traveled across the world to take back what's mine. There's no turning back now. "It disgusts me that they're living here happily ever after, while Cole and Mika and the rest of us are left to rot."

"I know." Daniel sighs, the reticence in his voice matching my own. "Do you want me to go with you?"

"No. I have to do this alone." I clamp down on my bottom lip, glancing down at the ends of my freshly bleached-blond hair. I hope my former best friend doesn't recognize me, but I can hardly recognize myself, so I feel confident that I can get away with this if I keep my head down and stay the course.

Just like in a tautly woven psychological thriller, Daniel and I plotted an elegantly simple plan for revenge. Nearly the complete opposite of the play Kip and Kerrigan tried to make, it would shock even the most seasoned reader.

And the beginning of the end starts now.

CHAPTER FORTY-THREE: KIP

Two weeks earlier

"Shh . . ." Kerrigan hushes the baby while she fusses and squirms. I'm feeling pretty fucking peckish myself after twelve hours of shuffling through airports to get to Greece.

"What's wrong with her?" I grunt, opening my laptop to check in with my email inbox.

Kerrigan turns the baby over her shoulder and tries to rub her back. "I think she's teething." Dani, or Zoe, as we're supposed to call her, only wails louder. "I don't think she likes me."

I glance across the small living room and roll my eyes. "She doesn't know you enough not to like you."

"She knows I'm not *her*." I can hear anger creeping into Kerrigan's voice.

I don't reply because there isn't anything I can say. When Ryleigh got pregnant, it didn't cause me an ounce of anxiety. I did what I always did and went into strategy mode. Kerrigan and I were headed for a divorce. Until Dad died.

With his passing, the ownership of Stonecliffe was suddenly on the table. Dad had spent years turning down offers from CanEnergy to buy Stonecliffe for a hefty cash price. The

Canadian oil company sent updated offers every few years with vague details about their plans to make Stonecliffe, which is almost equally positioned between Lakes Huron and Michigan, a home base for drilling into the lakebed to lay new pipeline with enough capacity to triple profit for shareholders in less than a decade.

"She'll learn to hate me," Kerrigan continues, "just watch. It's karma — karma for what we did."

"Life threw us some rotten lemons, babe, so we made lemonade." I take Dani from her arms, and she settles into the crook of my neck and sucks her little fist softly. "She just needs a nap."

Kerrigan sighs. "That last six per cent fucked us."

I don't have a response because she's right. I was prepared to handle Cole. Wresting his five per cent from him would have been easy enough because I knew the bind he was in after the accident with the tourist girl the summer before. If he ever had a chance of leaving the island to start over, he'd need to sell his shares to do it. But Ryleigh — I could never nail down her motivations. Getting to know Ryleigh at the athletic club and then more intimately only proved to deepen the mystery. Most people are motivated by the simple things — money, power, love. But Ryleigh pulled from something deeper inside her that I could never quite touch. She didn't care for expensive things, ego and power didn't impress her, and she never even said much about love or marriage or our future together. Ryleigh seemed to live in the moment and by her own unspoken code that I was never able to crack.

And then that last six per cent happened.

"I knew I'd have to use the baby to get her to give it up," I finally confess. "Dani was our only bargaining chip." I rub my daughter's back as she starts to drift off to sleep. "It took me months to convince her that preserving it for future generations is pointless if there's no money left to even afford the taxes and upkeep on an estate like Stonecliffe."

Kerrigan unlocks her suitcase and starts unpacking shorts and shirts. "Real estate is meant to be an investment.

If you don't cash in when opportunity knocks, you're doing it wrong."

That's my girl, ruthless in life and business. It's not that I didn't love Ryleigh — I did. I still do because she's Dani's biological mother, but Rye and I are not the same. Kerrigan and I are like two halves of the same whole — our minds think alike.

Apart, we are a force of nature, but together, we are unstoppable.

"I have a sinking feeling this isn't over." Kerrigan rubs her arms like she's caught a chill, even though it's well over ninety degrees outside.

"Oh, it's over," I affirm. "Ryleigh isn't going anywhere. You made sure of that."

"Did I, though?" She wrings her hands as she speaks. "We haven't gotten away with this yet. This entire ruse depends on the world believing I'm dead and it's Ryleigh's fault."

"Babe, there's an entire book outlining exactly how she did it . . . written by her former best friend."

"Yeah." Her features relax.

"Besides, she has no money. We were never legally married, so she can't come after me for anything. She sold her share of the island, but six per cent isn't much." I lay Dani down on the bed now that she's groggy enough to fall asleep. "Your real mama is basically handcuffed to poverty," I coo at my daughter.

"Don't say that." Kerrigan scowls. "I'm her real mother now."

"Of course you are, baby." I turn to face her warmly and take in her worried features. She's been an anxious mess since Chicago. She's always been so calm and collected under pressure, but I can tell the fallout from that summer at Stonecliffe is starting to weigh on her. I'd hoped a Greek getaway would help us heal, but leaving our old life behind only seems to be making her condition worse.

"You risked everything for our family, Ker. This entire plan to get our lives back on track is thanks to you." I rub her shoulders. "You were brilliant every step of the way. No one would suspect you if you were missing too — I never would have thought of that."

Kerrigan nods, but weary disbelief lingers in her eyes. "It was risky, but that's why you had to stay busy all week, always on camera with your head in your phone or a laptop. Your alibi was airtight from the beginning. It was just a matter of planting suspicion in Ryleigh to steer suspicion away from us." She's been doing this lately — spinning her wheels over what happened and what could have been different. "I know the plan wasn't to get rid of anyone," she continues, "but I was just so angry at Mika. I wanted to kill her after the things she said about you. And then she wouldn't even give you the time to make it right, just kept accusing us of being crooks. I mean, she threatened to go to financial regulators and report the hedge fund for fraud." Her voice falters. "I had to protect us."

"You did such a great job, baby. Hiding that scarf on the boat was the perfect distraction."

"Thanks." She wipes at her tears.

She's been getting lost in her memories a lot more these last few days. We've only been back together for a few weeks, but our emotional reunion, coupled with the added stress of a new baby, is definitely weighing on her. "It worked in our favor, either way. Remember how frantic Stavros was that day? Tearing up the seat cushions like he might find her hiding under them?"

Kerrigan nods, her eyes focus somewhere across the room. "I was so shocked when I stumbled upon Mika at the mouth of that cave. I thought she'd slipped and fallen on the rocks. I tried to help her at first, but she wasn't responsive, and then . . . then I saw an opportunity for us to get our lives back on track and scare the other shareholders. If Cole thought he was cursed by missing people on the island, and Ryleigh thought her life was in danger . . . Well, who *wouldn't* sell up for every last cent? My brain just went into overdrive with the possibilities, and I knew I had to act quick.

I had to make sure she didn't wake up, and I couldn't leave any evidence. Using a rock would have been so brutal and bloody . . . That old fishing boat was anchored just off the sandbar, so I slid her into the dinghy and rowed her out to it. I just kept thinking that I needed to hide her for a while. Long enough for the vote to pass and her shares of the island to be divided—" She covers her mouth in a silent sob as the memories of that moment overtake her. I hadn't considered that Kerrigan might need therapy after all she's been through, that she might not be the same woman she was when we were last together. I thought absence made the heart grow fonder, but in this case, it's left one of us with a disturbed, manic madness that lies just beneath the surface. Kerrigan's moods swing from cruel, cold, and detached to practically crazed with paranoia and accusation. I've never had a problem managing Kerrigan's shifting moods before, but the woman who sleeps beside me now is practically a stranger.

"I almost passed the edge of no return twice that week." Kerrigan's voice is thready and unnerving. "Twice in two days," she murmurs. "And poor Cole . . ."

"Baby, he's fine. It's a dog-eat-dog world out there. Sometimes people need to be kicked out of the nest to really see how far they can fly."

"Cole is better than that place," she agrees.

"Tell yourself what you need to," I say, "but it all worked out. And now we can count our blessings every day because we have back what was always ours." I think again about calling my private doctor to get her a prescription to calm her down or at least help her sleep at night, but I'm not interested in leaving a paper trail from our old life to our new one. "Ker?"

"Yeah?" Kerrigan's eyes find mine, and just like that, she's back — the woman I married.

"Why didn't you tell me you had the letter?" I finally ask the question that's been on my mind since she showed up on my doorstep — *our doorstep* — in Chicago with a bleached-blond bob and a smile two weeks ago. I didn't know it then, but something had changed in her, more than just the hair. Something broke in her in the time we'd been apart. The first time she held Daniella was that day two weeks ago, and while she said all the right things, their connection seemed cool at best. I thought the more Kerrigan got used to the baby, the more she'd warm up to motherhood, but it hasn't happened yet. I've been starting to wonder if it ever will.

Kerrigan leans into me, swiping at a tear with one polished fingertip. "I didn't tell you when I got the letter because the past belongs in the past. Because it does no good for Ryleigh to know we're sisters — that my father had a second family. It would only give her the power to take more from us."

"Your father's lawyer showed me the letter right after your father died," I finally confess. "Long before the will reading at Stonecliffe."

"What?" Kerrigan sits up.

"He thought when you finally found out, you might need emotional support . . . I'm sorry I didn't tell you sooner. I wanted to abide by his last wishes and wait until he wanted you to know. But when I found out Ryleigh — *your sister* — was working at the athletic club we belonged to just down the street from us, I couldn't resist going to see her. I had to know if she was someone who would be safe to welcome into our family. And then the hedge fund went into the red, and Mika started talking to the other fucking investors about getting their money out. I knew Ryleigh was gifted shares of the island because of that letter, and I realized it was the chance we'd been waiting for. I could woo the shares right out from under her and get the investors' money back in no time. I just had to pretend that I didn't know before anyone else found out that day the will was read. I saw an opportunity to keep us afloat and took it. Nothing went as planned, but to tell you the truth, Kerrigan, I'm not sure that we even had a plan. And you went rogue as well—"

She interrupts me. "We might have to go rogue again, you know."

"I don't think—"

"I know you think we've closed this chapter, but I know Ryleigh — we share blood. If she got even an ounce of the stubborn gene from *our* father, she will never give up until she gets what she wants." Kerrigan's eyes harden in a way I'm not used to. "I should have killed her when I had the chance." She glances up at me. "I should have killed her when I found out she was pregnant with my baby—"

"No, Ker, please. Then we wouldn't have our family. We have the best of all worlds. We have everything we could ever want now."

"I know . . ." Her gaze drifts somewhere far away. "I was so angry that day I just wanted her to feel pain, so I told her I was pregnant too." Kerrigan cradles her flat stomach. "I let myself believe just for a day that we'd done it — we'd created our own baby. I wanted so much to be pregnant." She wipes tears from her cheeks. "So I told her I was, and then I cut myself because I needed the scar. I needed the reminder of everything she took from me."

It occurs to me then that it's probably Kerrigan who needed to sit in a psychiatric hospital and be force-fed medications, not Ryleigh.

"I've come to terms that that's just not in the cards for us. Anyway, we should still have a plan for the worst-case scenario." Her tone vibrates with renewed anger.

I suck in a ragged breath. "I would kill for you — for both of you." I glance at our sleeping child. "I promise I will protect this family at all costs. Nothing can come between me and my girls." I squeeze her thigh to reassure her. "I promise, babe, if Ryleigh turns up, I will end her.

238

CHAPTER FORTY-FOUR: RYLEIGH

"New girl!" It takes me a minute to realize that the cook at the sidewalk café is talking to me.

"Yeah?" I spin just as I crack another egg into the bowl at my workspace. I've been working mornings here for the last three days, ever since Daniel and I arrived on Paxos.

"Bring the egg white omelets and grapefruit juice to the couple on the front patio."

I nod, dropping my current task to do what I'm told. In truth, I'm getting sick of putting the work in without payoff — I've even begun to wonder if Kip and Kerrigan are still here. Maybe they took off to another island or someone tipped them off that I was released.

Beelining out of the small galley kitchen, I make my way through the few locals who frequent the café and aim for the small patio at the front of the building. The patio anchors the corner of a main tourist walkway and a side alley that's relatively private. Until now, I've been confined mostly to the kitchen, and only on my lunch breaks or at spare moments throughout my daily tasks could I peek out into the dining area in the hope of seeing a familiar face.

It's never happened. Not until I turn the corner and see a woman with a bleached-blond bob that matches the one

Kerrigan has in the surveillance photos. My heart halts, my mind warring with the bone-deep knowledge that I've seen that exact angle of the shoulders before. And the delicate way the woman holds her spine taut as she sits in the wrought-iron café chair . . . It's all too familiar. My vision begins to tunnel, and the hairs on the back of my neck stand at attention.

It's her.

I gulp, tray of breakfast food tremoring in my hands as I halt in my tracks. I can't tear my eyes from the back of her head, and it's then I hear the soft chuckle that's been haunting my nightmares.

I think of the items tucked snugly in my bag hanging on the hook in the kitchen. I've been waiting for the right time. I'm not ready. My moment has come, and now that it's here, I don't know what to do. My heart thunders in my ears before I spin and weave through the tables and return to the kitchen.

"I'm feeling sick. I'm sorry. Someone else should deliver the food." I drop the tray in front of the cook and turn to head out of the kitchen and in the direction of the restroom. I push through the door of the ladies' room and lock it instantly behind me, crossing the room to the opposite wall and the ancient window that overlooks the alley. I crank it open gently and then hold my breath and listen.

Soft chatter from the street wafts in, and it takes a minute for me to filter through the voices to find the one I'm listening for. But it's not hers I hear. It's the last one I was prepared for right now.

"Stavros left a message at the Chicago office. I haven't listened to it, but Martha said something about 'Mika going home soon.'" It's Kip. My husband. I'm sure of it.

Where did he come from? When I saw Kerrigan, she was alone at the table. Now she's with my husband. So that begs the question, where is Daniella? I cringe when I realize they've probably changed her name by now. She probably wouldn't even know me anymore, that pure connection we shared now severed after a few weeks of daily interaction with Kerrigan instead of me. Daniella will be a year old soon and I've missed so much. They've stolen so much from me — and now her. I pray they haven't left her at their house alone.

"You're sure Martha won't say anything about where we are?" Kerrigan asks.

"I haven't talked to her. I just call in to the messaging service. She has no idea where we are. She just takes messages, baby," Kip says.

"Well, Mika may be walking, but she'll never be the same," Kerrigan replies.

"You never know," Kip mutters. "Why is the food taking so long?" Irritation settles in his voice. "It's not even that busy right now."

"I wish she'd died. I wish I could have taken care of this for us," Kerrigan gripes.

"It's fine, baby. You did the best you could. I'm stronger. I should have done it myself — just thought it would be more obvious because she's an investor in the fund."

"It would have been obvious. If there was any suspicion at all, the investigators wouldn't have stopped until they'd nailed you for it . . ." Kerrigan trails off, and just when I wonder if she's having an emotional moment of regret, she says, "I'm just disappointed that I couldn't finish the job. I spent all that time at the gym getting fit — who knew the lazy bitch was so strong?"

Kip grunts a laugh. I can just see the annoying smirk on his face in my mind. He waits a moment before assuring her, "You knocked it out of the park, Ker." I imagine he's probably reaching out to touch her lovingly, just like he always did to me. "You saved our family."

Kerrigan sighs. "I wouldn't have been able to get her into the fishing boat without all those workouts every week."

I freeze when I realize she's talking about the workouts at the athletic club — the place where we met. Where I met both of them. Was this all a grand scheme? Was I tricked by both of them in some greater game that I don't understand?

My blood chills as I listen to their version of events and the top-tier plan they had to take everyone down at Stonecliffe that summer — using the island against its guests, using the footage from the film crew as well-cut evidence in their stupid little true crime podcast. Everything was carefully orchestrated to deceive the shareholders just enough to get them to sign over their stakes in Stonecliffe. My stomach churns as I realize Daniel has always been right — wealth and friendships mix like oil and water.

"Ryleigh was the wild card," Kerrigan says so softly, I almost hear a trace of the friend I once knew.

"Rye was always the wild card," Kip says coldly.

As if I were just another step in the plan. A necessary cog in the wheel of their success. And now, I'm no more than a speed bump to overcome.

Besides, if Kerrigan was never dead, that means our marriage was never valid. It makes sense now why Kip was adamant we have a small ceremony on the beach just between us. He promised a grand affair after the baby was born, but I'm sure he knew that day would never come. Kip took care of everything for our wedding day — right down to the officiant who performed the ceremony. I imagine Kip never even delivered our signed marriage certificate to the county courthouse.

He's been married to Kerrigan all this time.

I curse myself for trusting him so completely. I should have asked to see the divorce decree from the court that he was supposed to file after Kerrigan went missing. I was so naive. I was so blindsided. I was so in love.

Kerrigan speaks again. "My mind just split when I thought of her carrying what was mine. The baby wasn't part of the plan, Kip."

"The doctor said it would be hard for me ever to have kids. How could I know—"

"Whatever. The past is in the past," Kerrigan says quickly. "I just . . . couldn't stop thinking about that woman raising my baby. My vision went black, and all I could focus on was getting what was mine. I almost killed Ryleigh. I didn't think I had it in me, but I do. I know now that I'm more powerful than I ever dreamed."

"You definitely are, baby," Kip agrees with his wife. His first wife. His only wife. I wonder what I'm supposed to call him now. I thought he was mine, but he's always been hers.

Our husband.

"I-I almost snapped and killed my flesh-and-blood sister." Kerrigan's voice is reedy and detached.

"Babe, you didn't know her. You weren't raised with her — she was your father's dirty little secret and nothing more." Kip's attempts at comfort make me cringe. Chills race up and down my spine, and my heart threatens to beat out of my chest. I rub at my sternum as my stomach churns and twists painfully. Is it true? Are Kerrigan and I really sisters? Shock radiates through me. I want to believe she's lying, but what if she isn't?

"The only silver lining I can find is that at least . . . at least the baby will look like me. We still share the same blood, the same DNA. In some ways, she's just as much you and me as if I'd made her myself. Right? I can almost convince myself that I am her real mom, not *her*."

"Ker. Dammit, I wish our fathers had died with this secret. What good does it do you, knowing that Ryleigh is your half-sister? None." I tune out the rest of Kip's reply as violent rage clouds my mind.

Tears chug down my cheeks as I back away from the window. I can't hear anything beyond my own anguish. It cries with devastated rage as I realize these two people used me as a pawn in their own selfish game. Just like Daniel warned, I should have kept my guard up around people like these. People used to having everything, entitled to their lifestyle more than I'm entitled to my own life.

I hated them before, but now my hate solidifies, and resolve strengthens my spine.

This is why Kerrigan and I were often mistaken for sisters, because according to her, *we are*.

I walk out of the restroom, wiping at the last trace of tears as I stop at my bag. I find my phone and send Daniel a quick text.

It's time.

He knows what to do next. We've talked about this. Kip and Kerrigan may have had an elaborate plan, but it can't compare to the steps Daniel and I are prepared to take next.

I move to the front of the café with a palmful of tablets from my purse clutched in my hand. My palms are sweaty as I go over and over in my head what's supposed to come next. Just as Kip and Kerrigan are in my line of sight, my husband stands and turns around, and for the first time, I see her.

My baby.

"Daniella," I utter and then clamp my mouth closed. While Kip and Kerrigan look different — different hairstyles and clothing than I'm used to — Daniella looks the same. She's wearing a soft, billowy white dress that falls at her chubby little knees, and everything in me wants to run to her. She seems comfortable in Kip's arms, and I have to admit, he looks good holding her. So good, I can almost convince myself that if I play this the right way, I can have my own little family back. Minus one Kerrigan Lange.

Daniella catches me with her eyes then, and I see her little eyebrows scrunch. My heart clenches with the hope that maybe she still remembers me. Daniel too. This will all be easier if she does. I could stare at her all day, but if I'm going to get her back, I'll have to stay away from her for a while longer.

Before Kip can turn and spot me, I slip behind the wall of the café. He passes the open front doorway a minute later, and I can hear Daniella cooing peacefully in his arms. The sound that warmed my heart for almost a year and has haunted me for the last few months.

If he leaves with her, the plan is ruined.

It's then I notice that Daniel has pulled up on his scooter, helmet still down. I see him look around, searching for me. I see the moment they land on *him*. Daniel's body remains frozen in place, my throbbing lungs the only muscle that moves

244

in my body. I step out of the shadows momentarily, and without knowing if Daniel is even looking at me, I point in the direction of Kerrigan sitting alone at the café table. Daniel nods imperceptibly, and that's when I know that whatever happens next is out of my control.

Kip continues his walk out of the café and up the sidewalk, right past Daniel on the idling scooter. Daniel's heart must be tightening in his chest at the sight of our girl — because at some point in our fight to get her back, in my mind, she became ours. Not Kip's and mine, as much as she has his soft dark curls and bright-blue eyes, it's Daniel who picked her up from daycare and attended playdates with me. It's Daniel who heard her coo "*ma-ma-ma-ma*" over and over for her first word.

Bile rises in my throat as I think about everything they've stolen from us since that summer. My anger reaches a climax when I see the opportunity I've been waiting for. The cook is shuffling out of the kitchen with drink refills on a tray. I gulp down my anxiety and force a smile on my face. "Feeling all better now. I can take that for ya."

He cocks an eyebrow at me and then huffs and drops the tray on the table between us. I pass him a polite smile, and he only grunts and turns away, heading back to the kitchen. I take a moment to check my surroundings to be sure no one is paying attention to me, and then I open my palm and slip one small tablet into the grapefruit juice.

I have no idea if this will work, but it's the only way I could think of to buy enough time to get back what is rightfully mine.

Without giving it a second thought, I come up behind Kerrigan and pass the glass of grapefruit juice around her shoulder. I say the word for *madam* in Greek, and before she can turn to see the hatred in my eyes, I'm weaving through the café tables and headed back into the restaurant.

If this works like it should, Kerrigan will be feeling drowsy in the next five minutes. Maybe even too tired to walk in ten. It's just enough time, if we move quickly. And if the worst happens and I've misjudged the dose and Kerrigan dies right here at the table? Well, I can't think about that now. Daniella is close, as close as she's been in months. I can't pass up this chance.

I will get her back.

Even if I have to kill my own sister.

CHAPTER FORTY-FIVE: RYLEIGH

"He won't put her down," is the first thing Daniel mutters when I approach him.

I don't say anything, only pause at his shoulder and watch Kip walk around the small living room of their rental. The front door hangs wide open, and I can hear him talking to her in that soft, gentle tone that a father reserves for a daughter. My heart pounds as it occurs to me for the first time that I'm taking something from him too — from both of them — but I can't stop to think about that now because what they have done is far, far worse.

Biologically, they are connected, but emotionally, he is nothing to her. At least, when I knew him. Maybe he's different with Kerrigan. Maybe together, they are the perfect nuclear family. Maybe with me out of the picture, Daniella's life will flourish, and she'll never be any the wiser. For the first time in months, I think that maybe the most selfless thing I could do is leave her here. With them. Without me.

Tears stream down my cheeks as I war with myself about the moral path versus the most financially stable one. In this instance, they are not the same. These two things have become mutually exclusive, and it's up to me to decide what path to carve for her sake. Kip can give her a big life — he gave it to me for a time — but then, I know the lies that will weave through her childhood like a toxic tapestry. The mountain of untruths between him and Kerrigan was staggering when I knew them, and with a secret like Stonecliffe festering, I can only imagine the baggage my daughter will one day carry.

"He should be putting her down for her morning nap anytime," I finally say, eyes trained on the familiar angles of his face.

He pauses and lifts a glass of grapefruit juice to his lips and sips. Daniella shrieks and then swats at Kip's head, and he chuckles softly and then tells her that it's time for her nap. Daniella seems to know exactly what this means because she begins to thrash her tiny body and cry until my ears hurt. Something in Kip's expression shifts then, and I recognize annoyance in his features.

He says something to her that I can't hear, and then he holds her at arm's length and gives her a soft shake. My heart halts as I realize that he's clutching her tightly, she's crying harder, and she's wiggling her arms and trying to slap at his face in an effort to get free.

"Dammit, fucking calm down," he growls at our daughter. "Don't make me give you more sleeping medication, okay?"

Tears sting behind my eyelids as I realize my child is being raised by an abusive monster. He is no different with her. No different than he was with Kerrigan or with me. I wanted to believe love for our baby would soften his heart, but he's the same callous asshole he's always been. Only now, he's more stressed. There's more on the line. Now, he's on the run from the law. And me.

My husband takes our daughter down the hallway and into the room I assume is her nursery. I know now what I have to do. My heart blooms with the promise of opportunity.

"We have to do it now," I say. Daniel doesn't reply. "And it has to be me."

"Rye — no, it's too risky. With Daniella missing, they'll suspect—"

"I don't care. I need to do it," I assert.

Daniel sighs. "Ryleigh . . ."

"If I make you do it, that makes me no better than him," I say. Emotions swell unexpectedly inside me at that thought. Just over a year ago, I was marrying the man of my dreams, and now I'm plotting his ruin.

Daniel groans. "I don't like this. It's not what we talked about."

"But it's the right thing to do," I insist.

"I'm not sure what's right or wrong anymore," Daniel admits.

"I know, but then I remind myself what this will look like in Daniella's eyes someday. She's the only person I need to live up to."

He knows me well enough to know that I'm right and, more importantly, that I've made up my mind. As far as best friends go, he's a pretty great one. I count myself lucky to have him, but I don't know if he could say the same.

"I'm going in," I husk before he can stop me, pulling out a handful of the little tablets and then moving around him to sneak into the house. Daniel doesn't bother holding me back because it's useless. I've never been more ready for this moment.

I move with deft speed, my gaze on the glass of grapefruit juice. When I reach it, my palm is already outstretched and ready to deal the deadly dose. I originally only planned to give him a single tablet, just enough to knock him out for a while, but now that I've seen him threaten our daughter with drugs to make her sleep, I can no longer pretend that his life is worth saving. Not now. Not after everything.

In the span of one second, I've dropped three tiny tablets into the glass of pink liquid — triple the dose I gave Kerrigan — and I'm already moving back to the front door. I hear footsteps, and my hackles rise. This is it. This is the moment where I'm caught, where the entire plan goes down the drain.

This is the moment I lose my daughter forever.

I slip around the doorway just as I hear Kip's footsteps in the kitchen. I hunker down in the place where Daniel stood just moments ago. He's executing his part of the plan, and while I should be following his path at this moment, I can't bring myself to move. I'm riveted, watching and waiting for Kip to take his last swallow of grapefruit juice forever.

He sets the glass back down on the table and then turns, Daniella's favorite baby blanket in hand. For a moment, he looks like the sweet, doting dad that I always dreamed he would be. Not the narcissistic nightmare he became. Kip winces and then rubs at his chest as if he's feeling some sort of discomfort. He blinks once, twice, then stumbles into the kitchen and plants a palm on the island. He gasps, then gags, and then clutches at his throat as if he's being choked. I smile quietly.

I know what I've done. I've just dealt him the deadly dose. That, coupled with the grapefruit juice, will slow his heart just enough to induce a massive heart attack. I simply have to hope that what I gave him was enough.

This wasn't the plan.

I was never supposed to kill my husband.

But sometimes, plans change.

CHAPTER FORTY-SIX: RYLEIGH

One year later

"Did you see what this little stinker just did?" I pull my baby close and tickle her until she erupts into giggles. Her belly laughs are food for my soul. The pure joy I get each day being her mom overwhelms me.

"Did she just bite you?" He laughs. "No biting, Dani. You're not helping, Rye — you're practically rewarding her bad behavior."

"I know, but she's just discovering her world."

"With her teeth," he chuckles.

"It didn't really hurt."

"This time," he grunts.

"Oh, stop being such a dad about it." I wave him off and go back to tickling our girl.

Daniel and I have been through hell and back to be here now, and I wouldn't have it any other way. I never planned to bring this little girl into the world, and I tried to make the best of it and give Kip the room he needed to become the dad she deserves . . . but I've learned that sometimes people can't be who you need them to be. Even if they think they want it for themselves. Sometimes, lies overwhelm the truth despite our own best efforts.

I struggle with the lie we now live just to be sure the past stays in the past.

Daniel has done his best to convince me that it's not a lie if we believe it. That's why we still call Daniella "Dani," even though we had to secure a new identity for her from the dark web. Thankfully, Daniel knows how to handle things like that. I haven't had to think about anything except being Dani's mom since the day Kip dropped dead in that kitchen.

After that moment, everything went exactly according to plan.

Daniel swaddled Dani into blankets and sneaked our drowsy girl out of Kip and Kerrigan's house in Paxos, carrying her sleeping form in his arms across cobblestone alleyways for multiple blocks to meet up with me at our rental. And from that moment on, we didn't waste any time. Daniel became her father because he saved both of us that night. I wouldn't have her without him. Because he made it right after he pointed the evidence at me and published it in *Murder at Stonecliffe*, by using the royalties to get us here. It's Daniel who bought the flights to Greece, Daniel who researched the toxin that would have a deadly interaction with the grapefruit juice that Kip and Kerrigan loved — and, per local newspaper reports, now have died by. He was the one who told me that we could pick it up over the counter if we stopped for a quick layover in Zurich.

Daniel made my dreams come true, even if it wasn't in the most traditional way.

He also purchased the small, rambling farmhouse on one of the most remote of the Ionian Islands. Our rural paradise is soaked in sunshine and peace, such a far cry from the getaway we last had together at Stonecliffe. Our island is a good place to raise a family and an even better place to get lost forever.

Adjusting to life off the grid and with new identities was difficult for me. While Daniel wrote the follow-up to *Murder at Stonecliffe*, Dani and I spent our days walking wildflower-lined paths and exploring the sandstone cliffs and cerulean coast-line. Local fishermen showed her the day's catch, and little old ladies shared pastries and candies with us as we got to know our new home. Now, I wouldn't have it any other way . . . but life in Greece is a world away from Chicago.

Daniel spoke to Stavros once shortly after our new lives started — to see how Mika was doing and also to get any news about Kip or Kerrigan. Mika is walking with a cane now and suffers migraines too severe to allow her to work again, but thankfully, she's made a solid recovery. And as for Kip and Kerrigan, Stavros hadn't heard a thing. Literally.

Kerrigan and Lyra's podcast went silent.

I chose to avoid the Greek newspapers, not that an over-dose of an over-the-counter medication by tourists is really newsworthy — but I chose not to engage with anything else from my old life. If someone were to ask me today if I'd ever heard the names Kip or Kerrigan, I would emphatically insist that I hadn't, and I would believe it.

Raina Matthews has never met anyone by those names. Raina Matthews has never been to Stonecliffe Island or Chicago. Ryleigh Lange couldn't sleep at night; Raina Matthews sleeps like a baby. Stonecliffe Island turned me into a criminal and a murderer, and if I try to leave our little Greek paradise, paranoia settles in my bone marrow like a cancer. Kip and Kerrigan left me with a lifetime of baggage and trauma and made me a prisoner on my own island . . . but at least I have my baby.

Raina Matthews would never kill her sister, but Ryleigh Lange had to save herself. And after Daniel requested a copy of the notarized letter that Kerrigan's father sent to Jon Caruso, revealing himself to be my father — revealing that Kerrigan and I were sisters by birth — I burned the letter and sent the smoke into the sky.

The day Mika threatened to expose Kip's and my affair to everyone at Grand Manitou changed all of our lives forever. Her last words echo on repeat in my nightmares. *I saw you and*

Kip last night. How could you have an affair with your best friend's husband? Where did Kerrigan find such low-rent trash for a friend?

Kip's words to me the night before Mika disappeared ring in my head. I didn't think much of them at the time, but now . . . now I think Kip chose his words very wisely. That night, Kip led me to believe that he could be scooped away from me before we even had a chance to make a life together. *Mika is threatening to report the hedge fund to the financial crimes unit at the FBI. I'll go under, Rye — they'll put me in prison for the rest of my life. There are millions unaccounted for — tens of millions.*

In hindsight, it seems obvious that he would also share this same sentiment with Kerrigan — planting the seed that Mika is to blame for the unraveling of all of our lives. Kip, always playing a next-level game in life and business, managed to have both Kerrigan and me doing his dirty work for him.

I lost my mind, and caged like a threatened mama bear, I lashed out to protect myself, my baby, my future. I couldn't raise a baby without a father, and so I snapped and shoved Mika, and then I watched in horror as blood streamed from her head wound. Kerrigan must have felt much the same way when she stumbled across Mika's body in the surf — an opportunity not to be missed. For as long as I've known her, it's always been Kerrigan against the world.

And in typical Kerrigan fashion, she chose Kerrigan.

I knew the moment Mika's head hit the rocks, I could never tell a soul what I'd done to save us. Not even Daniel knows that it was me who left Mika to die that day. But once I learned she was found in a fishing boat, I knew it wasn't *just* me. She was alive in that boat. But if not me, then who?

The more the pieces fell into place with the help of Kerrigan's podcast, the more I knew I'd need Daniel to help me. I knew he would never agree to lure Kerrigan out of hiding under the guise of helping him with his true crime book.

But I also knew Kerrigan could never resist the temptation of notoriety. A chance to go down in the true crime history books and leave a legacy beyond her struggling art gallery.

Kerrigan hid much of herself from many, but she could never hide her flair for dramatic narcissism.

Kerrigan orchestrated a brilliant plan to take me down. The only flaw in it was her own pride.

I didn't expect to be arrested the day of Daniel's book signing — that was never part of the plan — but I did expect my freedom to be stolen for a little while. At least long enough for Kerrigan to feel confident that the case was closed and she was safe to take over my life and my family for good. It was Daniel's idea that I threaten self-harm to keep myself out of jail — and I only agreed to do any of it if he promised to stay in Dani's life as much as Kip would allow. Life doesn't always go to plan, but I've learned that hardship sharpens my blade for the next battle. Not even my own sister could stop me from getting what was mine.

Some say blood is thicker than water, but that summer at Stonecliffe taught me you can drown in either.

THE END

ACKNOWLEDGMENTS

I'm so thankful for the team at Joffe Books for helping me make this story the best it could be. I'm so lucky to have such a great team behind me.

So much gratitude goes to Lisa at Silently Correcting Your Grammar — seven years and counting, baby! I couldn't make the books without your top-tier input and editing skills. You're the best!

Nelle Lamarr: you're the dearest friend a girl could ever hope to have. I live for our giggles and champagne moments in faraway places. Conversations with you always make my heart so big. If it weren't for us, I don't know if I'd still be doing this job.

The Private Island wouldn't be possible without the love and patience of my incredible family and some very dear friends. Thank you for listening to me ramble about the made-up stories in my head and giving me the grace and time to make books while the dishes pile up in the sink and the text messages go unanswered. And to my kids especially: thank you for understanding when we do takeout for dinner. Again.

To my Aldea Coffee family: your espresso and smiles keep me going when nothing else will. It feels like I stumbled in to write some words one day and never left. I'm so grateful for the warmth and community you bring to my world. You're never getting rid of me. :)

And to every reader that's ever picked up one of my books in these last 12 years publishing: thank you for your time spent with my words, enthusiastic cheerleading, encouraging reviews, and lifting me up on social media when the days get dark. I'm so lucky to have the opportunity to make books and it's all because of you.

THE JOFFE BOOKS STORY

We began in 2014 when Jasper agreed to publish his mum's much-rejected romance novel and it became a bestseller.

Since then we've grown into the largest independent publisher in the UK. We're extremely proud to publish some of the very best writers in the world, including Joy Ellis, Faith Martin, Caro Ramsay, Helen Forrester, Simon Brett and Robert Goddard. Everyone at Joffe Books loves reading and we never forget that it all begins with the magic of an author telling a story.

We are proud to publish talented first-time authors, as well as established writers whose books we love introducing to a new generation of readers.

We won Trade Publisher of the Year at the Independent Publishing Awards in 2023. We have been shortlisted for Independent Publisher of the Year at the British Book Awards for the last four years, and were shortlisted for the Diversity and Inclusivity Award at the 2022 Independent Publishing Awards. In 2023 we were shortlisted for Publisher of the Year at the RNA Industry Awards.

We built this company with your help, and we love to hear from you, so please email us about absolutely anything bookish at: feedback@joffebooks.com.

If you want to receive free books every Friday and hear about all our new releases, join our mailing list: www.joffebooks.com/contact

And when you tell your friends about us, just remember: it's pronounced Joffe as in coffee or toffee!